♡MARIANA

RHYTHM, CHORD & MALYKHIN

MARIANA ZAPATA

This e-book is a work of fiction. While reference might be made to actual historical events or existing locations, the names, characters, places and incidents are either the product of the author's imagination or are used fictitiously, and any resemblance to actual persons, living or dead, business establishments, events, or locales is entirely coincidental.

Book Cover Design by Letitia Hasser, RBA Designs

eBook Formatting: Jeff Senter, Indie Formatting Services

To Raul and Eddie, the two biggest idiots I will ever know.
For all the wedgies, the bruises, the insults and the pranks.
You're the best sisters I could ever ask for.

CHAPTER ONE

The last conversation that changed my life started with the words, "Gaby, we need to talk."

Exactly four minutes and fifty-five seconds later, I was apparently A) not in a relationship anymore, B) homeless and C) pathetic. Although the whole being "pathetic" part was only known by me... and my best friend... and my parents... and my brothers... and my sister... and my nieces.

Oh hell. Who was I kidding? Everyone knew I was pathetic when my best friend, Laila, told my parents I'd been dumped. She then told everyone else in my family that I had cried my eyes out for a week after my breakup and followed that up by watching *My Girl* every night for a month straight. The seven pounds and face full of acne I gained from stuffing my face with Spicy Cheetos and glazed donuts didn't help matters either.

So when Eli, who usually only called me twice a month and was drunk as a skunk each and every single time, called and started our conversation with "*Gaby-Gaby*" in a sing-song voice, I knew something was up. He never called me by my name unless it had a curse word before it. When he then asked me, "Do you have time to talk?" in a completely sober tone, I was pretty much expecting the apocalypse. Or at the very least, being asked to give up one of my major organs.

I shouldn't have listened to his offer. I should have known better, but Eli was my weakness in life, and the asshole knew it.

I couldn't count the number of times he'd wrangled me into doing something for him that I would never, ever do for anyone else. There were the occasions when I had to clean up his puke after he'd drank too much, because if our parents found out they would have flipped. Or when I ate ramen noodles for an entire month because I had to bail him out of jail, and he hadn't bothered paying me back. Then there was that time when he gave me bronchitis. I'd pretended to have my purse stolen while I was on antibiotics so that I could give him the extra dosage because he didn't have insurance and was too cheap to go to the doctor. In retrospect, I'm pretty sure that might have been a criminal offense.

I loved my twin brother, even if he was a restless bastard… and the bane of my existence.

"We had to let Zeke go," Eli explained in that

breathless voice so many stupid and oblivious women panted over. "Come on tour with us. Mom said you aren't doing shit this summer, so I know you don't have anything better to do—"

Umm... I didn't have anything better to do, but when someone else said it, it pissed me off.

I was lying down on my childhood bed with my knees to my chest when I rolled my eyes. The ceiling still had the glow-in-the-dark stars I'd glued on them nearly ten years ago; it seemed like they were mocking me, reminding me I wasn't a kid anymore, and that I needed to get my shit together so that I didn't have time to stare at them. "I've been applying for jobs, thank you very much."

"Aww, G, you've got the rest of your life to work. C'mon. It'll be fun," he insisted in that borderline-whiney voice that he used to get me to do his evil bidding.

He had a point; I knew it. I also knew how manipulative Eli was. He was almost as manipulative as he was full of shit, and he was full of a whole bunch of shit.

Go on tour with them, though?

I had a sudden flashback of all the scarring things I'd been through while in their company in the past. If I'd known back in kindergarten what I knew now about these boys, my life might have turned out completely differently. Getting detention at the age of five, right along with Eli, Mason and Gordo should have warned me of what was to come by simply being around them. Because seriously, who got detention in kindergarten? Not surprisingly, they were the three people I'd been with each and every single time I had ever gotten into any sort of trouble.

The problem was that I didn't like doing things to get into trouble, but it seemed to follow the trio wherever they went.

So yeah, I scoffed, admiring the teal color I'd painted my toenails the day before. "Fun? Hanging out with you on a bus is fun? Are you shitting me?"

Eli made an exasperated noise that got carried away by a gust of air in the background. He'd mentioned they were at a gas station getting fuel. "We're going to Australia and Europe..." He drew the words out and then paused for a second. "Nothing? You aren't going to say anything?"

I didn't say a word and that made him keep going because just saying the names of the two continents wasn't enough to black out my least favorite memories of going on tour with them years ago.

And he kept going. "Koalas, kangaroos... fish and chips, the Eiffel Tower..."

When I didn't automatically scream "yes!" he continued on with the bribes.

"Fine. We can pay you 10 percent of our sales plus whatever tips you get, you greedy prostitute," Eli offered.

Ding, ding, ding.

Ten percent? I could remember how much they

made when I'd last sold merch for his band, Ghost Orchid. They had sold fifteen hundred dollars worth of T-shirts and CDs during their concert. Ten percent of the total was one hundred and fifty bucks. One hundred and fifty bucks for six hours of work. Six days a week? And now they were making even more money? The asshole knew that I'd wanted to go to Europe forever, too, but it was the money that had me.

My bank account had taken a crippling hit when I'd quit my job to move back home to Dallas after I graduated.

Taking a look around my childhood bedroom with its robin's-egg blue walls and band posters plastered all over it, I sighed into the receiver. If I stayed, I ran the risk of looking for a job for who knows how long. I'd have to life with my parents until I found a roommate that didn't drive me nuts, and I'd have to deal with facing the Spanish Inquisition each time I left the house. On the other hand, if I went with Eli, I knew life would begin to consist of sweaty nights, an uncomfortable bed and dealing with three imbeciles that would sacrifice me to a group of zombies if it meant they would live.

Work.

Home.

Bus.

Travel.

Sweat.

Even more sweat.

Because, really, who likes to sweat? Who'd willingly sign up for a summer of sweating? It'd been fun when I was younger but now…

"C'mon, G, you're the only person I trust, and I miss you," he continued, sincerity stringing his words together.

"I don't know—"

"Three months," he kept going. "You'll probably never be able to do this again."

The reality of his words sunk in. I was single, practically homeless and jobless. Soon there would be bills, work and life in general that would tie me down and keep me down. I'd be a real adult with real adult obligations in no time.

That notion alone had me wanting to puke.

"Gaaaaaaby."

The one and only picture that I still had of my ex with a group of friends sat in the corner of the bedroom and seemed to wink at me, calling me a pussy.

"What are you doing with your life, Gaby?" Brandon, my ex-boyfriend, had asked thirty seconds into the conversation that had changed my life months ago.

"This is the hardest decision I've ever had to make, but this isn't working anymore," he'd said to me. The fucking dickwad. The hardest decision he'd ever had to make before that was whether he was going to use too much mousse or too much gel in his hair. Idiot.

Speaking of, why the hell hadn't I shredded that picture yet? I needed to do it before I forgot again.

Sure, it had a group of people in it but that didn't seem like enough of a reason to keep it any longer. I'd heard of things called "amicable breakups," but I'd never seen one in person.

It was the collection of posters right above the idiot's picture that finally drew my eyes away. They were posters I'd collected of Ghost Orchid on different tours over the years. Besides having to act like a babysitter and a nagging wife, and witnessing stuff no sister should ever have a front-row seat to, I'd had a lot of fun each time I'd gone out with them. I wasn't going to count the last day of the last tour I'd been on, but...

Was I seriously going to go on tour with my borderline-alcoholic brother for three months, all so that I could avoid the inevitable?

You'll probably never be able to do this again.

I pulled my legs back into my chest and hugged them with the arm that wasn't busy holding the phone to my ear.

Then I sighed. "Yes, damn it. I'll do it."

There was a pause before my twin asked slowly, "You will?" He sounded like he couldn't believe my answer.

"Yes."

"Have I told you lately how much—"

I cut him off before he had a chance to butter me up. "On two conditions."

∼

Six hours later, my flight from Dallas to Boston had finally landed.

Apparently buying a plane ticket exactly two hours before the actual flight took off didn't guarantee a good seat. I'd sat through a four-hour flight wedged between a mom with a really cute baby that had colic and a man who'd probably been smoking a pack of cigarettes a day since the eighties.

As soon as my bag came out of the conveyor in baggage claim, I caught a cab to make it to the venue where Dumb, Dumber and Dumbest were playing.

The fact that just a few hours before I'd been laying on my bed, watching television and debating whether I really needed to eat ice cream or not, didn't escape me. In the span of a twenty-minute conversation with my brother, he'd bought me the earliest plane ticket to Boston available and ordered me to "start packing, Flabby." I had no idea how much a last-minute flight like that would cost, but I hoped it was a lot.

It was a testament to my lack of shit-giving that I was able to get all my things together in less than half an hour. I pretty much flew blind as I threw clothes into the same suitcase I'd used a few months ago when I'd been forced to move out of my apartment. My wardrobe consisted of a handful of shorts, two pairs of jeans, T-shirts, a collection of tank tops and racerbacks. A bathing suit, underwear, bras, two cotton dresses, passport, neutral-colored sandals and as many books as I could fit, evened out my trusty vintage Samsonite and backpack. I figured I could buy whatever else I needed because there was bound to be something I forgot, for sure.

Mom and Dad were all-too-excited to have me tag along with Eli. They'd dropped me off at the airport with huge grins on their faces. I hated to think why they were so happy to have me out of the house, so I definitely wasn't going to go down that road of potential nightmares and nausea. I also think they secretly hoped I'd keep an eye on their beloved youngest boy, their wild child, but everyone knew there was no controlling Eli Barreto. The idiot had been born with hell in his veins.

On the cab ride over, I mentally braced myself for the insanity that was Eli, Mason and Gordo. Mason and Gordo had been in my life for as long as I could remember. I had a brief, blurry memory of being in kindergarten, watching Mason and Eli shove Play-Doh into their mouths while Gordo and I watched in both horror and fascination.

Even though I hadn't gotten to see them much over the last couple of years, I loved the hell out of them. So much of the first twenty years of my life included the three monsters, there was no way I couldn't. Once Eli and I got split up into different classrooms in elementary school to force us to make friends, one or the other had been in a class with me... usually sitting next to me, trying to copy my work.

Growing up, I'd been Flabby Gaby. Well, it

should be said that I'd been Flabby Gaby even up until the last time I saw them during Christmas. Except now they'd graduated past pulling on my ponytail constantly and intentionally doing things to piss me off. At this stage in our lives, they usually settled for just teasing me, but I wouldn't expect anything less.

The point was, you could love someone and still dread traveling with them, especially when it was going to be for three months straight.

It'd be fine. It really would be fine. *Right*. It sure would.

Yeah, I couldn't even find it in me to completely believe it.

I was wringing my hands nonstop on the cab ride to the venue, and I hoped like hell that my deodorant would hold up through the rest of the night. Glancing at my watch, I realized it was after seven. Eli had told me they didn't go on stage until at least nine.

When the cabbie dropped me off at the end of the block, I called my jackass of a brother.

He answered on the second ring. "Are you here?"

"No, I'm in Antarctica." I was already pulling my suitcase down the block.

The marquee was mounted on the opposite corner but I couldn't miss the lettering.

TONIGHT
THE RHYTHM & CHORD TOUR

SOLD OUT

Eyeing the massive bus parked on the street about thirty feet away, I couldn't help but remember Pepe, Ghost Orchid's old van. On the tours I'd gone on with them before, we'd stuffed ourselves into their Chevy fifteen-passenger van and their faded red cargo trailer. With peeling paint, duct-taped seats, and sketchy-looking rigged up doors—you couldn't help but love Old Pepe. He'd racked up more than two hundred thousand miles before he'd been retired. Some of my fondest memories came in thanks to his loyalty. Now that the band was making money, they'd upgraded to nicer things.

I couldn't say I wasn't excited to not have to sleep on a bench seat and pray every day that one of the guys wouldn't fall asleep behind the wheel on overnight drives, though.

"Flabby!" a voice that had begun haunting me from the moment I'd been born hollered.

I groaned but couldn't help but smile, excited to see my twin for the first time in more than five months, the longest time we'd ever been apart by far. His bulky and gigantic head popped out from around the corner of the green, silver and black touring bus as he made his way toward me in aqua-colored swim trunks, a white tank, and a flat-brim baseball hat. With hair the same shade of black-brown as mine except it was straighter, the same green eyes, and peachy-colored skin, Eli grinned like he'd just found out Sam Adams was endorsing him.

"Eliza," I sang out, calling my brother by the nickname I'd bestowed upon him at the age of four.

He flashed a big smile and held his tree trunk-sized arms forward, crooking his fingers in my direction. "Come to me."

I took Eli in for the first time in almost half a year. He still looked exactly the same... except it looked like he had a hint of a beer gut growing. That was only a slight surprise.

Ever since we'd been sophomores in high school, I'd sworn he used steroids but it didn't matter how much I looked, I never found any on him. Eli was built slightly shorter than six feet tall with biceps the size of my head and a neck I couldn't attempt to try to choke because it was too thick. I used to ask him when he was making his professional wrestling debut. He'd then ask me when I was planning on becoming the newest *Extreme Makeover* contestant. Jackass.

But the thing about him that was the most apparent was how clear his eyes looked. He hadn't started drinking yet—one of the stipulations I made when I agreed to come on tour. *I don't want to see you shit-faced*, I'd told him, and surprisingly, he'd agreed without arguing.

The instant we were close enough, we hugged and then hugged each other some more.

He held me against him for another minute before finally pulling away, resting a palm on each of my shoulders. "When was the last time I saw you?" he asked, eyeing me carefully.

I frowned before slapping his pooch with the back of my hand. "Five months ago, you douche." He'd been living in Portland for almost a year, and the last time we'd seen each other had been during New Year's.

He winced. "I've missed you more than I've missed Rafe," Eli offered with a smile before hugging me close again, a little roughly, a little too aggressive, and just like him and our relationship.

I snickered into his shoulder. "I'm going to tell her you said that."

He snorted, another trait we shared; our mom thought his snorts were cute while mine she considered disturbing. It was a real confidence-booster. *Thanks, Mom.* "I'll deny it." He would. Rafe was short for Rafaela, our older sister, who had terrorized us when we were kids. Hell, I think she still scared both of us.

Rolling my eyes, I squeezed his middle. While it was easy to get through day-to-day life when I didn't have a constant reminder that I missed him, now that I saw him, I realized how much I had. Being near him felt like home. "You're a little bitch, but I've missed you enough not to care you don't have any balls."

He hugged me back a moment longer, and then kissed my cheek unexpectedly before shoving me away. I didn't let the surprise of his affection register on my face. "Well, c'mon. Let me show you where the bus is. I still gotta warm up."

Pulling me in the direction of the bus's door, Eli explained what happened with Zeke. He'd been Ghost Orchid's merch guy for the last two years since my retirement. Apparently Gordo had began noticing that the band was occasionally a bit short on cash a few times in the past, but they hadn't thought too much about it until the same thing happened on the very first day of their current tour. Not a lot of money went missing but enough that Gordo, who was anal retentive about keeping track of their merchandise, noticed. That morning, Mason found that they were short more than three hundred dollars. According to the merch guy for the other band they were on tour with, he'd seen Zeke slipping bills into his laptop case.

What a moron.

So they left Zeke at a gas station with enough money for a cab and a plane ticket with an overnight layover.

My brother stopped in front of the bus and yanked the huge, heavy metal door open. He motioned for me to leave my suitcase outside.

"I sorta forgot to tell you that we're sharing a bus with the other band we're touring with," he coughed out in a quick sentence, climbing up the tall steps leading inside the bus. The driver's seat was vacant.

"Oh, yeah?" I asked, really not caring that we were going to be sharing fifty feet of moving vehicle.

I'd survived with them in the past in fifteen feet. Fifty wouldn't be a problem.

He pulled aside a heavy cream curtain that separated the driver's area from the living space. The space consisted of a flat-screen television behind the driver's seat. There was a long, narrow cloth couch on each side of the walkway that went straight down the middle of the bus. A small table for two was set up behind the seating area and a kitchenette was nestled before a doorway that led where the bunks would be. The set-up was similar to every other bus I'd ever been in before when I'd visited him on tour.

"Yeah. We've been sharing since gas prices started making my ass bleed," he explained.

"Are you sure the ass bleeding isn't from too much anal with Mason?" I cracked up, poking my finger into his back.

Eli flicked me off over his shoulder as he walked a little further inside. "I'm gonna fart on your pillow and hope you get stink eye," he muttered.

I couldn't help but laugh as I took in the living space, or rather what would be called "home" for the next few weeks. "You're awful."

Turning around to smile at me in that same sneaky way he'd done our entire lives, Eli winked, which was never a good thing. Him winking was a warning of trouble to come. "Oh, my tiny, eight-pound, six-ounce baby Gaby. I'm gonna show you awful."

CHAPTER TWO

"Jesus, Mary and Joseph! Is that my future wife?"

I'd been standing outside the bus, watching as my brother stashed my suitcase into the lower compartment of my temporary home for the next five weeks when the words pierced the Massachusetts air. I groaned, recognizing the voice that had been tainting my life for over twenty years. Then I turned.

Mason had his long, tattooed arms stretched in my direction, smiling like the demented fool he was and still more handsome than any jerk should ever be. "Come here, my bride."

I snorted and shook my head, already heading toward him. "Hey, you."

Even though we'd been friends since before I even knew what a training bra was, Mason had been telling me we were going to get married for as long as I could remember. Eli said it'd be a cold day in hell before he ever let that happen, and I couldn't help but agree. I'd been Mason's pretend-girlfriend at least a hundred times, his sister, wingman, wrangler, voice of reason and prom date.

That was just the tip of the iceberg with our history.

When you know the worst things about the people you care about and still managed to love them anyway, it sometimes turned into a brotherly type of affection. At least that was the case with this guy. Not that it stopped me from thinking Mason was attractive.

Because he was. Good gracious, he was. It was undeniable.

I felt his arms wrap around me and squeeze; all I could think about were his perfectly sculpted biceps.

With sky-blue eyes and a haircut that left him looking like a clean-cut Calvin Klein model, Mason was the reason why the band had so many female fans. If you asked my mom, she'd insist Eli was the attractive one, but yeah, no way. Mason was around my brother's height, muscular enough but not as bulky, and he had this grin that was deceptively sweet. He'd also slept with more women than I could count, smoked weed at least once a day, and showered only when he felt like it, which wasn't often enough; yet somehow he managed to pull off being a vagina magnet despite his hygiene issues.

And today was my lucky day because by the way

he smelled—or I guess *didn't* smell—he'd taken a shower recently. Praise Jesus.

"I just about shat my pants when I heard you were hopping on tour with us," he murmured against my hair. Hugging me to him again, he pulled on my ponytail just like old times.

"According to E, I don't have anything better to do this summer." I laughed but it was a little forced. The reminder that I didn't have a job, my own place or even any prospects for either was like a nail right to the eye.

Mason pulled back and grinned down at me. "I haven't seen you in forever. Have you been hiding at the Chocolate Factory again with your Oompa—?"

I poked at his nostril with my index finger. At five-foot-two, I'd heard countless jokes about my height for the last ten years. "You're an idiot."

His only response was an unapologetic shrug.

Eli yanked on my belt loop a second later, distracting our conversation. "Your bag is in the bus. Let's go sell some shit. Gordo's phone is dead, and I bet my fucking balls he's been giving out the wrong change for the last hour without his calculator app."

I nodded, remembering the time I'd witnessed Gordo trying to give a cashier change at the gas station. Painful didn't even begin to cut it. I'd ended up giving the poor lady money out of my own pocket to put her out of her misery.

Mason laughed. "You know he only volunteered to go out there so he could scope out the sausage scene in the audience tonight."

My brother groaned. "Let's go, G."

"I'll see you later, Flabby. Make Daddy some money tonight," Mason winked with a laugh, pulling on my ponytail one last time before he made his way toward the front of the bus.

Following after my brother, he led me through the building's rear entrance, which opened to the venue's floor. As soon as we walked out, insanity ensued and it caught me completely off-guard. I was more than familiar with the kind of crowds Ghost Orchid brought out, from traveling with them in the past. Since then, my parents, my older siblings and I would drive out to any of their shows within a five-hour trip from Dallas. I thought I'd seen it all.

This time there were so many more people than I ever remembered seeing in the past. The place was already packed. It wasn't that I didn't think they could draw a crowd; it was just rare so many people would show up hours before the main act.

Eli elbowed me. "Crazy, huh?" He could sense my surprise at the hundreds of people crammed into the venue so early in the evening. More often than not, he and I didn't need words to communicate. "We got really lucky they chose us for this tour."

"Who's the headlining band?" I finally asked, putting my hand on his shoulder to follow him through the crowd. The last few hours had been so hectic I hadn't gotten a chance to ask, not that it really mattered anyway. I'd gone with them back when they'd played with everyone from a rap-metal band to a straight-up indie-pop group.

People stared as my brother made his way through the crowd ahead of me, apologizing to each person he shouldered past. It had always seemed strange to me that people would get stars in their eyes when they saw him in person. Because this was my Eliza. He wasn't anything special or better than any other person. His crap smelled just as bad, if not worse, than anyone else's, and I had a million other humbling stories about him if anyone wanted to hear them.

"The Cloud Collision," he answered.

I wracked my brain for recognition of the name and only barely came up with a vague mention in the past. The band had to be well known if they were the headliners, but I still couldn't come up with a solid memory. Not a song title, album name, band member, or even what they sounded like. Anonymity wasn't necessarily unheard of for bands that weren't mainstream acts. There were easily tens of thousands of bands that wouldn't be known by the masses. Groups didn't need to be played on the radio or television to be successful, even if they were considered unheard of.

It didn't help that I'd really fallen off the bandwagon of searching out new music in the last couple of years. I'd been so busy with school and a full-time job that I hadn't really kept up with almost anything.

"I have no idea who you're talking about," I admitted.

He shrugged his big hammy shoulders as we kept walking. "You'll like them. They're good; Sacha's spot on every night too."

Sacha? I felt myself brighten up a little. "Oh, that's cool. I didn't know there was another girl on tour." She might be a raging bitch, but maybe not.

I missed the way Eli slowly turned his head to look at me, this weird expression on his face. Slowly he nodded, like you would nod at someone who asked a stupid question.

That had me frowning. "What?"

"Nothing." He made his eyes all wide, like I wasn't familiar with each and every one of his facial expressions and what they meant.

"Why are you making that face?"

"No reason, Flabs. I'm not allowed to smile?"

"No." I stared at him a little longer, suspicious.

But my brother just shrugged and didn't say another word.

I'd keep my eye on him. I knew he was up to something.

In no time, we were at the merch table where Gordo looked like a deer caught in the headlights. A small group of people surrounded him, half of them wanting to buy something and the other half wanting nothing more than to talk to the singer and guitar player of Ghost Orchid. A blind person could tell how uncomfortable Gordo was. The poor bastard had sweat running down his temples and he looked twitchy. As soon as he spotted his bandmate and then me hovering behind the overgrown human sausage, he visibly sighed in relief.

I'd never totally understood how Gordo managed to put up with my brother and Mason. He was the sane one. The thinker. Soft-spoken. He was the kind of guy who didn't talk much or relish getting into trouble. He was usually the voice of reason, where the other two morons acted first and thought things through second—if ever. When we were younger, Gordo and I would usually sit back and watch the other two get into all kinds of shit while we shook our heads and judged them the entire time.

After a quick hug, an explanation of how to use their credit card swipey-thing, how much each shirt, poster, drink koozie, CD and tab book cost, I was left on my own to face a firing squad who wanted to buy something. Eliza and Gordo disappeared as quickly as they could to go warm up backstage. Even though I hadn't sold merchandise—or merch, as it was shortened—for them in years, it was like riding a bike. You gave the fans what they wanted and they gave you money. It was that easy. Knowing that I'd get paid depending on how much merchandise was sold, I may have brushed the cobwebs off my best flirtatious smile and purposely not pulled my shirt the inch higher it could have gone. I wasn't one to usually show off Lucy and Ethel because I was self-conscious of them, but money was money.

A girl's gotta do what a girl's gotta do.

Plus, selling merch had gotten me my girls, so I wasn't going to hate on the job that had given me so much.

As soon as the line dwindled down, I finally turned to look in the direction of the table next to mine. The set-up mirrored the one I was manning. A large, collapsible table was set up with a flat metal rack leaning against the wall behind it. On the rack were T-shirts and zip-up hoodies pinned to it. On the table were stickers, CDs and vinyl. Cluttering the floor and stashed below the table were boxes and containers filled with the products on display. The band name, The Cloud Collision, was printed on a large banner that was mounted above the rack.

I plopped down onto one of the large plastic bins where some of the T-shirts were stored, and took in the guy working behind the other band's table. He was possibly a few years younger than my twenty-six. He was slim, with long straight hair in the front and a buzzcut from ear-to-ear in the back; he was busy at work with a line that was ten people deep.

The moment he got through with the line, just as the local opening band went on stage to start setting their instruments and gear up, he turned to look at me and gave me a shy smile—small and cute, highlighted by a hoop lip ring at the corner of his mouth. Worming his way through the maze of plastic bins and boxes that separated us, he thrust out a hand.

"I'm Carter," he introduced himself. Now that he was up close, I realized he was possibly half a foot taller than me. He also had another piercing through his eyebrow, a black ball, that I hadn't noticed initially. "You're Eli's sister?"

I nodded, shaking his hand. "Yeah, I'm Gaby. It's nice to meet you."

"Nice to meet you too." He gave me another shy smile, even blushing a little, before pointing at me. "If you turn around, I can take the sign off your back."

The sign...?

"Ah, Gordo taped it to your back when he gave you a hug," he explained.

I groaned, not surprised at all, and turned around to let him pull it off of me. Gordo was the quiet one, sure, but he was still a prankster. How else would he survive with the other two if he didn't have any in him? The guy named Carter handed me the bright yellow Post-It note lined with the same clear packaging tape I'd seen in one of the bins I'd rummaged through. In Gordo's awful cursive, the note said:

Hi, my name is FLABBY.

I burst out laughing.

"He would," I mumbled to myself, pressing the adhesive to the top of the lockbox for a memento. Glancing up at the other merch guy, I shot him a smile. "Thanks for taking it off, otherwise it would have stayed on there all night."

Carter nodded and lifted his thin shoulders. "Anytime."

I smiled at him. And then, we just stared at each other for maybe ten seconds. I didn't know what else to say and neither did he.

"So… is this your first tour?" I finally asked, raising my voice a little so he could hear me as the band members onstage banged their equipment around in preparation for their set.

"No. This is my… twelfth one."

Twelfth? He looked fresh out of high school. "Whoa."

"I like touring," he explained simply. "It's good money, too."

He had me there. I grinned at him just as the band onstage started their soundcheck, making talking nearly impossible unless you were yelling. No thanks.

It was then that it hit me. I hadn't grabbed any earplugs. A dumbass. I was a dumbass. Not wearing earplugs for the duration of a concert was a newbie mistake. You were asking for severe hearing loss without them night after night; I'd never forgotten before.

Out of my peripheral vision, a hand waved. Carter held a balled-up fist out in my direction, a "take it" expression on his clean-shaven face. I got to my feet and opened my palm under his as he dropped two orange foam earplugs in it. I mouthed "thank you" to him along with a thumbs-up with my free hand.

Not even a minute after those puppies had gone in, the guitar player on the stage accidentally hit a note that screeched through the speakers, making everyone in the audience cringe. What followed was some of the longest twenty minutes of my life. I made it through two songs before I took my phone out and started to send Laila, my best friend, a text message before more Ghost Orchid fans approached the table, and I gestured my way through a few sales.

Once that band finished their set, my favorite three idiots on the planet went on. Eli brought pieces of his drum set onto the stage while Gordo and Mason carried their guitar and bass, along with their power amps, cabinets, pedals and cables. Gordo adjusted his microphone, and the band went through a quick soundcheck despite the earlier one they'd already gone through.

Ghost Orchid began playing.

The group had been together since freshman year, annoying everyone in the neighborhood when they practiced in our garage most days of the week. They'd driven me nuts back then, especially when I couldn't hear myself think while I was trying to study. But I'd faithfully gone to every show and dragged my friends along with me. Back then it would have been considered a good show if there were twenty people in the audience, even if they were all family members.

Eleven years later, here they were. Playing in

front of what had to easily be around nine hundred people cheering and screaming.

I couldn't help but smile through the entire forty-minute set.

Fifteen minutes after they went offstage, nothing could have prepared me for what came on.

I didn't believe in love at first sight.

Lust at first sight? Sure. I'd seen Michael Fassbender in *X-Men: First Class*. Hello.

But what happened fifteen minutes after Ghost Orchid got off the stage, after I'd screamed my throat raw cheering for my brother behind the drum kit, Gordo on guitar, and Mason on bass, was unexpected.

I fell in love with the voice in the dark. No joke, no exaggeration. It was a pure, raw love.

The stage had been cleared when the headlining band's sound guy scurried about one last time, checking on the two guitars, bass, a microphone and a drum kit that had been set up hours ago. When the lights darkened, the crowd that had swelled to fill the venue's capacity, at what I estimated to be over a thousand people by that point, went bananas. They were animals, and it was as scary as it was exciting. In the pitch-black auditorium, a wispy voice began singing softly, making the fans shriek even louder.

With a flash of elaborate, multicolored LED lights on a huge panel behind the massive drum kit, the stage lit up like fireworks in July, illuminating two guitar players who had come out of nowhere, a bass player and a drummer already onstage.

The lyrics and the song floated through the air in a whisper, the notes the singer was hitting unidentifiable, and it was over—in an emotional sense, that is.

While Gordo had a good, deep voice that was rounded and almost hoarse, the singer onstage was the complete opposite. His tone was slightly higher, breathy and incredibly strong, piercing through the air with its clarity and tone. And the range he had… good grief.

I could only see an outline of a man walking on the stage with an energy and charisma that every person in the audience including me, couldn't tear their eyes away from. I focused on everything going on: the explosion of yellows and reds on the LED panel behind all the music equipment, that beautiful melodic voice and the catchy instrumentals that flared after the opening verse.

It was love. Plain, easy, uncomplicated love.

Unfortunately for me, a ton of fans decided to come buy merchandise during the set. Trying to hustle about and sell as quickly as possible, I kept an eye and an ear out for the singer's dynamic presence. He was so good. Well, the entire band was. Catchy, a mix of pop rock, indie and prog—they were a genre of their own. During the quick glances I could take when I wasn't busy, the long, sinewy figure in black dress pants and a gray button-down shirt and tie moved and jumped in time with the rhythm constantly.

The next hour and half blew by in a mix of amazing music and sales. Watching the old pickle jar on the corner of the table fill up with bills kept me shooting smiles at all the people buying stuff, even though a part of me wanted them out of my face so I could enjoy the band playing.

During brief breaks between their set, the singer would talk to the crowd, thanking them for their presence and support, or he'd introduce the next song. At one point, a bra went airborne and smacked him in the arm in the middle of a song. The singer picked it up by the strap without missing a note and draped it over the microphone stand, letting it stay there for the remainder of the set.

It was a beautiful kind of insanity watching The Cloud Collision and their audience interact. It was easy, then, between the smiles I'd share with the guy "next door" named Carter, and the screaming, earplug-to-mouth chats I had with Ghost Orchid fans, to forget about why I was going to spend the next few months of my life with my three male best friends and eight strangers.

In the madness that ensued once the band finished their encore performance, in his swanky, tenor voice, the singer thanked everyone for coming out. I relished it all. The nonstop hustle to pull shirts out of one of the bins, while making sure I marked down every sale on the tally sheet correctly, was old and familiar. Before I knew it, the security in the venue was trying to usher fans out while Carter and I packed up the bins and tore down the racks. Usually the band would be trying to load the trailer at the same time so I wasn't too sure who was going to come and help me take the bins out. In the past, one of the idiots would come inside and help me carry everything.

Carter must have read my mind because he waved a hand as he rounded his table. "I'll get the dolly," he said.

Well, that explained a lot. Over the course of the concert, I'd seen the size of Carter's wrists and biceps. I was more muscular than he was and that wasn't saying much; I was a runner, not a weightlifter. By the amount of bins and boxes he had stashed on his side, there was no way he was going to be able to carry those things all the way to the bus. I finished tearing down Ghost Orchid's display while Carter came back. We helped each other carry our backbreaking bins onto the flatbed dolly before he took it upon himself to wheel them out while I pushed both of the tables onto their sides and folded the legs in.

"Flabby!" Eli hollered from across the empty auditorium, skipping around the employees busy mopping the floor. "You need help?"

I rolled my eyes and shook my head. "You're like thirty minutes too late. Carter and I are pretty much done."

The asshole had the nerve to snap his fingers as if he was disappointed he missed out. "I'll help you carry the tables so we can get going."

As we walked out, I told him how good the show had been and even mentioned how well he played. After more than ten years of drum lessons and an intense practice routine, he really was good. Eli had somehow managed to avoid doing any actual schoolwork in middle and high school using his drumming skills as an excuse with our parents. Copying my homework when I was asleep or copying whatever girl was dumb enough to share with him, helped too. Luckily for him, it paid off. My dance classes as a kid had only afforded me the opportunity to not look like a complete ass at prom.

Once we made it outside, Eli steered us toward the huge trailer hitched to the back of the bus. My shoulders began burning from carrying the two tables in an uncomfortable position. Four other men stood inside the massive trailer, trying to arrange the protective flight cases of musical equipment in an orderly manner. I recognized two of them from The Cloud Collision's performance and the third man was their sound guy, who had been checking their equipment before they'd played. Gordo's presence rounded out the four men packing the trailer.

"We're stopping at a travel center on the way out of here, so if you wanna shower, grab your shit from your suitcase," Eli said. He leaned toward me before taking a quick sniff and pulling back with a frown.

"Take a fucking shower. I'm begging you."

"Shut up," I laughed, taking a step away from him.

I wasn't going to lie. I had taken a whiff of my armpits when I'd been breaking down the tables and it hadn't been pleasant. Not at all. I had a feeling I was going to end up buying some men's deodorant soon or I'd steal Eli's. Whatever was easier.

Walking toward the front of the bus, I saw someone bent over at the hips, looking through the compartment where the suitcases were stashed. The bare upper body, shadow of dark hair and a full-sleeve tattoo caught my eye while I stopped behind him. "Mason."

He stopped moving around for a second before continuing to push things over in his endless search for his luggage.

"Mason."

Nothing.

"Mason, you dick," I said again.

When he laughed from inside at the same time that I took a step forward, I frowned. I would swear on my life it happened in slow motion. My foot went up on its own, eyeing the target—his ass—at the same time I spotted someone stepping out of the bus. It was another bare chest with a full-sleeve tattoo and a dark head of hair. And as the tip of my foot connected with the black dress pant-covered ass, I realized that it wasn't my supposed future husband, Mason, I had kicked in the ass.

Mase was the one coming out of the bus.

CHAPTER THREE

Mason—the bastard, asshole, prick, dick—that he is, doubled over in laughter when he saw my face turn bright red at the same time I squealed, "I'm so sorry!"

No!

No!

When my Mason-imposter-clone turned around with wide eyes and a gaping mouth, I wanted to fall on the floor and die. Or blame it on Eli. But I couldn't… because he wasn't anywhere near me.

"Did you just kick him in the ass?" Mason cackled, holding his stomach with the palms of his hands.

I was mortified, beyond mortified, so far into the realm of mortification I couldn't see the starting line; so it wasn't too strange when my face got so hot it rivaled the maximum heating temperature my straightening iron was capable of. I was one of those people who acted like a complete ass when I was nervous. According to Eli and Laila, I acted like a complete ass all of the time, but when I was nervous it reached epic proportions.

"It was an accident!" I told the guy in front of me. I couldn't look at him directly, not even close. Somehow, at some point, I'd linked my fingers together and covered my forehead with my palms without even noticing it. My eyes went wide as I dragged my hands down the sides of my face until I was cupping my cheeks. "I thought you were Mason" wheezed out of my mouth.

The real Mason only laughed harder from his spot ten feet away.

Out of nowhere, the guy in front of me, whose ass had just become friendly with my foot, laughed. It was a sweet, clear sound.

And it reminded me of the guy who had just finished singing.

No. Please, no. *Don't let it be him.*

"It's fine," the warm voice chuckled.

Grumbling deep in my chest, at myself more than anything, an awkward smile covered my face as I finally started to shift my gaze, because what the hell else was I supposed to do? "I'm really—"

Tattoos.

All I caught at first was the thick swirl that painted his pectoral, followed by the tattooed bands of black ink that striped the length of his arm. Then there were the tattoos on half of his neck, located on the same side as his full-sleeve tattoo. *Hello.* Yeah, after the first quick glance I realized his imposter only had one full-sleeve tattoo versus two. *Way to go, idiot.* My friend didn't have any tattoos on his chest, but it wasn't like I'd seen him from the front beforehand anyway.

My eyes strayed back to the hard, flat muscles that packed his chest and checkered abs, and then the narrow hips that flowed seamlessly into the slim-fitting black slacks that had paraded around the stage less than an hour before.

Fuck my life. It was him. The singer for the band. *Whyyyyyy.*

"I'm so sorry," I breathed out, forcing myself to drag my eyes all the way up. If I kept on looking at his bare chest any longer, I'd officially earn my Hussy Merit Badge.

The guy was smirking at me, folding long, muscular arms across his chest. It was right then that I asked myself if I'd died. He was... I don't think a proper word exists to describe the face above the body I'd been just short of ogling. Mason was a specimen worthy of all the attention he received, but this guy was... just... *oof.* Just as good looking in a completely different way, mainly because he wasn't my lifelong friend whose looks I'd become almost desensitized to.

Most importantly though: I had just kicked a hot guy, a stranger, a man I was going to be spending the next three months with, in the ass.

Again I asked myself why. Why. Why hadn't I just kept my foot to myself? All I wanted was to pull a turtle and hide in my shell.

As much as he looked like Mason from the neck down, their faces were very different. While Mase looked like a model for a cologne line, with his almost androgynous features that had gotten him called a pretty boy hundreds of times in the past, this other guy wasn't so classic. His bone structure was a little harsher and his eyes deeper set. They both had black hair but it was cut differently. This man's was shaved down at the sides, the top just a couple inches long, while my childhood friend's hair was a good length all over. But still, the faint resemblance was there.

"E! Flabby kicked Sacha in the ass!" Mason cried out, basically cackling as he bent over from how hard he was laughing.

I felt Eliza's heavy hand on my shoulder before I heard his snort. "Fucking Flabby," my brother laughed, slipping a heavy and sweaty arm over me. "Does that mean I don't have to introduce you after all?"

The man I could safely assume was Sacha—a guy, for the record, not the girl that the dumbass I'd shared a womb with led me to believe he was— shook his head before extending a hand out in my direction. "Sacha," he said after I dropped my hands from my forehead and took my outstretched palm in his. "It's nice to meet you, Flabby."

The elbow I brought up to jab Eli in the rib was an after thought. "It's Gaby, actually," I tried to correct Sacha AKA hello-how-are-you-sexy, shaking the warm hand a little longer than I needed to. "It's nice to meet you, too."

Eli snorted again. "Don't listen to her, her name's Flabby, man."

Sacha smiled again—a pull of sensual lips and straight white teeth—before he dropped his hand, eyeing Eli and me. "Are you two—?" He drew a straight, horizontal line in the air between us.

"Eww…" Eli and I both groaned out at the same time, shaking our heads quickly. It didn't make us pull apart, though.

"I just barfed in my mouth," Eli gagged. "This is my baby sister."

The slow nod that Sacha gave us in return made it seem like he wasn't entirely sure whether Eli was lying or not. Smart guy. You could never trust Eli Anthony Barreto. Ever.

"We're twins," I explained. "I'm filling in for Zeke the rest of the tour." When Sacha quirked an eyebrow—a very dark one on his smooth, almost pale skin—I remembered that tonight would only be the bands' fourth tour date together. He might not know who exactly Zeke was. "He was the old merch guy."

By the way he nodded and snapped his fingers, it was obvious he hadn't known Zeke's name. "Right."

Someone yelled from inside the bus, telling us to hurry up. Eli squeezed my shoulder. "Grab your stuff, stinky, and I'll meet you inside."

My stuff. The stranger's butt. Ugh. My face got all hot again, and I found myself smiling nervously.

I nodded and watched my brother and Mason retreat into the bus, leaving me with the man whose ass I'd just kicked. He smiled and gestured toward the open compartment. "I'll get your bag if you promise not to kick me again."

Throwing my hands up in surrender, I shook my head. "No ass-kicking, I swear." I couldn't help but choke a little before adding, "I won't call you a dick again either." What was wrong with me? What I'd done was bad enough, and then calling him—well, Mason really—a dick was the cherry on a shit sundae.

He tipped his head back and laughed, the sound uninhibited and wonderful. "Deal." A moment later, he was asking me which suitcase was mine prior to pulling it out. I started yanking out clean underwear, a shirt and sweatpants while he finally managed to retrieve the big black suitcase he'd been rummaging through when the ass-kicking incident happened.

Dread knotted my stomach as I remembered what I'd done. Humiliated, I zipped up my suitcase and shoved it back inside the compartment. "Your show was amazing," I squeaked out, keeping my eyes toward the trailer hitched up to the bus. "I wasn't sure what to expect, but it was great."

"Thank you," he murmured softly. It was impossible not to absorb the tone of his voice when he thanked me. There wasn't a hint of superiority or conceitedness in it at all. He sounded pretty genuine. "First time?" he asked.

"Yes." I found myself toeing the ground, feeling awkward. "I hadn't heard of you guys before tonight." For a split second, I thought about telling him that I thought his voice was beautiful, but I didn't want to sound like a suck-up.

"I'm glad you liked it." Sacha zipped up his suitcase, holding a bundle of clothes to his chest. He turned to look at me, a kind smile on his five o'clock-shadowed face. "Did you get what you needed?" I nodded and followed after him silently before he waved me into the bus first with the towel in his hand. He winked. "Don't want you to forget about our deal so soon."

Ugh. I was never going to live this down.

"I'm really, really sorry," I insisted, still feeling horrible as I climbed up the steps into the bus. My face was getting red all over again.

Why the hell had I done that? My subconscious answered: *because you really believed he was Mason, and if it had been, no one would have thought twice.*

"Ladies and gentlemen!" my twin bellowed the moment I stepped a foot past the curtain and into the living space.

I stopped like an idiot, or better yet, like a deer caught in the headlights. Eli clapped loudly until the

40

low buzzing of chatter inside stopped. I couldn't help but notice that there really weren't any ladies on the bus besides me—unless you counted Mason and Gordo—and I knew my twin well enough to accept that he wouldn't refer to me as a female. "Everyone, now that the asshole we kicked off the bus earlier today is gone, I want to introduce y'all to our newest addition."

He reached out to grab my hand, throwing up both our arms like I'd won a boxing match. "This is my baby sister, Gaby. She'll be with us for the next few months." He shook my hand, still in mid-air. "Flabby, say hi," he instructed me as if I was a little kid. Fucking Eli.

I grinned nervously at the five new faces looking me intently, and let my brother wave my hand for me. "Hi, guys."

A low murmur of multiple "Hi" greetings were spoken while I yanked my hand away from Eli's grasp. At that very instant a hand landed on the small of my back. Turning my head over my shoulder just barely, I saw that it was the only person it could have been—Sacha. Up close and under the decent lighting of the bus, his skin looked clear and a little glossy from how sweaty he'd become during the concert. He really was good-looking, and a little taller than Mase as well.

"Don't bend over in front of her. She likes to kick people in the ass," he laughed, giving me a sly smile before shimmying his way around us to walk to the back of the bus.

I groaned to myself while Eli and Mason laughed like it was the funniest thing they'd ever heard. Minutes later, I found myself squished between Mase and Gordo while the bus driver steered the traveling hotel and trailer to where I'd been informed we'd be showering that night. The couches on either side of the bus were long, but it seemed like everyone was crammed into that front area closest to the door, including the narrow kitchen and bathroom. After the mini tour Eliza had given me hours before, I knew that past the door by the bathroom were the twelve bunks we'd be sleeping in, and at the farthest end of the bus was a small room with a U-shaped couch along the walls.

Mason introduced me to two of the guys from The Cloud Collision, a big muscular guy named Julian and a lanky one named Isaiah that I recognized as being the guitar players for the band. I caught Sacha standing in the kitchen, drinking something steaming from a ceramic mug, still half-naked. Still unbelievably hot, if not hotter than before. The yellow lighting in the bus did wonders for the lean cut of his chest and for his narrow hips with their cut oblique muscles, all of which then did wonders for my panties—I mean my hormones.

"You should wear shirts like that more often."

I slid my gaze over to Mason, whose entire side was pressed against mine. I shouldn't have been as surprised to see his eyes on my "shirt," and by my shirt, I really meant my breasts. The tank top had begun to ride low enough so that the edge of my lavender bra was visible. Instead of replying, I frowned and tugged my shirt up enough so at least the girls weren't hanging out so much… since half an inch of boobage was apparently too much to begin with.

When I met Mason's gaze again he was smirking, looking entirely too pleased with himself. "I can still see them."

"No way." I rolled my eyes, trying not to be too self-conscious. It wasn't like I didn't get the same reaction from him every time we saw each other over the last three years. Well, it was the same reaction from just about every guy that wasn't my brothers or dad. I'd spent ten years of my life trying to keep people's attentions away from my chest and now, after everything, I still didn't want people looking there for longer than a quick glance.

Gordo nudged me from his spot on my other side. With hair so dark it was almost blue, a beard that was so thick and wiry it could pass as pubic hair and his naturally dark skin tone even tanner than normal, his face was one of the most familiar things in my life. "Are we going to be on the same team together?"

"The same team…?" And then I remembered what team he was talking about. "Hell, no." No, no, no, *no*.

"Oh come on, Flabs," Gordo insisted, his dark,

nearly pupil-less eyes narrowing.

Mason, who was still leaning forward, rested his forearm on my knee. "You're already trying to choose teams, asshole?"

"I'm not playing, so he can't be trying to choose teams." I made sure to look both of them in the eye so that they would know I wasn't playing around. I wasn't going to play ever again.

"You have to play," the man whose real name was Luis Alberto claimed. "It's our tradition."

What it really was, was a yearly tradition of humiliation and physical pain. I shook my head at Gordo. "It's not happening, Gordis."

"You're playing," Mason reiterated, eyeing my boobs again in a gesture that was intentionally meant to annoy the shit out of me. Really, I didn't think he liked my breasts *that* much, it wasn't like I had a D cup size, much less the Double-D size he usually salivated over, but irritating me was definitely at the top of his list of things he enjoyed. "I need those puppies on my team."

I smiled at him sweetly.

There was a time, immediately after my surgery, that I had really tried to get him to quit making comments about my chest. For about six months straight he'd revolved between calling me Hooters and Twin Peaks. In typical Mason fashion, me complaining only made him do it more often. So I stopped telling him anything because I knew he really he did it to get a rise out of me. Instead I just began handling it differently.

I reached under his arm to twist his nipple, an easy thing to do because he was shirtless. "I'm not playing and if I was, I definitely wouldn't be playing on your team, jackass," I said, turning the beady pink nip sharply as he leaned away with a grimace and an ugly "*Nooooo!*"

The words had barely left my mouth when the bus pulled into a brightly lit travel center with a gas station, twenty-four-hour restaurant and restroom facilities. Eli tossed me a towel before everyone except Mason, who had his arms crossed over his bare chest like that would protect him from me, piled out of the bus with our belongings and headed inside. It was then that I realized I'd forgotten to bring shampoo and soap with me from home. I groaned and peeked inside, realizing that if I went into the showers after I paid, I couldn't come back out for free.

I waited outside the men's bathroom for a few minutes, hoping Eliza or Gordo would hurry up and come out so I could borrow their soap and shampoo. Less than ten minutes later, the smacking of flip-flops on the floor got louder and louder.

But it wasn't Eli or Gordo coming out.

It was Mason 2.0 in basketball shorts, a T-shirt and flip-flops, making his way out with a backpack over his shoulder and black dress shoes hanging off his fingers. He smiled genuinely the instant he saw me standing there looking like a hobo asking for a handout.

"Everything okay?" he asked, making me feel like a total mess.

I nodded, my face immediately flushing at the memory that I'd kicked this poor guy in the ass just minutes ago. I cleared my throat when my ears got hot too. "Yeah, I'm just waiting for Eli."

Sacha raised a dark eyebrow, giving me a chance to take in the smoky, nearly transparent gray of his eyes. He glanced at the clothes in my hands before pursing his lips. "Did you forget your soap?"

I was a little hesitant to admit it, but I did, fighting the urge to rub at my ears. "Yeah."

He smiled.

"I want to borrow his," I explained.

Sacha didn't hesitate a second. "Here," he said as soon as I'd finished talking. Thrusting a bottle of some 3-in-1 shampoo, conditioner and body wash at me, he shrugged. "It isn't for girls—"

This man had another thing coming to him if he thought I cared what I used for toiletries. I'd even be willing to share with Mason—the disgusting ass of the year—if I knew he didn't borrow someone else's on the rare occasion he decided to shower. I took the bottle from him and smiled, the embarrassment that had been swimming along my spine earlier from what I'd done disappearing at his kindness. "I have invisible balls, it's cool," I told him like I would have told Eli… and immediately regretted it. It wasn't like I thought we were flirting or anything, and the fact I definitely wasn't looking my best didn't escape me, but that didn't mean I wanted him to think of me as… well, I didn't know what. Unattractive, I guess? Manly? It didn't help that I was still mortified over the kicking incident.

Sacha laughed that cute, bright laugh that made me smile despite everything. "All right, invisi-balls. Have at it."

"Thanks. I owe you," I said a little more shyly than I normally would have. Walking backward toward the entrance to the bathroom at his command, I gave him another awkward wave I immediately regretted. Good God, I was on a roll and needed to quit while I was ahead.

He simply nodded at me before I ran into the area where the showers were. I rushed through mine as quickly as I could, not caring in the least that I smelled like a clean guy. As soon as I finished drying off and dressing, I hustled out feeling way better than before. Luckily, my brother was waiting for me right outside the restrooms.

"I was gonna give you five more minutes before I went in there," he warned. "I thought somebody kidnapped you." Those green eyes so much like mine, peered at my feet, earning me a frown. "Where are your flip-flops, and why are you holding men's shampoo?" A smirk covered his mouth a second later. "You finally decided to go through with that surgery, huh?"

I snorted and socked him right in the stomach as I

walked by him. "That Sacha guy let me borrow his shampoo because I didn't bring any and you were taking forever douching in there." I hiked my thumb toward the restroom as Eli rubbed where I'd nailed him. "And I didn't bring flip-flops with me. Why?"

He grimaced, eyeing my feet again. "You stepped on that floor without shoes on?" When I nodded in response, he shuddered. I glanced at his feet to see he was wearing a pair of rubber thong flip-flops. "You better pray tonight."

When Eli gives you a reason to pray, you better pray. I just didn't know what I was supposed to be praying for. Back when we toured in Old Pepe, we always showered in hotel rooms. This travel-center-showering was a new experience for me.

We made our way into the bus, where I handed Sacha his shampoo back with a "thank you" while my brother made us three packets of ramen noodles to share, sixty-forty style with pieces of grilled deli chicken thrown in. He promised to take me to buy groceries, cheap sandals and shampoo the next day. As soon as we finished eating, I walked by another member of The Cloud Collision, who had some Middle Eastern ancestry in him. He was on the phone, so I raised my hand in a wave and he did the same back before I followed Eli into the bunk area.

"Mine is that one," my brother said, pointing at a top bunk with its curtain pulled all the way back. There were twelve total bunks with crimson curtains, three stacked on top of each other, six on one side of the hallway, six on the other. He then pointed at the bottom bunk, below where Gordo was sleeping at the top. "Zeke slept on that one. It's yours now. I put my backup sheets on there for you earlier."

I immediately thought of Zeke drooling over the bed—or worse. Yuck.

"Thanks."

It was then that the curtain on the bunk above mine slid open, and I fist-pumped in my brain because sane people don't do that in real life. Sacha looked at me from his spot in the bed above the one I'd be taking. "Hi, neighbor."

CHAPTER FOUR

The next two weeks went by before I could ask what the hell I had gotten myself into.

One day we were in Boston and the next thing I knew, we'd gone through Florida, Alabama, Indiana, Ohio, Michigan, Illinois and Missouri. The routing made absolutely no sense but it never had. Booking agents usually didn't care how long the drives were between dates as long as they scored bands the highest guarantee possible.

A handful of fans had asked me so far, "How awesome is it to be on tour with them?"

With them. *Them.* Eli, Mason, Gordo, Sacha, Isaiah, Julian, Miles, Mateo, Carter, Freddy and Bryce. Ghost Orchid, the members of The Cloud Collision, their merch guy, front of house slash tour manager and their lighting guy.

I showered in gas stations. I had some kind of

fungus thing on the bottom of my toes from the one bloody shower I took without flip-flops. I'd eaten more pizza over the course of two weeks than I had in my entire life.

On top of all of that, summertime was a vengeful, rude bitch that didn't care about your comfort.

I sweated all the time. I stunk at the end of every night. I spent countless hours rolling around in a bus from town to town, and I hung out in venues for nine hours a day minimum. I lived in a bus with ten men who were like every other twenty-something-year-old guys in the world. They farted, they burped, some of them had smelly feet, some of them didn't brush their teeth enough, or the only thing that really drove me nuts: some didn't cover their food in the microwave.

This life wasn't glamorous. At. All.

On the other hand, to be fair, no group of people made me crack up like they did. It had been a long time since my stomach had cramped from how hard I laughed at or with them.

Eli and I had been acting more like conjoined twins than fraternal twins, as if we were trying to make up for all the time we'd spent apart over the last few years. I'd met a lot of twins in my life; some were close and others couldn't stand each other. We weren't like that, though.

Before high school, we'd been inseparable. Two peas in a pod. Each other's security blanket. My mom liked to tell people that when we were toddlers, sometimes she would walk into a room to find us on opposite sides, totally silent, as if we were having some kind of telepathic conversation. What she wouldn't tell everyone was that if she stood there long enough, we'd randomly start laughing our butts off for no apparent reason, which in turn scared the crap out of her. Yeah, I didn't blame her.

Even during high school, there was never any doubt that we were still more than best friends. We didn't spend as much time together by that point, but it didn't matter. I'd woken up plenty of times in high school with Eli on my bed, his feet way too close to my face as he slept on top of the comforter with his own blanket over him. We might not have come from the same egg, but no one knew me, understood me or made me feel as comfortable as my brother did.

I guess I hadn't realized how much I'd missed having him around over the years as we'd each gone our own ways.

When we were in the bus, I was constantly with Mason, Gordo or Carter. When we were off of it, Eliza went everywhere with me. I'd spoken to the guys with The Cloud Collision a few times, but we hadn't been anything more than friendly in passing. They were all always on their phones or their computers, so I didn't take it personally. We had three months ahead of us to get to know each other; it wasn't a big deal.

I was enjoying my time, and that was all that

really mattered.

And besides the couple of times a venue had been playing one of Brandon's songs between sets, I hadn't thought about killing that piece of crap once.

~

"Shouldn't you go eat something soon?"

I finished setting the last cymbal on the stand and tightened it down, glancing at my brother over the top of his drum kit. He was closing the travel cases since we were mostly done setting up his stuff. We usually tag-teamed putting together his drum kit to save time; I'd done it so many times I could do it with my eyes closed. Most of the time he helped me bring most of the merch into the venue right after we got to wherever the tour package was playing, and then I'd help the guys set up their equipment to do soundcheck since it wasn't like I had anything better to do. There was usually so much time before doors opened that I'd rather keep busy than sit around.

But today we'd gotten to Little Rock almost three hours late, thanks to a major accident. Now, everything and everyone was running behind schedule, including soundcheck.

I pulled my phone out of my pocket and took a peek at the clock with a wince. Doors were opening in two hours. "Damn it, I didn't know it was so late."

Eli turned to look at me over his shoulder from where he was kneeling. He raised his eyebrows. "I mean, you could go without a meal or two—"

He should have known better than to talk shit when he was on his knees. I shoved him.

"Whore!" he cried as toppled over like a chopped-down tree.

"Your mother," I muttered as I kept right on walking past him to sit on the edge of the stage before hopping down. By the time I was back on my feet, Eli was again on his knees, glaring over in my direction. "I'm going to grab something to eat."

He was still giving me a dirty look when he said, "I can't go with you. We gotta do soundcheck."

I shrugged both shoulders; it wasn't like I didn't already know that. "Okay. I'll be back."

He blinked. And then he simply raised a fist with his middle finger fully extended.

I stuck my tongue out and went to look for the only other person that might be able to go out to eat with me.

The venue hadn't provided us with food and instead had opted to give the tour members buy-out money to fend for ourselves. The TCC tour manager, who was also doing sound for them and Ghost Orchid, had walked around a few minutes earlier and passed out everyone's cash. For once in his life, Eli had been right. If I waited any longer to go on the hunt for food, I wouldn't make it back in time for the start of the show. According to Mason, I had something called a job. Like I didn't know what the hell that was.

In no time, I found my new friend Carter, the TCC merch guy, sitting outside of the trailer surrounded by a huge pile of boxes. Clenching a clipboard, he shot me a tight smile, scratching at one of the legs of the knee-length cutoff skinny jeans he'd put on that day.

"Still busy?" I asked, looking at the cardboard boxes that had been waiting outside when the bus had rolled in an hour ago.

Carter let out this long sigh straight from his belly. His normally passive face was clearly exasperated. Even his ponytail was limp. We'd gotten to know each other over the hours of free time we shared at the merch tables. He wasn't much of a talker unless you prodded him, but he was hardworking and kind. Mostly though, when the people I usually spent time with were louder than howler monkeys, I really enjoyed his company. "I'm only halfway done with inventory, and I need to get it all done before the show." He shot me a flat look that drew his lip piercing tight. "By myself."

I grimaced, knowing all too well how frustrated he got with The Cloud Collision guys. They all basically left him on his own to do everything. According to Carter, it was pretty normal for bands at their level to feel entitled to do that, but I still pointed at him and said "ha" when he'd first told me. It was occasions like those that made me appreciate playing the sister card on Eli.

"I was going to get food, but I can help you if you

want," I almost told him how I'd wanted him to go with me, but what was the point in rubbing the situation in? The poor guy was stuck working outside in a trailer with next to zero air circulation, counting T-shirts. That sucked.

The corners of his mouth tilted up just enough in what could be considered a sad, resigned smile. "Don't worry about it. I can get it done; go get something to eat," he said.

I didn't think he was trying to do reverse psychology on me, but I'd spent too much time with people who did. "Are you sure?"

He nodded.

"Are you really, really sure?"

Carter's smile tilted up a little more. "I'm positive."

I felt bad but... "Want me to bring you something?" I offered.

His brown eyes lit up and he finally smiled, suddenly forgetting how irritated he'd been a minute before. "Please." He began fishing through his back pocket for his wallet. Handing me a twenty-dollar bill, he paused and made a thoughtful face. "Who's going with you?"

Even though we'd only met two weeks ago, apparently he was going to worry about me. I liked it. "No one. My brother's busy, and I can't wait any longer if I want to get back here before doors open. I'll just walk somewhere close by, no big deal."

"Gaby." Carter's long face was already telling me

he thought my idea was terrible. He was only twenty-one, but he was such a mature guy, he seemed older.

"Yes?"

He shook his head. "This isn't the best side of town. Find someone to go with you," he insisted.

"There's no one." There wasn't. The guys were more than likely about to start soundchecking.

Carter scratched at his chin, he hadn't shaved in a couple of days and though he wasn't capable of growing in a beard—his words, not mine—he had some stubble going on. "TCC isn't doing anything. They're around here somewhere."

I almost crossed my eyes. "I don't want to bother them. Honest. I can go by myself."

Just as he opened his mouth to argue, someone cut in.

"Where do you want to go?" The voice I'd come to recognize as Sacha's, from our handful of conversations and from listening to him talk to the audience every night over the last fourteen days, floated through the air.

I turned to find him in his black basketball shorts, ASICS running shoes and a T-shirt. He didn't even look like the same man who went onstage every night in a button-down shirt and dress pants with his hair gelled or moussed into perfect place. I thought he looked even better when he wasn't in that persona, but that was probably just me.

We'd only spoken a couple of times about how

the most recent show went, and he still seemed like a really nice guy who brought up nearly every day how I'd kicked him in the ass. Twice already he'd walked by me with his hands splayed out behind him like he was protecting his butt cheeks from attack. I also tended to go to bed before he did, so it wasn't like we got to gossip in our bunks or anything.

"I want to go get something to eat," I explained a little awkwardly, eyeing the piano keys I'd come to recognize were tattooed on his neck.

He smiled easily, making those black and skin color keys tighten. "I'll go with you."

What? "You will?" We'd spoken a few times but really, it hadn't been more than ten or fifteen minutes total. There was also the fact that every time I spoke to him, I thought about how we'd met and it made my insides cringe. We were friendly but we weren't friends exactly. At least, not like how Carter and I were. We were at the point where I knew he liked Dr. Pepper and sour candy, disliked the same music I did, and he had a girlfriend who hated him going on tour. You knew you were friends with someone when they grew comfortable enough around you to let you read psycho text messages from the person they were dating.

"Yeah," the tall man agreed with a dip of his chin.

I didn't miss the pleased look Carter had on his face.

Just like that, Sacha and I were walking across the

parking lot at his guidance while I pocketed my younger companion's twenty dollars.

The black-haired man walking alongside me looked down from over his shoulder, his eyes such a pristine shade of ash they were nearly a clear blue. "Are you craving anything?"

I scrunched up my face. "As long as we aren't eating pizza again, I'm game."

Sacha laughed, his gaze still on me. "It's the worst, isn't it?"

There was a reason almost everyone on the tour crossed their fingers and toes that pizza wouldn't be the meal of choice wherever we happened to be that day. Venues were responsible for providing the tour package with food every night. Each band had a rider, or a list of requests, of items they wanted. It wasn't anything crazy like all red Skittles, Oreos without the filling or anything. Ghost Orchid's rider consisted of a case of Dr. Pepper, some kind of vodka, a large bag of barbecue chips, a sandwich tray and Oreos. They were a vision of health.

Apart from their riders, the two bands were either supposed to have dinner provided or if that wasn't available, each person on the tour was given a certain amount of money to supply their own food. The problem was that when the venues did have dinner available, more often than not, it consisted of pizza. Not the good kind of pizza either, at least so far, but the kind that had cheese that tasted like the off-brand individually packed crap, suspicious-looking pepperoni, and no sauce. It made me want to puke.

If you thought there was a food you could eat every day without getting tired of it, you were lying to yourself. Everything got old.

"I haven't had pizza on tour in almost ten years," Sacha continued. "There's a Thai place about five blocks away…" He trailed off and I didn't miss the hopeful look he shot me.

He gave me the type of innocent smile as he raked a hand through the hair at the top of his head that reached into your soul like a puppy's lick could. "I swear it's great—"

"Okay." I shrugged up at him, meeting his gaze. "I'm game."

Sacha paused for a second. His six-foot-one-ish height towered over my five-two. "You don't mind?" He asked it so hopefully even if I hadn't wanted to eat Thai, I would have still done it to keep the grin on his face.

The question earned him a snort. "Food is food."

He hitched a shoulder up, the sleeve of his T-shirt sliding back to reveal more of the thick, black bands of his tattoo that went from wrist to shoulder. "That was easy."

I didn't even miss a beat before blurting out, "I'm easy."

I slammed my mouth closed. And I blinked. Then I stopped blinking all together and just stared.

If it wouldn't have been for Sacha stopping again

and turning to look down at me, his mouth pulled tight at the corners, I wouldn't have known he'd heard what I said. His dark eyebrows were halfway to his hairline. His eyes were huge as they flicked to the side.

I narrowed my eyes at him, heat crawling up my neck. "Don't... say... anything."

He coughed the fakest, most forced cough in the history of coughs. "Say anything about what?" he asked slowly, hesitantly. He even added a little questioning shrug at the end.

It was a lot harder than it seemed to not laugh. "Exactly." I shrugged back at him, wanting to kick myself in the ass for having such a big mouth.

Sacha gave me a low-lidded glance before visibly pursing his lips together and coughing one more time. I didn't miss the way his mouth pulled up into a tiny, short smile before he managed to wipe it off his features altogether. Sacha scratched at the bridge of his nose and glanced at me out of the corner of his eyes again before finally grinding out, "You're sure you're fine with eating that, then?"

At that point, it wasn't like I could say no even if I wanted to. I nodded, which earned me another smile from him.

We walked a block in silence, each of us giving the other a few curious if not a bit awkward glances, like neither one of us could think of what to say until Sacha broke the silence. "Are you having fun on tour?" he asked as we came to the first crosswalk.

"Yeah, besides dealing with the heat." It had been hot in every single venue we'd been in over the last two weeks, and me complaining about it said something; I'd lived in Texas my entire life.

He groaned. "It never gets easier to handle, trust me. I've been touring six months out of the year for the last ten and it hasn't gotten any better than that first summer the band spent in a van with no AC." Sacha shuddered at the memory, and I think I could have exploded at his cuteness.

"Ten years?" I asked him, looking up. He didn't look twenty-one or even twenty-five but he didn't look over thirty either. His face was still relatively unlined, except for these deep laugh lines on the sides of his mouth. How old was he?

"Ten years in August," he reiterated. Sacha turned to look at me with those clear gray eyes. "Is this your first tour?"

I snorted as a dozen memories of the five years I spent on and off with Ghost Orchid blew through my brain in the span of a second. "No. I used to leave with Eli, but about two years ago, I decided to go to school full time and stopped. This whole bus thing is new to me. We used to get around in a van," I summed it up, leaving out a few details that didn't seem important.

Sacha grinned at me slyly. "I guessed that when you didn't take shoes into the showers with you." He looked down at my tennis shoes and waggled his eyebrows. "I heard you got fungus from it."

I wasn't even going to bother trying to guess which asshole spilled the beans on my foot problem. It could have been any of them. Pricks. I'm not sure where the action came from, but I bumped his arm with my own. He was so much taller than me, I was hitting closer to his elbow than his shoulder. "I don't want to talk about it."

And just like that, he was nudging me back with a big grin on his face. The corners of his deep-set eyes crinkled. "I bet your skin looks raw, huh?"

Just at his mention of raw-looking skin, that crease between the balls of my feet and toes started doing this weird itchy-burn sensation I'd become familiar with. I'd been smothering my feet in cream for two weeks and changing my socks twice a day per Mason's instructions. What no one tells you in those athlete's foot commercials is how long those creams take to work.

"Sucking ass" just barely began to describe the experience.

"It happens to everyone," Sacha added when I didn't respond immediately.

I snickered, remembering the last time I'd heard those exact same words. "I'm pretty sure Mason has said the same thing about having The Clap."

The laugh that exploded out of him in response was so unexpected that I jumped a little at first.

It was so infectious it made me snort.

"That is... that's absolutely not true," Sacha snickered in between bouts of clear, loud sounds of enjoyment.

"That's Mase for you."

He slapped a long-fingered hand over his mouth as he laughed. "I thought I heard him say last week something like 'it's all fun and games until someone gets crabs.' But I thought I imagined it."

Oh god. I burst out laughing just as loud as he'd been going at it a few moments ago. "Yeah, that sounds like something he would say."

His head tipped down enough so that our eyes met. Very intently, he asked, "Is he serious or does —"

"Oh, he's serious most of the time. I went with him to a free clinic when we were seniors because he'd gotten crabs from a girl on the drill team." It had been our secret until he got drunk one night and told everyone willing to listen about his previously itchy privates. I'm pretty sure the staff had assumed I'd given them to him but who knows.

Sacha's mouth gaped in amusement for a second before he stopped abruptly in front of a storefront. "The restaurant is in here." He gestured toward a glass door to our right, opening it and waving me inside.

The small restaurant was homey with burgundy walls, round black vinyl-covered tables and a counter directly in front of the door with a menu mounted above it, written in chalk. There wasn't anyone in line and I took my time looking at the various items listed for that day. Sacha stood next to me, deciding what to get as well. After a couple of minutes, an older lady in an apron and a hairnet made her way out of the kitchen and took our orders.

With our drinks in hand—some tea drink for Sacha and water for me—we took a seat at one of the empty picnic tables.

My unexpected eating buddy took a sip of the yellow drink in a clear red cup and raised his eyebrows. "You've known Mason for a long time then?"

"I've known him and Gordo since I was five. We all grew up together," I explained. "They're like the brothers I never wanted."

He smiled. "But you and Eli really are brother and sister?"

"Oh yeah. He likes to say he shoved me out of the way to come out first."

Sacha blinked. "No shit? You two really are twins?"

I knew he hadn't believed me! Then again, most people didn't. My brother had more physical traits in common with Bigfoot than he did with me. "Yup."

He still made a face that said he wasn't entirely convinced. "But he's twice your size."

Twice my size. I could give him a hug for being such a terrific liar. "Yeah. I'm pretty sure he tried to eat me in the womb."

Sacha burst out laughing again, making the lightly tanned skin on his face glow. His complexion was so clear it almost radiated; it made him even more attractive. "Jesus. They said you were funny, but I didn't believe them."

Funny Gaby. I smiled and held back the sigh creeping around in my chest. How many times had I friend-zoned myself by joking around? A dozen? It wasn't even that I tried to be funny; I just grew up around smart-asses. You either learned to adapt or you died. Well you wouldn't really die, but you'd get verbally eaten alive by the folks that were supposed to love you; apparently they just loved making fun of you an equal amount. My siblings and the two idiots could find the smallest things to tease me over.

I pushed all five of them out of my head and smiled at the man sitting across from me. That longer hair at the top of his head and the shorter buzz cut along the sides were really flattering even when he didn't have it perfectly in place.

"What about you and your band? Have you been together a long time?" I asked.

"Isaiah—do you know Isaiah?" he asked, and I nodded. "Isaiah and I have known each other since middle school. We started playing together in high school, doing some cover band stuff, and then we met Julian. He's the big guy," Sacha explained, like I didn't know the names of the people I'd been on tour with for the last two weeks, but I didn't correct him. "The three of us started TCC when we were sixteen, and then slowly added members over the years."

Was asking his age considered flirting? I wasn't positive, but I decided that I didn't care. "So you've been together…?"

"Eleven years."

He was twenty-seven. Huh. That sounded about right. I whistled. "That's a long time."

"It is." He shrugged. "But I wouldn't want to do anything else… most of the time."

I smiled at him, his words hitting home. I had no idea what I wanted to do with my life now that I was done with school. The only thing I did know was what I didn't want. That didn't exactly help any, but I guess that's what this tour was for. To give me some time to figure things out.

What was the rush, right?

The same woman who had worked the counter came over with our order. Sacha's bowl was shades of green and brown while mine was a red curry dish. It must have been a sign of how hungry we both were that neither one of us said a word as we tore into our food. When I finished before him, I got up and ordered Carter the same thing I'd gotten.

He smiled at me from behind the rim of his glass as he finished off the last of his tea when I sat back down. "Thanks for being a good sport and eating here. I usually have to pay one of the guys to come with me."

"Why? They don't like Thai?" I asked. I wasn't a picky eater. You could put a vegan dish in front of me, or fried chicken, and it was going to get devoured.

"Not at all. None of them like spicy food," he

said, setting the glass on the table.

"But not all of the food is spicy…"

He blinked. "I know."

"Babies," I muttered, a little unsure how he'd handle me calling his friends that.

He beamed at me. "Huge babies."

"They don't know what good food is."

"Right? If it were up to them, we'd get fast food every day. All I'm asking for is a little Chipotle at least."

"Chipotle's high class." I smiled.

He lifted a shoulder. "I'm a high-class kind of guy."

Yeah, I couldn't hold the joke back despite how inappropriate it might be considering we didn't know each other well. But screw it. Kicking him in the ass was like jumping ahead three months in a friendship. "You know who else is high class? Hookers. Hookers are high class."

Sacha didn't even miss a beat. He blinked those clear gray eyes at me and asked very seriously, "Do you know from experience?"

Was he seriously calling me a hooker on our first expedition out?

By the smile on his face, I would say yes. Yes, he was.

I think I'd found a friend.

CHAPTER FIVE

Where are you today?

I had to refer to the list of dates we had on the wall. Every day felt like a near repeat of the one before, and after the first week of The Rhythm & Chord Tour, I'd lost track of what city was next. Since there usually wasn't enough time to go sightseeing, one place looked just like the rest; maybe one venue was nicer than the other but since that was really all we got to see, it didn't make a difference.

I texted Laila back:

New Orleans.

A minute later, I got a response from her:

> Don't flash anyone. It isn't Mardi Gras no matter what anyone tells you.

> That's all you, hooker.

She knew exactly what I was referring to: her twenty-second birthday, Mardi Gras in Galveston, two in the morning. If I tried, I could still hear my screams at her flashing an unsuspecting crowd after one too many Long Island Iced Teas.

> OMG. STFU. If I don't remember it, it didn't happen.

I'd helped her change out her catheter more than once in the past, so it wasn't like I was horrified or anything remotely close by her bare boobs. But still. I felt obligated to give her a hard time over it.

> I wish I didn't :P

LOL. I'm about to teach a class. LY.

Have fun. Love you too.

I set my cell back down and sighed.

It was only about three in the afternoon, and we'd been parked at the venue for close to two hours. My brother, Mason and a couple of the guys in The Cloud Collision had decided to go "hang out with some friends in town." In reality what this meant was that they were doing something they couldn't do in the bus.

As much as I loved Eli and Mason, I hated seeing them high or drunk, so I opted out of tagging along. Instead I plastered myself in the back room of the bus with one of the books I'd stuffed in my bag before leaving home. I was on *The Boy in the Striped Pajamas* this week. Even though I was having fun spending time with my three idiots, still getting to know Carter, and sucking at Mario Kart when I played against Mason in the morning, the whole living-with-ten-other-people-thing was difficult.

Even though I missed my parents, Rafe, Gil, their kids and Laila, I missed the lumpy bed at my parent's house even more. It was the things I took for granted, like showering without shoes and hanging out in my room half-naked, that I missed the hell out of.

But I knew it wasn't any of those things that were really bothering me right then. I was a little bit aggravated with Eli for still doing the kind of shit that had gotten him in trouble in the past. We'd agreed before I joined the tour that he'd tone down the drinking as one of my conditions. He'd been holding onto his end of the bargain so far, but I wasn't betting on the streak continuing today.

There was also the chance I wasn't giving him enough credit, but I wasn't going to hold my breath.

"Can I come in?" a soft voice asked, the door to the back room cracking open.

"Of course," I answered, recognizing Sacha's low timbre on the other side.

His dark head of hair peeked in before he swung the door open. "I wasn't sure if you were doing something." His eyes flickered around the room cautiously before he plopped down onto the length of the couch opposite the one I was sitting on.

"I'm just reading. What are you up to?" I asked, eyeing the lean muscles beneath the tank he was wearing. Sacha had on shorts that were riding up his thighs, showing off what seemed like meters of nearly pale skin beneath dark leg hair. He was also wearing a scuffed pair of running shoes, not his normal set of clean black ones.

He scratched at the short hair on the side of his

head. "I'm waiting for Julian to come back," he explained, referring to the guitar player for his band.

"Didn't he go with my brother?" I swore I saw him get into the taxi with the other morons. If that was the case, there was no way the group was coming back anytime soon. Much less coming back sober. I wouldn't bet any money on the chances of them being able to stand on two feet when they returned.

Now that I thought about it, I should probably try and have my camera app open on my phone just in case something ridiculous happened during the show.

"He said he was only going for a couple of hours."

I hated people telling me that they would do something and then not. Disappointment was bitter. It wasn't like it was my fault Julian had taken off, but I felt bad he'd left Sacha hanging. I would much rather take someone being blunt and hurting my feelings in the process, than let me down.

I sighed before breaking it to him. "They're not coming back soon."

Those translucent gray eyes that bordered on sky blue blinked in my direction.

"Were you planning on doing something?" I asked.

"We were going to go for a run," he explained with a shrug. "It isn't the end of the world."

Slipping my legs off the couch to plant my feet on

MARIANA ZAPATA

the floor, I raised my eyebrows at him as I set my book on the seat next to me. "I'll go with you if you want."

"Yeah?"

"Yeah." I nodded. "I used to run track."

"You did?" He made it sound like the idea was preposterous. Rude. It may or may not have been because I complained about the bus being too far from the venue back in Birmingham when I was moving merch bins, but in my defense, it had been raining.

Either way, I couldn't help but scratch my forehead before amending my answer. "In high school."

Sacha flashed those perfect white teeth on display. "What you're meaning to tell me is that you're pretty much a professional track star?"

I made sure to keep my features even as I nodded. "Exactly."

His eyes widened playfully. "I'm pretty fast," he warned.

"We'll see how fast you are," I said and immediately felt a little weird for inviting myself. "But only if you want the company. If you don't, I completely understand." And I might cry a little, but I kept that part to myself.

Running was one of the only things I'd kept up with over my life, especially in the time since my breakup; I made time for it a few days a week on the treadmill or when I didn't mix it up with the

Stairmaster. I figured my ass and thighs could thank me when I was forty. But it had been more than two weeks since the last time I'd made an effort to put my legs to use.

But Sacha was the same person who took me accidentally kicking him in the ass like a champ, and had gone out to eat with me so I wouldn't go by myself. He hadn't given me the smallest impression that he was anything but a nice guy. "Come with me," he said, already waving me forward.

"Are you sure?" I asked,

The singer rolled his eyes. "I'll wait for you outside."

"Let me change," I looked at the thin sweatpants I'd had on since the night before, "and find sunblock. I'll be quick."

Sacha tipped his head to the side. "I have some —"

Of course he did, with that clear skin that somehow managed not to be pasty.

"—get dressed and I'll grab it."

Grabbing semi-clean shorts and a sports bra from my backpack, I changed into them as quickly as I could and threw my T-shirt back on. I also grabbed some cash that ended up getting stuffed under a bra strap. If we were going to suffer from heat exhaustion, I was stopping to get something to eat at some point afterward; he just didn't know it yet. After letting Gordo know that I was leaving since he was the only one who hadn't taken off, I found Sacha waiting outside of the bus with a small tube of aloe vera-based sunblock in his hand that he tossed over.

I'd like to say that I focused on putting the sunblock on my own body, but I didn't. Correction: I couldn't.

When Sacha peeled off his shirt and began smothering the cream onto his freckle-spotted shoulders, arms, chest, neck and even the shell of his ears... I was entranced. It was like seeing a meteor shower. Or having candy for the first time after you'd tried going on a diet.

Except way more magnificent.

Sacha even had these small light-brown moles dotting his abs and back. He had a trim, muscular frame that I admired from the corner of my eye every time he was shirtless. He had the body of those swimmers that Laila and I groaned over every four years, and he was putting lotion all over himself. It was better than watching porn. Hell, better than watching Robby Lingus porn. Good grief. I finished slathering myself sloppily while he put his shirt back on.

"Do you know where you want to go run or are we figuring it out as we go?" I asked as I bent over to stretch my hamstrings.

"East. There's usually less people in that direction," Sacha said.

I hummed like I knew what direction east was without searching out the sun and chirped up an, "okay."

Five minutes later, we were both stretched and ready to go. He tipped his head to the left with a playful smile and asked, "Are you ready, Jesse Owens?"

I snorted. "I was born ready."

Sacha snickered before nudging my forearm with the back of his hand.

We started off with a slow jog to warm up for what seemed about a mile. He tempered his step so that he wasn't twenty feet in front of me considering his legs were almost a foot longer. He shot me a glance over his shoulder once and I nodded. Then we took off.

He wasn't kidding when he said he was fast. He really was. He had the stride of a long distance runner but the potential, restrained speed of someone who possibly ran sprints for fun. Luckily for me, I'd been a sprinter in high school, so it didn't kill me too much to catch up with him.

At first.

One mile.

Two miles.

Three, four and five miles.

My lungs started to get tight.

Six miles.

Seven miles.

My calves began cramping.

By the eighth mile, I was struggling with my breathing and my cramps passed "aching" and went straight to "cramping."

Honestly, I had no clue where we were, much less where the venue was. What made it worse was that Sacha looked sweaty but not nearly winded enough. What the hell was he? A cyborg?

It was probably another half a mile before I decided... that was it. I couldn't keep going without dying.

"Hey, hey," I wheezed as I came to a stop.

It took a second for him to slow down and turn around. His face was pink, perspiration dotting along his temples. "Are you all right?" he asked sounding just slightly out of breath.

I was sucking in air through my nose raggedly as I nodded, pressing a hand flat to the part of my stomach that was the most deprived of air. "I can't... I need to stop."

Those gray-blue eyes swept over me for a second as I stood there, one hand on my hip, the other over my belly button. My loose shorts were clinging to my legs and my shirt was definitely plastered to me. Then there were the pit stains. I didn't even want to think about the pit stains and the damp spots on my shorts. Whatever. Who cared. Sacha saw me after the show was over every night when my mascara was runny and I smelled like week-old socks. Plus, it wasn't like I was trying to get a boyfriend or anything.

"I don't... run... for distance," I panted.

He took a big visible inhale through his nose and nodded. "That's okay."

"You… can keep…" I didn't think I was out of shape but apparently, I was. "You can keep going," I rushed out. "I can get back by myself."

Sacha shot me a look as he moved closer to the side of the building to get out of pedestrian traffic. "No. I'll walk back with you."

"Walk back?" That came out sounding as panicked as it was meant to. "The entire way?"

"Yeah."

All I could do was stare at him. Did he not know I was on the cusp of death?

The sheer terror on my face earned me a laugh from the tall man. "I'm fucking with you. Let's walk a little, and then we'll catch a ride back."

"If… I… wasn't so…"

He grinned, cutting my threat off. "Let's go. Are you hungry?"

I nodded.

"Want to get something to eat?"

I managed to nod again.

We walked for almost twenty minutes in silence, taking our time. I was still too out of breath to talk so I focused on calming down. Eventually Sacha hailed a cab and we both climbed in.

It was the choked laugh from the other side of the backseat that had me turning my attention toward him. He was sitting with his back to the corner, a smug smile on his face. "Are you gonna live?"

"Barely."

His eyebrows went up as he smiled even wider.

"You went a lot further than I thought you would."

Wait a second.

"Julian and I usually only do five miles," he explained.

I stared at him; there could be no other way to describe what I did besides maybe referring to it as a glare. I sat there with my chest expanding and retracting while still trying to recuperate, processing what the hell had just come out of his mouth. "Are you joking?"

He shook his head.

I kept my gaze on him for a brief second longer, extended my middle finger against my thigh in plain view and turned to face out the window.

Sacha laughed.

Okay, I smiled. A little but not much.

Neither one of us said a word until he instructed the driver to drop us off at the end of a block that didn't look particularly familiar. "This place is pretty good," he noted pointing at a decorated glass door as we climbed out of the cab after fighting over how to pay the fee.

I still wasn't on speaking terms with him, though I'd caught my breath and followed him inside the restaurant, which wasn't as cool as I would have liked. The smell of roasted chicken made my stomach growl.

He raised his eyebrows at me from the other side of the table after a waitress brought two glasses of water over. "Still mad at me?" he asked.

I narrowed my eyes at him as I took a sip, taking in how he still looked relatively put together and not at all like he'd tackled eight miles half an hour ago. "You run marathons, don't you?"

"Nah." He put the glass to his lips, but I could still catch a glimpse of the corners of his mouth. "Half-marathons."

Half-marathons. "Thanks for telling me that now," I snorted.

"You didn't look winded, and I figured you would tell me when you couldn't go any further."

I grumbled and shook my head just as the waitress came by to take our order.

She had barely left when the dark-haired man sitting across from me asked, "So, are you on summer break?"

"Nope, I finished school about a month ago. I just... haven't been able to find a job yet."

Saying it out loud was weird. I knew it wasn't unusual to not find a job right after graduating. Half the people that had finished school at the same time as I did were struggling to land one. It didn't help that the degree I'd gotten wasn't exactly bursting with employment opportunities either, but it still made me feel a little raw. When I first told my family I wanted to study history, the first thing out of my dad's mouth had been, "What are you going to do with that degree? Why don't you do accounting? Or nursing?"

It was a sore subject, to say the least.

Sacha asked what I studied and I told him.

"Are you planning on teaching?" he asked.

"No…" For a second, I thought about telling him that I wanted to do research or work at a museum, or *something*. But I couldn't. I'd gotten my degree in it because I liked learning about history; that was all. "I don't really know, to be honest. I'd rather not teach, though. I think I'd be pretty terrible at it. The kids would probably laugh at me if I tried to be firm about something."

Sacha nodded solemnly. "You'll find something, just give it some time. I used to get shit thrown at me onstage when I was younger; if I would have given up every time I heard 'you suck' being screamed at me, who knows where I'd be right now."

This guy used to get stuff thrown at him? He had one of the best pitches and ranges I'd ever heard and he killed his performance every night. "You really had people throw things at you?"

He snickered. "Yeah. The first time was at a high school talent show. This asshole threw a Coke bottle at me and by the end of the song, I'd pretty much been booed offstage. I only stayed on because I'm stubborn."

I had to slap my hand over my mouth so that I wouldn't laugh. "If it makes you feel any better, one time, I had a dance recital when I was probably seven, and I threw up all over the stage. I was so nervous. I remember telling my mom I didn't want to do it but she made me anyway." There was footage of it too that someone in the family dug out every couple of years when they needed a laugh.

Sacha covered the lower half of his face with the bottom of his T-shirt, and closed his eyes simultaneously. His shoulders shook with restraint. "What did you do?"

"I cried my eyes out," I laughed.

"I fell off the stage once," he added, smiling huge.

"You didn't!"

"I did. I just walked right off of it—"

Yeah, I burst out laughing, picturing it.

"—It's the single most embarrassing moment of my life onstage," he said right before tossing his head back and laughing his ass off. "That's what I get for not paying attention."

It was the "onstage" that got me. Once I got myself under control, I raised my eyebrows at him. "And *off*stage?"

He ran a hand through the loose hair at the top of his head and closed one single, gray eye. "I had to take a crap into a plastic bag once. The bathroom on the bus was clogged, and we were in the middle of nowhere during a thunderstorm."

For the record, there's no way in hell you can hold back a laugh when someone tells you that they took a crap in a plastic bag. Especially not when the story is told in a matter-of-fact voice. It wasn't possible. On the other hand, it didn't help that Sacha's face took 'striking' and 'handsome' to a different level. I've always figured that people in the upper echelon of beauty—sans Mason—were incapable of doing the ridiculous things that semi-attractive people like myself do; like fart or burp in front of others, smell or have stinky shit. But apparently Sacha, whose last name I still didn't know, was the anomaly.

He'd taken a crap in a plastic bag.

When I had to hunch over and press my forehead against the vinegar-and-lemon smelling table, Sacha poked me in the shoulder. "When you gotta go, *you gotta go*," he said with another laugh that didn't hold a lick of embarrassment in it.

I looked up to see that his grin was telling me a story about an incredibly handsome man that didn't take himself too seriously.

It was like finding a four-leaf clover.

"Did I gross you out?" he asked when I didn't immediately respond.

I scowled and shook my head. "Are you kidding me? Have you talked to Eli?" He nodded, but there was no way he'd interacted with him enough to not be fully aware of my brother's mental impairment. I couldn't see Eli talking to someone for longer than twenty minutes without making some rude and/or inappropriate comment.

"There's four of us kids in our family, and Eli and I used to have to ride the bus to school together in the morning, so we had to wake up earlier than everyone else. He'd make sure to get up before me every single day for years so that he could purposely leave me 'presents' in the toilet," I snickered. "You can bring on the brown pickles with me anytime."

Sacha chuckled, his index and middle finger pressing against his temple. "What you're trying to say is that Eli's to blame for making you this way?"

"Hey!" I cried. I wasn't sure whether to be insulted or not.

"I mean it in a good way. You're beautiful—" I'm not sure how I managed not to fall off my chair. "—And you don't have a problem talking to me about The Clap, diarrhea and vomiting. You're fun, Gaby."

My ears went red. Too worried about saying something dumb, I held out my hands at my sides in a "what can I say" gesture.

Sacha smiled and opened his mouth right before the sound of loud beeping coming from his pocket tore his attention away from the table. Pulling his phone out, he asked me to hold on before answering the call. "Hey... I just finished going for a run... yeah... I'm about to eat." He shot me a smile when he glanced up. "I'll see you soon... I miss you too... okay... bye."

The chances that the person he was talking to on the other end was a family member could be pretty high, but my gut feeling said otherwise. Someone that good-looking had to have a significant other in the picture.

"Girlfriend?" my mouth spewed without a second thought.

He simply shook his head, and I missed the way

one of his eyelids lowered in denial. "Old friend."

Friend?

Sure. I almost snickered. I'd grown up alongside three boys, two of them becoming manwhores right before my eyes. I understood how they worded their sentences. An "old friend" that you told you "missed" was more than likely an ex-girlfriend or an ex-buddy you used to do things with that you probably wanted to do more things with in the future. Sacha didn't seem to be like my brother or Mase, but still. An "old friend" was an "old friend."

It wasn't my business, though, so I pushed Sacha's friend and conversation out of my head and smiled over at him, close-mouthed.

He only smiled back at me. The silence settled around our shoulders in a weird fit.

"Are you ready to go?" I asked him.

Sacha nodded and we got up, making our way out. Neither one of us spoke up as we walked back to the venue. I didn't know what to say, and I guess he didn't either. We smiled at each other a couple of times when we'd stop at a corner and wait to cross the street.

I heard the guys before I saw them. We were rounding the nearest building to the venue when Eli's booming laugh mixed with two other boisterous ones. Immediately, I felt this big ball of dread form in my stomach, my shoulders tightening.

I knew Eli inside and out. I could recognize his laugh when he thought something was kind of funny, really funny, not funny at all but he was attempting to be nice, and I was all too aware of the texture his laugh held when he'd either drank too much or smoked pot. And while he was a grown man and I had no right to tell him what to do, there was a reason why one of the conditions I made before coming on tour with him was that he kept the drinking, and by default the partying, to a minimum. Especially when I was going to have to put up with his crap afterward.

Eli laughed again, and I took a deep breath, already palming my chest for the tour laminate I had on a lanyard so I could go into the building through the front instead of the back door.

Sacha's hand nudged my arm. "You all right?" he asked when I looked up at him.

"Yeah, I'm fine." I forced a smile onto my face when Mason's voice pierced through the air.

He frowned. "You don't look fine."

We were getting closer and closer to the corner of the block where I would either go in through the front or walk a few more feet and make my way to the back where the bus and trailer were. "I just..." I blew out a shaky breath I hadn't realized I was holding and shook my head as if I wanted to shake off this entire situation with the idiots. "I don't like being around Eli when he's on something." I had a sudden flashback of the night that had finally been my breaking point, when I decided I didn't want to keep going out with GO. I'd been so pissed that I didn't speak to any of them for months after that tour ended.

"He's that bad?" Sacha asked.

I lifted up a shoulder, fighting off the anxiety trying to make a home in my chest. "Not *bad*, he just… says really stupid stuff. They all do." Hurtful, personal stuff that none of them had any business sharing.

He nodded as if he understood, and maybe he did. Most people had that one friend that turned into a wrecking ball once they had drunk too much or done something else that changed their personalities or thinking process.

When we got to the corner in front of the venue, I touched his side. "I'm going in through the front."

Sacha tipped his head down. "I should start getting dressed so I can begin warming up." He flashed me that bright white smile one more time. "If you ever want to go running again, let me know. You're a better running buddy than Julian."

I couldn't help but smile and nod.

The dark slashes of his eyebrows went up. "I'll even let you off easy with only seven miles next time if you want."

I fought the urge to push him away like I would have if he were one of my demons and snorted instead before backing away. "Go put your make-up on and warm up, Celine."

I could still hear my brother laughing when I entered the venue less than a minute later.

CHAPTER SIX

I knew something was going on when I found my twin and Gordo smiling sweetly over at me from their spots in the living space of the bus. The fact that all of the members of TCC and their crew were surrounding them didn't help any. I usually didn't sleep in, but a stuffy nose had kept me up. I grabbed a plastic cup from the cabinet over the microwave and then fished out one of the gallon jugs of water that were stashed in the lower kitchenette cabinets, all while watching the group closely and trying to listen to what the hell they were talking about.

The scent of bullshit was strong in the bus.

"I'm in," Julian said first, looking at Freddy. "You?"

"I'm in," the TCC tour manager agreed.

What exactly were they *in* for?

Slowly but surely, the rest of the members sitting

on the couches all nodded or verbally agreed to whatever it was they were talking about. I slowly slid in to the only seat available across from Carter, which was one of the two chairs belonging to the small table in the kitchen.

"Carter, what about you?" Eli asked the man I spent a lot of time with.

Still in his pajamas and looking only slightly more awake than me, he shrugged. He had his hair down and parted down the middle, the ends brushing his thin shoulders. "I'll play."

I'll play?

Oh *no*.

"How many people is that, then?" Gordo asked. I didn't miss the smug look he threw my way after he asked.

"Eleven," one of the TCC guys answered.

Gordo let out the most exaggerated sigh I'd ever heard in my life, even going as far as to make his eyes go wide. "*E-lev-en?* That's an odd number. We can't have an odd amount of players in the game."

This motherfucker.

My brother turned to look at me and shrugged his shoulders. "Flabs, I guess that means you have to play."

"The hell that means I have to play. I'm not playing," I said in a careful, controlled voice before taking a too casual sip of water, making sure to keep eye contact with him.

"You have to," Eli repeated.

"Odd numbers," Gordo piped in like a little shit.

I shook my head, making sure to keep my features even. If I was careful and really nonchalant about it, my chances of getting out of this were higher. Eli knew too easily how to pull my strings at the right time, and I sure as hell wasn't going there. "It's not happening."

Carter shot me a curious look. "You don't like to play?"

I glared at the two idiots when I answered. "I don't like to play with *them*."

The scoff that came out of Eli and Gordo was impossible to miss.

"C'mon. Don't be a party pooper," my twin muttered.

"I'm not being a party pooper. I just don't feel like getting the crap beat out of me," I explained to them. Glancing back at Carter, I sighed. "Every time we've played in the past, I end up getting hurt. My lip got busted last time, and I'm pretty sure my tailbone was fractured. I also had this bruise bigger than Eli's head—"

"We need you on a team," Gordo insisted.

I just shook my head.

"Quit being a baby and play. Gordo promises not to knee you again, don't you, Gordo?" Eli asked.

The dark-skinned man next to him nodded almost enthusiastically.

They were so full of shit.

"I promise not to knee you either," Eli amended

next. "We can be on the same team if it makes you happy."

Well, that was part of the problem when we'd played in the past too. I wasn't usually a competitive person—a game was just a game and if it made someone's day to win, so be it—but when it came to doing things against Eli, that was a whole different story. We'd been competing for attention, love, food and just about everything else from the moment we'd been born. Arguing and fighting over stuff was second nature for us.

But still. The memory of my bloody busted lip was still fresh in my mind two years later. Before that there had been a visit to the dentist for a new filling, a bloody nose, a sprained back, an ankle I couldn't walk on for two weeks... the list was endless.

Then there was whatever crap the losing team had to go through. It was the whole purpose behind playing: to embarrass the loser.

"I'll tell Mason not to purposely trip you anymore," Eli finally added with an expectant look on his face. "Deal?"

I hesitated. Along with the bloody lip in the past, there had also been a black eye, an elbow to the center of my chest...

"It'll be fun," Bryce, the TCC light guy, suggested.

～

It'll be fun, they said.

Just a friendly game, they said.

Well, they were fucking liars. All eleven of them.

Two hours after I was finally guilt-tripped into agreeing to play, the bus made a detour on the journey from the parking lot it had sat overnight to the park it dropped us off at. The drive had only been four hours long, and in the middle of the night, we arrived in Houston, Texas. Unfortunately, there was more than enough time to kill before we needed to get to the venue, so I couldn't use that as an excuse as to why we couldn't play. We all piled out, dressed in shorts, T-shirts and an array of tennis shoes.

A few of us, including me, were busy putting sunblock on when Gordo went around passing out pieces of torn-out notebook paper folded into small pieces. There were two papers with stars on them for whoever won team-captain duties and nine pieces of paper with either a "1" or a "2" on them, the deciding factor for which team each person ended up on. We'd already agreed in the bus that Eli and I would be on the same team, so I would choose a paper for the both of us.

That part of it went fine. There was no problem.

Julian ended up the captain of the "1" team and Freddy, the tour manager/sound guy or front of house, got the other piece of paper to command the "2" team.

Julian, Mason, Sacha, Bryce, Isaiah and Mateo were on team one.

Freddy, Carter, Gordo, Miles, Eli and I were on team two.

Still, no problem.

Then they decided they were going to go over ideas as to what the losing team had to do as their punishment. This wasn't unusual, either; every time I'd played their stupid Soccer Death Match in the past, there had been some bet going on. It had always been something humiliating, so my standards weren't too high. I was pretty much ready for something involving bare asses or being someone's slave for a day.

And then Mason's dumb-dumb-dumb-ass blurted out, "Losing team has to shave their heads."

Uhh…

"YES!" I wasn't sure who first yelled out their agreement, but I wish I had so I knew who to nut-punch.

"No!" I threw my arms out and looked around at the group of idiots who weren't screaming at how dumb his idea was. "Are you shitting me?"

They weren't.

Why almost all of them thought this would be an excellent punishment for the losing team was beyond me.

"Majority wins," they said. Carter and I seemed to be the only people against it, and that was more than likely because we had the most hair out of everyone on tour by far. Everyone was so confident that the team they were on would win, they didn't mind taking a risk.

All the boys were too scared to accidentally break a finger that it was decided there wouldn't be goalkeepers on either team. Fine, all right.

We split up on opposite sides, team 1 deciding that they'd go shirtless so everyone would know who was on what team. I may have ogled the guys that were in great shape—Mason, Julian and Sacha— a little more than necessary, but I had no regrets. We started playing.

The first fifteen minutes were good. We were all being respectful of each other, happy kicking the ball back and forth as we jogged up and down the field. I exchanged smiles with a few of the guys on the other team as I tried to defend against them in case the soccer ball made its way over in their direction.

Good. Fine. It was going well.

Then Mason, who had played varsity soccer in high school, scored a goal for his team and it was like a small animal had been slaughtered off the coast of South Africa. The sharks came out to play and the aggressiveness on the field multiplied.

My resolution to win didn't come out of nowhere. There was no way in hell my head was getting shaved, and I was going to do whatever I needed to do to make that happen. Apart from running track, I'd played two years of soccer in high school, plus on and off with these guys most of my life.

In the fifteen minutes after that initial friendly beginning, each player began hustling back and forth across the grass. When Sacha got ahold of the ball and it seemed like everyone else on my team had their fingers up their butts instead of trying to keep up, I started going after him to steal it away. His legs were longer than mine but apparently no one on my team knew what cardio was, and I got stuck chasing after him. Sacha started putting his hand in my face when I got too close, and I had to whack it out of the way each time he did it.

"Stop hogging the ball!" I yelled at him, trying to futilely steal it.

"If it bothers you so much, get it away from me, then," he teased before passing it to Mateo.

Between the thirty to forty-five minute mark, every player started running as fast as they could. No one wanted to be on the team that lost. The ball travelled from player to player faster than it would have normally. I was getting desperate. Sweaty as hell, thanks to the humidity and the sun that didn't seem to care I'd put on sunscreen not that long ago, I started digging my shoulder into Sacha's side to throw him off balance every time the ball got too close to him. The idea of losing my hair—because I sure as hell didn't have the bone structure to pull off a shaved head—made the beast come out.

The ball came straight at us and I tripped him. Then I tripped him again and again.

And again.

As I ran with the ball at the tip of my left foot, I heard Sacha in the background calling out, "What the hell? That was a yellow card!"

"Suck it up, Sassy!" I hollered back at him.

And then, it really got out of control.

Even though we were laughing our asses off, I started elbowing him—somewhat gently—in the ribs, and I kicked him in the thigh another time. Not-so-innocent-Sacha pulled the end of my ponytail and would use his shoulder to push me away.

The last time I managed to trip him, he grabbed the back of my shirt to pull me down too. Unfortunately, his weight made me fall down hip first, bumping the shit out of my side as I landed next to him, still laughing. Sacha was smart enough to hop up and take off running to get the stray ball.

My shirt was soaked in sweat, my arms and neck ached with sun exposure, and I had dirt all over me. So, it wouldn't have been a big deal when Sacha dipped into our half-limping, lazy-running time by hip-checking me so hard I lost my balance and fell on the ground once more.

At the last minute, before the one-hour timer went off on Gordo's phone, Carter scored a goal that I didn't completely understand.

What I did understand was what happened next. Tied, and with everyone on the verge of dying because only three of us ran on a slightly regular basis, no one wanted to add more time to the clock. So the game went to penalty kicks.

Penalty kicks.

It was Eli that said, "One of you merch losers and

Bryce should be goalies. I vote you do it, Flabs."

I was sitting on the grass when I tipped my head back and scowled at him. "Excuse me?"

"You three are the only people that can risk getting hurt," he said like that made total sense.

I guess it sort of did. Did I really want to leave the fate of my scalp to Carter's goalkeeping skills? Not really.

"Does that work?" Julian asked.

I nodded, thinking of my bra-length hair. "Fine." I glanced at Carter and widened my eyes. "I'll do it."

"Can I go first? We can alternate," Bryce, the TCC lighting guy, asked without even putting up a fight.

I rubbed the back of my sunburnt neck and nodded. "Go for it."

Eli went first and missed. Cold dread went down my spine, and I had to bury my head between my hands when I realized how screwed we were.

I got to my feet and said a prayer under my breath while I marched toward the net-less, lopsided goal.

"Don't let me down, Flabby!" Eli yelled.

I shook my head at him as I walked backward, mouthing and pointing "This is your fault." I was going to end up bald. I fucking knew it.

The first person to come up to do a penalty kick was Mason. He winked at me as he got into position. "I love you, Flabbers, but this ball is going in."

"Shut up and kick." I waved him on, ready to get this over with.

"Your wish is my command, my bride." He then blew me a kiss.

I only just barely managed to deflect the ball a half-inch with the tips of my fingers when he nailed it. His team was screaming from the sidelines while Eli and Gordo hollered at me for missing. Dickwads.

Freddy on our team went next and managed to score. Nerves stirred my stomach, but I pushed them aside and focused on what I needed to do as I walked back to the goal.

Next on the opposing team was Julian, who didn't talk any shit and simply went for the shot. The ball went up high and I was too short to reach it.

"Goddamnit! Why aren't you taller?" Eli's bellow came out at the same time I yelled in frustration with myself.

Miles, on my team, went last and scored.

Carter came up behind me and squeezed my shoulder. "Gaby, I won't be mad at you if we lose."

I patted his hand and smiled sadly. "Thanks, remember you said that later on, okay?"

The last player to kick was…

Sacha.

He smiled over at me as he took a dozen steps away from the ball and got into position. "You ready to lose?"

I crossed my eyes and nodded. "Bring it on, Sassy Pants."

He raised an eyebrow before smiling huge. "You said it," he replied, getting into position.

Sacha's goal: getting the soccer ball into the goal.

The ball's goal: breaking my damn face.

It wasn't *really* Sacha's fault the ball curved at the last minute and that my hands were in the air when the ball got intimate with my chin.

I'd never gotten into a real fight before, and I suddenly realized why. Getting hit in the face was… not cool. At. All. I know for a fact I squealed, grabbed my chin with both hands and possibly wailed, *"Why would you do that to me?"* before collapsing to my knees on the ground.

Sacha—as I quickly learned—was a jackass. I could hear him laughing as he ran up to me, getting down on his knees somewhere close by. The hysterical laughs coming from my brother and his friends were background noise I couldn't ignore.

"Gaby, oh my God, I'm so fucking sorry!" Sacha's unmistakable voice was at my ear, both horrified and amused at the same time somehow. "Are you okay?" A hand landed on top of mine and another clasped the back of my head.

"No!" It was the truth.

My face.

My face was broken.

He had the nerve to laugh harder, wiggling closer so that his bare, dirty knees pressed against my own bare, dirty knees. "I'm so sorry."

Him practically giggling didn't make his apology totally believable.

I'm not sure how long we sat there, me squeezing

my eyes closed with my chin between my hands, Sacha holding my hands in one of his and the back of my head with his other. It took everything in me not to cry because seriously, my chin was throbbing so bad my brain hurt. Even my teeth felt rattled. When the urge to cry finally managed to pass, I blinked up to see those translucent eyes peering at me in concern. Isaiah, Carter and Gordo were standing behind the man who had just kicked a ball at my face, visibly worried.

"Let me see," Sacha said gently, prying my hand away one digit at a time. Once he prodded with his fingers and made me wince, he let his hand fall to his lap.

"Are you all right?" Carter asked, palms cupping his knees, his face pink and distressed.

I nodded over at him, still holding my face and telling myself grown women didn't cry from humiliation.

"Are you sure?"

I nodded again.

He didn't look convinced. "I'll go grab you some ice, okay?"

Yeah, I didn't hold back my sniffle. "Thank you, Carter."

Sacha patted my back. "Let's go sit over there, Princess." He stood up first, holding his hand out for me to take. After pulling me up, he led me toward one of the benches nearby. "I'm sorry," he kept repeating, smiling more than he should have, but I could tell he felt remorseful at least. If it had been either of my brothers who'd done that, they would have been on the floor dying laughing.

Out of my peripheral vision, I could see Eli arguing with Mason and Julian. By the time we made it to the bench, my brother was gesturing wildly and pointing in my direction.

"Are you sure you're okay?" the man sitting next to me asked, his entire body angled toward mine.

I went back to holding my face. "Yeah. I'm okay."

"Positive?"

I nodded.

"I'm not joking. Are you sure?"

I gave him the same answer. I was fine. Mostly.

The corners of his mouth pulled down just slightly, his eyes roaming my cheeks and jaw. After a minute of silence, he smiled gently at me, his dark eyebrows slightly rising. "That was pretty fun though, wasn't it?"

"Yeah," I sniffed again, "until you tried to break my jaw."

"It was an accident!" He frowned, reaching over to put his hand on the top of my head gently. "I am so fucking sorry, I can't tell you how shitty I feel. Do you want to hit me?"

I shook my head.

The corners of his mouth twitched up again. He was still fighting laughing no matter how bad he felt. "I really do feel awful. I can't believe that happened."

I made sure he watched me as I rolled my eyes but smiled afterward. "It's all right. It isn't the first time I've had a ball kicked at my face."

Sacha had this expression that was a perfect mix of a frown and a smile. "If it makes you feel any better, you kicked my ass a few times on the field." We both looked down at him. Brown and green splotches covered his shirt and shorts, and I swear there was even some mud tangled in his leg hairs. If he weren't so handsome, he'd look like a homeless person. "You play pretty fucking dirty."

I just shrugged at him. What was the point in denying it?

"Will you forgive me?"

"No." I frowned and blinked at him from the corner of my eye. "Yes."

Carter came jogging up to us a moment later with an ice-filled plastic baggy. "Here you go," he said, handing it over.

I thanked him and took the bag; my hand had barely left my chin when both men hissed. I froze in place. "Is it that bad?"

Carter said "no" at the same time Sacha grimaced and tipped his chin down just enough for it to be counted as a nod.

He didn't even try to bullshit me. The "yes" that came out of his mouth was loud and clear.

Ah, hell.

CHAPTER SEVEN

I saw the cinnamon roll first—of course I did—before I saw the long masculine finger pushing the small plastic plate my way. I didn't need to look up to know whom it belonged to. I closed my book slowly —this week I was on *The Story of Edgar Sawtelle*—and set it down on the merch table.

Sacha stood there, still in his everyday clothes though the doors were about to be opened any minute. His face was contrite and hopeful and way too sweet-looking to stay pissed off at. "Eli told me they were your favorite," he offered.

Cinnamon rolls weren't my favorite; they were Eli's. I was more of a glazed donut kind of girl. But I didn't tell him that, and I didn't make a face either, mostly because it would hurt too much. The truth was, everything ached, but it was mostly my face that bothered me. I once worked with a woman that never smiled because she said she didn't want to waste the collagen in her face. Back then I didn't understand how the hell that even seemed like a sensible idea but with the way my face was hurting... yeah, I was keeping my facial expressions to a minimum.

"Thank you," I thanked him like a mature woman that wasn't hung up on the huge bruise on her jaw because I really wasn't. It'd been a total accident. Plus, it wasn't like I hadn't had worse done to me.

My brand-spanking-new haircut, on the other hand, was a different story.

Subconsciously, my fingers began reaching up to touch the section of my head directly above my right ear, until my brain reminded them that there wasn't hair there anymore. There was fuzz. There was fucking fuzz where my long hair used to be. Twenty-four hours ago, my merch buddy had taken clippers to part of my head.

Carter had become the chosen one because I trusted that he wouldn't have an "accident" that would lead the clippers across my eyebrows. Also, obviously, because he had experience shaving the back of his own head like a boss every week. In the time since the haircut, I'd rationalized that there were worse things in the world than having a third of your head shaved. Like root canals. Cancer. Charley horses in the middle of the night.

I'd gotten off easy.

The words that had come out of Julian's mouth once we'd all piled back into the tour bus after my near facial reconstruction went along the lines of, "We decided you don't have to shave all of your head since... you know," he pointed in my direction, tracing the shape of a circle with his index finger.

He said it as if I should have gotten down on my knees and kissed their feet for making such an accommodation.

Then he added, "Are you sure you don't need to go to the hospital?"

Realistically, I wasn't surprised. If anything, I was surprised they weren't going to make me *V For Vendetta* my scalp. Fortunately, Eli wasn't on the opposing team, otherwise I'm sure he would have petitioned for them to shave off my eyebrows too... maybe even said something about shaving my upper lip to be a smart-ass. When they buzzed off all of Carter's beautiful, long black hair without him batting an eyelash, I tried to calm myself down. Eli grumbled through his entire cut but did it. Then the rest of the guys went through with their shaves with only minor complaints.

Was I going to be the one to pitch a fit when everyone else went through with it? Nope.

All I heard when I sat down in the chair they'd set up outside the venue, the clippers connected to an extension cable, was Mason asking Carter, "Can you do this?"

To which Carter answered, "Yup." Then he

paused before asking, "Gaby, do you want a mirror so you can see what I'm doing?"

"No." Absolutely not. "Just remember how much I like you, okay? Remember."

And that was how I ended up with what they jokingly called the 'Viking Girl' haircut. One-third of my hair was shaved off above one ear, from my forehead to all the way to the back of my neck. All in all, it could have been worse but still. I wasn't that vain but a girl's hair—whether it's short or if it's long —is her hair. I hadn't suffered through those painful hair ties with balls at the ends as a kid for nothing. Plus, it wasn't as if I had fine cheekbones and a long face. On a good day, someone might say it was heart-shaped.

"I'm really—" Sacha started again, bringing me out of my memory of the day before.

"It's fine," I assured him, watching his face as his eyes went over the big reddish-purple spot that reached from my chin to halfway up my jawline on the way to my ear.

He frowned but plopped his butt onto the corner of the white table, hands on his lap. "I feel like shit." Those gray eyes drifted down to my chin, the wince on his face was more than noticeable.

"I promise it's okay. I know it was an accident." I smiled at him that was all lips, ignoring the twinge of pain coming from my jaw. "You aren't on my hit-list."

Sacha blinked very seriously. "Who's on it?"

Wiping my hands on my shorts, I tore a piece of cinnamon bun off. "Mason—"

He nodded, understanding off the bat why I'd put Mase on the list. He'd been way too eager about making sure my head got shaved.

"I'm still on the fence with Freddy for missing his shot—"

That time, Sacha shrugged.

"And my brother." Definitely my brother.

He bit the inside of his cheek. "I thought he was going to try and fight me after I kicked the ball at you."

Yeah, that made me laugh. "I'm surprised he didn't high-five you or try to give you a hug."

He paused.

And the pause said it all.

I opened my mouth. "He did, didn't he?"

To give him credit, he nodded, a sheepish expression on his face. "He gave me a hug and said he owed me a drink."

I would call my brother a traitor-ass-bitch if I didn't know Eli any better than I did. But I did, and if he'd gotten all bent out of shape in my honor, I would have asked him if he was dying or something.

On the other hand, it wasn't as if Sacha knew how ruthless he was. "I should have smothered him with a pillow when I had the chance, I swear."

Sacha cracked a big smile as I tore off another piece of cinnamon roll and ate it. "You said he's only a little older than you?" I nodded. "You're the youngest?" I nodded again. "I'm the youngest of five by a lot. It's a baby thing. They still call me Sasquatch."

My mouth gaped for a second before I remembered there was bread inside of it. "Sasquatch?"

"Sasquatch," he confirmed. "They've called me Sacha maybe twice in my entire life. The rest of the time is 'that damn Sasquatch' or just 'Sasquatch.'"

"Girls or boys?"

"Four sisters." He shook his head as if having a flashback of going through something traumatizing with them. "They were the same way with me as Eli is with you."

"They used to take craps and purposely not flush the toilet?" I asked with a snort.

Sacha grinned, raking a hand through the longer hair at the top of his head. His tattoos popped against the pale skin beneath the wide bands of ink striping the length of his arm. "Just as bad; they'd leave their tampons all over the place. When I was really young—my oldest sister is almost fourteen years older than me—they'd put dresses on me and tell me that our parents named me Sacha because I was really a girl."

Somehow I managed to hold back the snort rising through my nose and keep my features even and serious as I asked, "What you're trying to tell me is that you're *not* a girl?"

He stared at me. "Remember when I told you I

MARIANA ZAPATA

thought you were funny? I changed my mind. You're not."

All I could do was just smile despite the pain that shot through the lower half of my face.

The effort he was putting into not laughing was completely obvious, especially as he raised his dark eyebrows. "Don't think I didn't hear you call me Sassy either before you pushed me on the ground."

What was I going to do? Deny it? "Ask me how many regrets I have?" I didn't wait for him to answer. I made a circle with my thumb and index finger and held it up for him to see. "Sassy Sacha."

Before he could reply, a voice I was way too familiar with filled the empty Dallas venue. "GABRIELA!"

"It's my mom, run," I whispered under my breath as I leaned to the side to spy the woman who never let me forget how hard it had been to carry twins for almost nine months. On one side of her were my dad, Rafe and two nieces. On the other side of my mom was Eli with his arm around her, our oldest brother Gil and my other niece.

I put my hand up and waved, mentally bracing myself for the shit storm that usually went hand in hand when the entire Barreto family was together. Insults, wedgies and yelling were essential parts of a family that was half Brazilian and half Italian.

"You don't remember you have a mom?" my mother yelled over at me as the whole family kept walking across the venue in my direction.

110

"Like I could forget!" I hollered back at her with a weak smile.

She visibly shook her head at the same time my dad flashed me a grin and a silent wave. While my parents were great and you could tell that they loved each other, a lot of times, I wondered how they made things work for them the last thirty-eight years. Mom and Dad were polar opposites who frequently disagreed on everything from what car they should take to church, to whether the lawn could go another week before it needed to get mowed or not.

Rafe's two daughters screamed, "Aunt Gaby!" a second before they took off running. I made sure that Eli saw my smirk at our niece's reactions since we were always arguing over whom they loved more.

Izabella and Heidi, four and six-years-old, shrieked until they were five feet away when they suddenly stopped… and gawked.

It wasn't either one of them who verbally reacted to my makeover.

It was Gil. "What the—," he glanced down at his daughter, "you-know-what happened to you, Demi?"

My siblings, Gordo and Mason really brought out the worst in me. I stuck my tongue out at him. "The important question here is: why do you even know who that is?"

He tilted his head over at the reserved nine-year-old by his side. "Disney Channel all day every day."

It was the loud smack of a palm meeting flesh

that had me glancing over at Eli, who was holding the back of his head with both hands, scowling at Rafaela. "What the hell was that for?"

The second oldest Barreto kid, when in reality she had always seemed to be the most mature, scowled at her little brother. "Why would you do that to her?"

"I didn't do that!" Eli frowned, edging closer to our mom who was fussing at Rafe for hurting her baby boy.

"Did you fall again?" That was our dad that asked.

"Again?" Sacha whispered under his breath, and I couldn't help but poke him in the side.

What really got me about the question was that they either expected Eli to be the culprit or my own clumsiness to be the cause of blame.

"We had our Soccer Death Match yesterday," I explained, walking around the table so I could hug the entire clan, wincing every time one of them touched the side of my body that had taken the brunt of the impact when Sacha had tackled me playing.

The "ahhh" that came out of them was on the spot. They'd all heard about it, even the little girls, whom I went to hug first.

Izabella, Rafe's youngest, pulled away from me after I kneeled down to hug her. Her little eyes, the same shade of green as my dad's and mine, focused on the bruise on my face. She put up her little hand as if she wanted to touch it but was too scared to.

"Did it hurt?" Iza whispered, her fingers curling in the air hesitantly.

"Yes." Why pretend like it hadn't? It had, and I'd be a damn liar if I tried to play it off. Either way, I had a feeling Iza knew me too well. She'd call me out on my lies and it wouldn't be the first time.

She then looked into my eyes. "Did you cry?" Testing me. She was testing me and I was fully aware of it.

I heard Sacha make a noise behind me but kept my focus on my niece. "A little bit."

Then she did it. The little girl I'd spent countless hours with, my mini-partner in crime, threw my ass under the bus. "Like when your boyfriend broke up with you? Or not like that?"

CHAPTER EIGHT

The moment the bus rolled to a stop, I elbowed Gordo out of the way with a "Move it, sucker," spat with the single intent that I be the first one out of there. Laila had texted me to let me know she was already waiting at the venue in San Antonio, and sure enough, I spotted her making her way across the parking lot.

After the Houston date with our soccer match and my head shaving, then Dallas with my family, and another stop in Austin—I was ready to get away from the guys that drove me nuts and see my best friend.

At four-foot-eleven and with a smile that took up her entire face, Laila was like a breath of fresh air after being surrounded by so much testosterone. The second we were close enough, she wrapped her arms around my middle as I hugged her above her shoulders where she could fit perfectly under my chin. The pedals on her wheelchair dug into my shins, but I didn't give a single crap.

There was something about Laila's hugs and warmth that always radiated understanding and comfort. There was also the fact that she didn't judge me when I laughed at things I shouldn't. Even though I would never ask for another sibling to replace the three I already had, I loved Laila fiercely.

We'd survived high school together. Stayed friends even after she and her mom moved to San Antonio for her to go to school, and I'd gone on tour with Ghost Orchid. Then she'd let me live with them when I'd had to move out of my ex's place.

She was still hugging the hell out of my middle when she finally spoke. "I'm so happy to see you!"

"I'm so happy to see you too, you lazy broad." I gestured to her wheelchair before giving her another bone-crushing hug.

"I didn't feel like dealing with my braces all day," she explained.

I made a face at her just to give her a hard time, but really, I knew how hard it would be for her to be on her feet for such a long period. Someone just needed to bust her chops so she'd keep walking around as much as she could handle. Pulling away from her, I took a step back and looked her over. Slim, with dark hair and a unique light caramel color to her skin that she'd inherited from her Cuban mom and Caiman dad, I'd always thought she had the face and personality that belonged to a princess in a cartoon movie.

It took me all of a second to realize that her hair had been cut to her shoulders. "When did you get your hair cut?"

Laila blinked back at me. "When did *you* get your hair cut?"

"That was the surprise I was telling you about," I explained, touching that shaved section with gentle fingers. The rest of my hair was in a low-side ponytail but it still couldn't hide the obvious buzz cut. "Surprise!" I muttered, wiggling my fingers in the most unenthusiastic way possible.

She just stared at me before slowly asking, "Holy bologna, Gabba. Was this Soccer Death Match loser crap?"

I nodded. I'd already told her about the ball to the jaw I'd taken. In person, the huge bruise confirmed the story.

She tilted her head to look at me and finally nodded, almost sagely. "You got lucky they didn't do your whole head at least. You look cute like that, but if it was everything…" She let out a little whistle and flared her nostrils. Sure, she was sweet, but the honesty that came out of her mouth at times was candy-coated brutality at its finest.

Laila opened her mouth for a split second before shutting it at the same time she went bug-eyed. I turned my head just a little to see who she had her eye on. Sacha, Freddy and Julian had all gotten off the bus and were looking in our direction intently from their spots twenty feet away.

"Those guys are on the tour?" she whispered.

"Yes and stop drooling, you horny biatch."

"I'm not drooling." Laila shifted in her wheelchair, her small hands gripping the arm rests. "I changed my mind, I need to call my mom and tell her to bring me my braces after all."

I snorted and went to pop the strap of her bra peeking out from under her tank top.

She didn't even make a face when the material snapped back against her skin; she was so focused on the three men standing around. Her brown eyes flicked up to mine. "Which one of them is the Sacha-guy you've been telling me about?"

"How do you know it's one of them?"

"Because if I remember correctly, your text message said, 'I just kicked the hottest guy I've probably ever seen in the ass.' And I asked you what he looked like and you texted me back, 'Like a double bacon cheeseburger I'd take a bite out of.'"

Apparently, she had gobbled up the information like a hooker would a penis. Because okay, that sounded about right. I gave her a look. "He's the one in the middle with the sleeve tattoo," I muttered.

Laila let out another little low whistle. "That's the same guy that kicked the ball at your face?"

"Yep."

"Introduce me," she demanded with a smile, looking up at me.

The little slut.

"Yes, mistress." I bowed to her, earning a pinch to the back of my knee. "Follow me, Wheels." She pinched me again even harder.

Under normal circumstances, I would have offered to push her wheelchair but we'd been friends for more than ten years, and I knew her like the back of my hand. I could tell you all of her favorite foods, her pet peeves, what size and style her clothes were, and even what kind of tampons she preferred.

And I knew she wouldn't want me to push her wheelchair when we were going to meet new people she found attractive. She'd been battling for her independence her entire life, and I was behind her every step of the way. Because of her spina bifida, most people tried to tiptoe around her. I couldn't say I hadn't tried to smother her in those first few years we'd become friends, but now we'd figured it out. She liked it when I gave her shit and teased her since most people didn't.

The moment we were close enough, I smiled at the TCC members.

It was Sacha that spoke up first. "Hey."

"Hey. This is my friend Laila." I think I did this weird thing with my hand, drawing a sloppy line between the two of them, but I wasn't positive since I wasn't paying attention when Sacha thrust his hand out to shake my best friend's hand.

"Nice to meet you," he said after giving her his name.

Freddy and Julian did the same.

Honestly, I was relieved they didn't start acting weird or talking loudly. People had done that to her before for some reason I didn't completely understand. Did they think she had hearing problems because she was in a wheelchair? I wasn't sure, and it aggravated me a lot more than it bothered her.

It was the little things like that—how people treated one another—that mattered the most to me. I appreciated how normal they were being.

"What are you up to today?" Sacha asked.

"Hanging around here," I answered. "I need to unload the trailer and then we'll go grab something to eat."

The man I'd come to think inspired the creators of Hungry, Hungry Hippos brightened up at the mention of his favorite word, *eat*.

I didn't even need to ask Laila if it was okay to invite him—them—because I knew the answer. Plus, it would be kind of rude of me to not invite the man that had gone to eat with me in the past every time I'd asked. "We were going to get *pho*."

"I love *pho*," he replied.

Of course he did.

"He's really cute, Gaby," Laila stated as she helped me fold shirts behind the merch table a few hours later.

"Who? You were flirting with all of them except Gordo," I snickered with a laugh. Eli, Mase and Gordo had tagged along to go eat at our favorite *pho* joint, too.

"It's pointless to flirt with Gordo," she said like I didn't already know that. "And you know who I'm talking about."

Of course I did. She'd been pinching me under the table every time he spoke. The bruises were going to be happening later.

"Does he have a girlfriend?" she asked when all I did was groan in response.

I bent over to grab another pile of shirts that I'd messed up during a rush of customers the night before. "I don't know; I don't think so."

"Have you heard him talking to anyone for long periods of time?" Investigator Laila inquired.

"No." I glanced at her out of the corner of my eye. "It isn't like I get to spend all day with him or anything, Lai. I'm in the venue most of the time; I don't know what goes on when I'm in here and everyone else is out there."

"I guess, but I think you'd know." She paused, handing me the two shirts she'd finished refolding. "I'm just saying, he's really cute and he seems like your type."

That had me turning my entire body around to give her a look.

"Okay, okay. He's just about everyone's type, but

you two were flirting."

I choked. "We weren't flirting, we just joke around." A lot.

"That was flirting, you friggin' liar."

"Maybe a little bit—"

"He threw a balled-up straw cover at you and called you Princess twice," Laila stated.

I coughed. "We're always messing with each other—" I tried to explain before realizing that I was digging myself into a deeper hole. She just didn't get it.

She sighed and touched my knee. "That's not helping you win your case at all. I love you, and I want you to be happy, Gab. That's all."

"I am happy."

"You know what I mean."

I nodded at her, and nudged her hand back with mine. "I know, I know, and I swear I'm a lot better now than I was before I left."

Laila raised an eyebrow that she quickly covered by shaking a shirt out in front of her face. "You don't want to kill Brandon anymore then?"

"I'd settle for him getting a really bad case of hemorrhoids."

Laila threw her head back and laughed. "Bleeding, inflamed hemorrhoids."

There was a reason why our friendship had survived so many years. We high-fived each other.

When I pulled back, I had a big smile on my face.

"If I never see him again, I'd be perfectly happy."

~

Hours later, I knew something was going on when Eli texted me.

Do u want to take the nite off.

Mason, Gordo and him loved their fans, but selling merch was something that none of them were particularly fond of. They couldn't get anything done because people wanted to talk to them more than they wanted to actually buy anything.

When I sent both Mason and Gordo messages and didn't get a response, my gut feeling was confirmed. Those two bitches kept their phones on them like the end of the world would be set into motion if they missed a call or a text message. Laila was sitting behind the merch table with me and offered to keep an eye on it after I showed her the message. I tried my best to get through the crowd as quickly as possible without having to elbow too many people. I'd barely made it to the hallway behind the stage when I spotted Gordo pacing outside of the green room.

His dark, nearly black eyes, widened when he saw me approaching. "Are you leaving?" he asked, scratching his eyebrow with a single index finger.

I shook my head in response. "No. What's going on?"

"Nothing," the son of a bitch answered too quickly. He was worse at lying than I was.

I narrowed my eyes at him. "Gordis."

He winced and immediately sighed in defeat. The man was the easiest person in the universe to break. I would never trust him with a secret because he'd crack in no time. "Brandon is here."

I think that if I'd heard those words two months ago, more than likely I would have gone ballistic breaking things while on a war-path to destroy his face—wherever it was.

But the surprising part was that I found myself without the slightest urge to do just that. I mean, what kind of nerve did he have coming to a show he knew my brother was playing at? I never took Brandon to be that much of a dumbass, but I guess I'd misjudged him. I didn't want to see his face, and I definitely didn't understand where his balls came from.

This tour was my house. My family. My place.

And I sure as hell wasn't going to let him make me cower in hopes that I wouldn't see him. I'd given him too much power over my life in the month immediately after we broke up, and I would never give him or anyone the same again. I hoped.

Screw. That.

I nodded at Gordo and even smiled as his face took on an "oh shit" expression. "Okay."

I was fine, and that fucker would learn just how fine I was. Maybe I'd been completely caught off-guard when he broke things off, but I would bet he'd be way more surprised before the night was over. I made a beeline for The Cloud Collision's green room next door, knowing that they were the reason why Brandon was at the show.

He hated going to shows. He'd said that to me at least a hundred times in the two years we were together.

When I made it to the back room, I found Sacha and Isaiah inside preparing for the show. Sacha was standing in the corner of the room pulling things out of a small nylon bag I'd seen him go through before after the show. Inside of it was some kind of massager, tea, and an oil he applied to his throat before starting his vocal warm-up. He was already halfway dressed for the night in his slacks and undershirt. Isaiah ,on the other hand, had his guitar in his lap, plugged into a small practice amp. When Isaiah noticed me standing there, he motioned me inside.

"Is everything all right?" he asked.

I cleared my throat and nodded. "Yeah, everything is fine. I was just wondering if you've seen Brandon?"

Sacha turned around. The expression on his face was one of pure curiosity.

"The guitar player in Screaming Ivy?" Isaiah asked.

It was an immediate response to want to gag at the mention of that terrible band but I held it back. What the hell had I been thinking, dating someone who played in a band with such a stupid name? "Yes."

"I think he's on the bus with Julian and Miles," Isaiah replied. Miles was the name of the bass player of TCC.

Sacha's lips twitched as he walked over to where Isaiah was sitting and parked his butt on the armrest. "Do you know him?"

I swear I couldn't help but snicker as I steeled my spine and prepared to go rip my ex a new asshole. "Yeah. I do." I rubbed my hands over my thighs and gave them a smile that was probably more vicious than it needed to be. "Thanks for telling me. Have a good show tonight, okay?"

I'd barely made it three steps out of the room when I felt a hand on my elbow. Without looking I knew it was Sacha who was tugging me back toward him. His eyes were wary. "Why do I feel like you're about to go do something bad?"

"Because I am," I chuckled, taking a step forward, a step closer to my mission. "I'm kidding. I swear I'm not going to do anything bad. I just need to go talk to him for a minute."

Those gray eyes swept across my face. "Are you friends?"

I cleared my throat and fought the urge to scratch my ear. "We used to date."

"That guy is your ex?" he asked after a brief pause.

He'd heard more than enough about my infamous ex from my family the night before. Especially from traitor Iza. Damn it.

I nodded completely unenthusiastically. "Yep."

He raised an eyebrow. "But you're not friends?"

I shook my head. I should have focused on the fact that he was so insistent on asking if my ex and I were friends or not, but I didn't. "No. I'd kick my own ass if we were friends."

Sacha smiled at me, this big, grand smile that could have lit up Main Street at Disneyland. "I'd help you if you want."

"You already have." I grinned at his flirty butt. "I promise I'm not going to do anything bad, you can go back and warm up."

"And miss whatever you're going to do? Nah."

The security guard in the back winked at me as we made our way out of the back door toward the bus. Sacha grabbed my forearm that time, easily matching my quick stride with his natural, normal one.

"What exactly are you planning on doing?"

"Ask him what the hell he's doing here." I think.

His large, warm hand tightened its grip. "Were you together for a long time?"

"Around two years," I mumbled, reaching for the door handle to the bus before flinging it open. I don't think I had ever run up those two steps faster than I did right then. I heard the voices in the bus before my foot even landed on the first one.

"—get the fuck out." I recognized Eli's voice immediately.

"It's not a big deal," the voice I hadn't heard in months greeted me in return when I made it to the top of the steps. The curtain was pulled closed so I couldn't see anyone at first.

"What in the fuck would make you think showing up here wouldn't be a big deal, you dumbass? Gaby's here, pickle dick!" my twin bellowed.

I don't think I had ever loved Eli more than I did in that moment standing at the top of the stairs with Sacha's warm body directly behind me. He was talking so loudly it could have been considered yelling, but I knew that Eli only genuinely yelled when he was excited about something, and he was definitely not excited to see Brandon.

"I invited him out," the voice I recognized as Julian's deep one spoke up.

"This has nothing to do with you, man. This taint stain knows he had no business coming here but he did anyway," Eli explained before pausing.

My ex let out a sigh that I'd heard one too many times over the years. "Look—"

"Shut the fuck up and get out. I don't want to see you, and Gaby doesn't want to see you either." I swear to God my brother growled. "Go hide or die, I don't give a shit what you choose. Otherwise I'm going to take a shit on your face right after I knock you out for breaking up with my fucking sister over the phone, mangina."

Sacha poked me in the back at that moment, snickering quietly, and I couldn't help but snort a little too. Leave it to Eli to come up with *mangina*.

"Gaby's a big girl, Eliza," I thought I heard my ex say.

But he couldn't be that stupid, could he?

"What the fuck did you just call me?" Eli snapped, and I had my answer.

This asshole just called my twin by the nickname only I could use. If I wasn't going to murder him for simply showing up to the concert, I was now going to do it because he messed with Eli. Nobody messed with my brother.

Pulling the curtain aside so roughly I might have torn it, I spotted my ex sitting on one of the long couches with his arm draped around a pretty brunette. What struck me first was the fact that the bastard had on a shirt I'd bought him for Valentine's Day a year ago. Seriously?

"Gaby," Brandon muttered with wide blue eyes.

I felt my ears start to heat up from how angry I was getting each second that passed by. "Brandon."

It was only when I felt Sacha's fingertips dip into the band of my jeans, brushing at the small of my back that I calmed down enough to think rationally.

In months past, I'd thought of a hundred messed-up things I would have loved to happen to Brandon. Everything from hooking up with a transvestite, to losing his dick from some kind of strange man-eating bacteria, had waged its war through my imagination. I didn't hate him, really, but he would always and forever have a spot on my Shit List. But when I felt my new friend tug on the back of my jeans, I realized that I wasn't the same person that I'd been a few months back. Even a month back.

Though the flesh and the flakes that comprised the shell of skin were the same, I felt stronger than before. I didn't need Brandon, and I really was better off without him. We'd had a good relationship but in hindsight, he wasn't the kind of man I wanted to be with forever. Our interests were too different and… I guess something had been missing. We didn't have that easy camaraderie that came so naturally to my demons and I. Hell, even Sacha and I had instantly taken to each other's humor. He'd loved me, I think, but it wasn't enough to erase the fact that I'd always been second—sometimes third or fourth—in his life after his shitty-ass band. It was just that our breakup had come out of the blue. I'd asked myself a thousand times if the signs had been there that things were falling apart, but no matter how much I over-analyzed it, there really hadn't been a sign.

Really, it was okay. Whatever his reasons were, I didn't care anymore. I cried, I grieved, and like every Barreto before me, I was going to move the hell on with my life. I was happy, regardless of whether I knew what I wanted to do with my life or not.

But more than ever, I wanted Brandon's ass torn

up by a dozen hung porn stars.

"Let's go outside," I told my ex in a voice so calm I didn't know I was capable of.

His eyebrows furrowed as his face went a little pink. "What?"

"Come outside with me, Bran," I said, indicating with my head toward the exit. "We should talk."

Those eyes that I'd once cared for narrowed in my direction. He knew me; he knew that even if I was calm, he'd crossed the fucking line calling Eli my nickname for him. Some things were unforgivable. His brunette girlfriend tugged at his hand as she shook her head.

I shot my brother a smirk; he was standing there with a flushed face and rigid jaw. All signs of the devil inside of him were visible, waiting to burst out and destroy. "Come on, Brandon. Let's go. I'll only take a minute."

"Baby," the girl whined softly.

I'd never been clingy with him and maybe that was my mistake, but I couldn't find it in me to bother wondering if that had been a factor in our split. If Brandon had wanted to talk to someone, talk to one of his fans, I'd never cared. I figured if he wanted to cheat on me he could do so any time he wanted and there was nothing I could do about it. But this bitch was going to learn that I definitely didn't want his pimple-butt ass. "I don't want his pickle dick." I glanced at Eli when I said it. "I just want to talk to him for a minute, and I don't want to embarrass him in front of everyone."

Sacha tugged at the back of my pants again, his fingers dipping deeper into the area between the denim and my panties. "Gaby," he warned.

"I didn't know you'd be here," Brandon cut off Sacha. "I figured I could avoid—"

I couldn't help but roll my eyes. He thought he could avoid Eli? Oh, please. "I don't care," I piped up in a sing-song voice. "Get off the bus and talk to me. You owe me." I wanted to add a "motherfucker" at the end but I kept it to myself.

He knew he owed me. I didn't bother waiting to see him get off the couch; I glanced over at Eli once more before I turned around. He was clenching his fists and staring at Brandon like he could kill him by looks alone. I passed Sacha on the way out, circling his wrist quickly with my thumb and index finger as best as I could. I didn't meet his eyes, but it wasn't because I was embarrassed that he'd learned that I'd been dumped, much less over the phone. It happens to every girl. I think. Maybe without the phone part. Touching Sacha was more to just tell him that I was fine. That I wasn't going to do anything I'd end up regretting.

In no time, Brandon was tumbling out of the bus after me, closing the door behind him. Four months had passed since the last time I'd seen him and of course he looked exactly the same: his dark hair was perfectly styled, the facial hair that he kept just long enough to be called a beard the same as always, and his body was still just muscular enough to be considered fit. Was he good looking? Yeah, but who cared? I could go online and find thousands of guys that were just as equally, if not more, attractive as him.

I could look at the guys on tour with me.

Brandon stopped and crossed his arms over his chest, his eyes boring into mine. "Gaby, I'm—"

"Shut up."

Brandon's eyes widened at my snappy tone, and I didn't miss the way his shoulders reeled back in surprise. "Why are you being like this?"

Why was I being like this? Seriously? "Are you joking? Or are you really asking me why I'm pissed off that you're here?"

"This isn't a joke," he replied.

"Of course it isn't a fucking joke. You're here, and you shouldn't be. What's difficult to understand about that?" I snapped.

"Baby, you've always been so sweet—"

My vision went red. He'd gone there with the b-word. Holy fuck.

"This isn't how you usually act—" he kept going, oblivious to the fact he was *this close* to getting shanked.

Honestly, if there wasn't steam coming out of my ears, I would have been surprised.

This isn't how you usually act.

Baby, you've always been so sweet.

Gaby, what are you doing with your life?

I can't do this anymore…

Everyone had his or her breaking point, and I'd reached mine.

"You broke up with me! On the phone! Out of the blue! All you said was that you didn't want to do this anymore and some shit about me not knowing what I want to do with my life and how it affected your artistic vibe, you prick. I spent two years with you—two years! And in five minutes you kick me out of the place *you* had asked *me* to move into with you six months before. I'd told you I didn't want to live with you and you told me how much fun it would be, how much you loved me, how it was inevitable. Six months, Bran! What the fuck?"

Under normal circumstances, I wasn't one to go on a rant or a tirade of any sort. Well, unless it was around my family members or Laila. But the words had been bottled up deep in my chest for months now. All the questions and the frustration over what had happened to my doomed relationship just exploded out of me in this hateful, screaming demand.

To give him credit, Brandon put his hands on his forehead and sighed, his gaze going down to the ground. "I did love you. I'll probably always love you, in a way. You're great—"

I put my hand up to stop him from continuing on with a list of traits he admired because, frankly, I didn't give a shit what he liked about me. "We hardly ever fought, and we'd talked on the phone the night before like everything was normal. You just cut me perfectly out of your life after so long, and I never heard from you again. Then a week or two later, I find out you have another girlfriend already? It just caught me out of the blue, do you understand why that pisses me off?"

"I'm sorry. I'm really sorry, babe." He slid his hands down his face with a shaky exhale. "I didn't mean for things to go the way they did. I swear I didn't have sex with her while we were still—"

I had to rewind the words that came out of his mouth and go through them again.

When I did, my ears went hot and my brain just kind of short-circuited for a split second. Not once had I even thought that he'd cheated on me. I really hadn't. Brandon thought he was a catch but not once had he ever been the type of guy that I imagined texting eight other girls while he had a girlfriend. That wasn't like him. We'd gone on a date the day after we'd met. I guess I had just thought he'd done the same thing again.

But this...

"You didn't have sex with her while we were still together...? But you started talking to her while we were...?"

Anxiety crossed his features so quick it was amazing. He might have even stopped breathing before he began stuttering. "Well..."

I wasn't even mad, per se. I wasn't. What was done was done and whatever. I cleared my throat and got the knot out of it. "It doesn't matter." The words came out of my mouth a little rough, a little weird. *He'd started talking to other people before we'd even split up.*

But my pride, my pride couldn't handle it.

I picked up the imaginary pieces and balled them up.

"It really doesn't matter anymore, but I will cut your balls off with my eyebrow trimmers if you ever talk to Eli like that again. You walked out of my life, and I don't care if I ever see you again. My brother doesn't want you around, and you better believe that the only reason your face is still intact is because you came out here with me."

"I'm sorry, baby," he said quietly, using that same damn nickname that was stabbing a spike into the back of my neck. "I didn't mean to hurt you like that."

I shrugged because how else could I respond that didn't include me punching him right in the eye for being a piece of shit? "I don't care anymore, Brandon. But I want you and your girlfriend to get off the fucking bus. Go watch the show from wherever you want but stay away from me."

He opened his mouth to say something else but he must have understood how serious I was because he closed it. Nodding, Brandon looked away. I took a second just to look at the guy I'd been with for two years.

Brandon was good-looking and tall and lean, but

now, I didn't look at him the same way that I used to. None of the physical crap really mattered in the long run. A part of me wanted to focus on everything that he wasn't, but there wasn't a point.

He'd made me look like an idiot. More than anything else, that was something I couldn't ignore.

I sucked in a breath and smiled in his direction, letting the anger bubble inside of me. It was in that moment that I asked myself what I would regret more later on sitting in my bunk: being an adult or making myself feel better.

And I knew. I knew deep in my heart what exactly I would regret more. A smile easily crawled across my face as I said, "Thank you for seeing things my way."

He eyed me suspiciously for a second before nodding, his own little smile tugging at the corners of his mouth. "I'm sorry for everything."

I nodded.

Then I took two steps forward, holding my arms out at my sides as if I was going to give him a hug… and when he started to lean in, I went onto the tips of my toes and punched him almost as hard as I could right in the throat.

He made this choking, puttering noise as he bent over at the hips, but I wasn't looking at him any more.

When I pivoted around to head back toward the venue with vindication in my veins, I happened to look up at the windows of the bus to see my brother and Sacha with their faces pressed up against the glass, looks of amazement on their faces. I waved.

There. Now I could go to sleep tonight. Otherwise I would have lay in my bunk with my hand fisted and called myself a coward for not going for it.

The rest of the night went by pretty uneventfully. Laila had apparently made friends with Carter, from the way I found him behind the Ghost Orchid merch table, sitting right next to her. During a break between songs, she asked me loud enough for Carter to hear, "What happened?" All I said in response was, "I punched him in the throat," which made her burst out laughing and led to Carter asking if it was Mason I punched.

Once she got herself under control right around the time Ghost Orchid went onstage, she kept slapping my shoulder when she got excited. It was a slower night than usual so I had a lot of time to watch their set and The Cloud Collision's. Sacha moved across the stage so effortlessly and with so much energy it was electric. Even if he wouldn't have one of the most striking faces I'd ever seen, it would have been impossible to keep my eyes away from him. He was a performer in his blood.

Most importantly, he was my friend. When Gordo had stayed inside after he found out Brandon was around, Sacha had been the one to go find him with me because he was worried I would do something bad. If that wasn't friendship, I didn't know what was.

At some point in the middle of their set, when he usually got chatty with the audience, telling them some short story about the road or his life, I realized that if anything—Sassy, in his black pants, light blue button-up, and skinny navy tie—was a loyal bastard.

"Do you know what I hate?" he asked the roaring audience in front of him. They screamed all kinds of things in response.

"Pussy!"

Sacha shook his head and pointed in the direction of where the person had screamed. "Nope. I like that."

"Guys in skinny jeans!"

He shrugged dramatically. "Whatever, man."

A couple other people screamed other random things until he waved them off, pressing the microphone really close to his face like he was going to tell the thousand-plus people in the audience a secret. He held up one finger, which he pointed straight ahead almost as if he was pointing at me in the back.

"Pickles," he screamed and then extended his middle finger, still pointing straight ahead. "And dicks!"

Immediately, the loud bang of the bass drum picked up, signaling the start of another song.

I almost pissed my pants from laughing so hard.

∿

I was in love with the world and with the men in my life the rest of the night.

Why hadn't anyone told me that being loved and cared for—albeit in a strange way—could be so awesome? I felt like someone pointed a wand at me and cast a spell that was all rainbows and unicorns. My brother called Brandon a mangina, and Sacha followed that up by calling him out in front of a thousand people. What more could I ask for?

As soon as Carter and I got done loading the dolly with bins and tearing everything down, we made our way out of the venue. Laila had left minutes ago, explaining that she had to be up early for a class she was teaching and her mom didn't want to pick her up too late. With a flurry of hugs and promises to text me the next day, I said goodbye to my best friend for the next two months.

I saw Eli first, standing with his back to me after loading his drum cases into the massive trailer. With three long steps, I launched myself on top of his back, wrapping my arms around his neck to kiss his cheek. "I love you," I told him, pinching his cheek.

"Fuck, I'd love you if you lost ten pounds before jumping on my back again," he huffed, hoisting me up higher on his back with one hand.

"Whatever," I muttered, pinching his cheek again. "Thanks for standing up for me, Eliza."

"Somebody's gotta do it, Flabby. If I would have known you were gonna punch him in throat, I would have taken it easier on him, you fucking psycho." He laughed. "I swear to God, seeing you do that almost made me cry."

I snorted, the curiosity killing me. "What happened after I left?"

"He sure as hell didn't say anything when he got back in the bus. He waved at his girl and got the fuck outta there, but not fast enough because I made sure to laugh right in his face. Sacha had to go into his bunk from how hard he was laughing." He snorted. "Mason was pissed off he missed it."

It hit me right then that I hadn't seen Mason all night. He'd gone out of his way to ignore my text messages, but then he also hadn't been on the bus when the Pickle-Dick incident went down. I knew that son of a bitch. There's no way he would have just sat back and done nothing. "Wait. Where was he?"

I could feel the rumble of my brother's chuckles from beneath me. "I think it's better that you don't know just in case the cops ask."

"E!"

A hand smacked my ass really hard and I yelped. Not surprisingly, Mason stopped right next to us, smirking. "That's my payment for tonight, my ball-and-chain," he said with a fake leer.

"What did you do?" I hissed, but really I was obscenely interested in what he'd done. I'd gladly trade a bruise on my butt to find out.

He shrugged. "Let's just say Brandon is going to need three new tires and a car wash, Flabs. He had it coming."

My small Grinch heart swelled and swelled.

Eli turned us around so that my butt was in front of Mason one more time before the jerk slapped it even harder than the first time. I jumped off of him, rubbing my poor cheek in hopes the sting would wear down, and then called them both dicks that I loved. Grabbing clean clothes from the compartment beneath the bus, I overheard yelling coming from inside. Since I didn't know exactly who was involved, and I definitely didn't want to make it awkward by walking in during the middle of an argument, I waited until the voices lowered.

Once inside, I spotted Julian and Miles sitting in the living area looking pissed off, the frowns they shot my way were anything but nice. Yet I didn't give a single shit.

In the back area, I found Sacha and Isaiah in the bunk space, going through their backpacks quietly. It didn't take a genius to figure out that it'd been Sacha and the two in the living area who were fighting just a minute before. It was my fault—well, Brandon's for being an idiot—that it had happened.

"I'm sorry about all that," I told him from the door.

Sacha's gray eyes shot over to me as he tossed his backpack inside his bunk. His facial expression softened and he shook his head. "Don't worry about it." His cheeks pulled up into that crooked smile that made my insides turn to goo and the sensation made me feel weird. What the hell was going on? "It was worth it," he continued.

I shoved the gooey feeling aside and focused on him and what he'd done. "It was pretty awesome," I laughed. "Thank you."

He lifted a shoulder but kept those hypnotic eyes on me. "Anytime, *Streetfighter*."

I snorted before closing the distance between us and throwing my arms around the middle of his chest, hugging him. It took him all of two seconds to realize what I was doing before he wrapped his arms over my shoulders, squeezing me to him tightly. I didn't care that he was sweaty, that his undershirt was drenched and clinging to him like a second, wet skin, and obviously he didn't care that I'm sure my hair smelled like it could use a wash, because he hugged me for a minute that seemed to stretch ages and eons. This was my friend, my friend who got into an argument with people he had a more important relationship than the one we had, and he didn't care.

I hugged him even tighter.

It was in that moment, when I was hugging him as if my life depended on it, that I recognized the strange, gooey emotion that had been floating around in my belly the last portion of the night.

I liked Sacha.

CHAPTER NINE

"Let's play Twister."

"No."

"C'mon, Gaby."

"No."

"Please?"

"No."

"Please?"

I sighed. "Fine."

"Naked?"

I set my book of the moment on my lap and nodded over at Mase with a straight face. "Okay. I've always wanted to see what a hermaphrodite's body looks like."

Gordo snickered from his spot across the living space from his bandmate and me. We had a day off for the first time in nearly three weeks thanks to a twenty-hour drive between cities. At the eighteenth-hour mark, the cabin fever and boredom was beginning to reach epic proportions. Not even Mario Kart could ease the hysteria bubbling up through all of us—or at least those of us who were awake.

"You know I'm a man," Mason objected, yanking on my earlobe in retaliation.

I smirked in his direction, eyeing the black hair that was in need of a good washing. "If it looks like a woman and screams like a woman—it's probably a woman." Tapping the tip of his nose as he scowled, I smiled slyly. "You sure sounded like a lady when you screamed bloody murder when that rat ran across your foot yesterday." I pinched the tip of his nose.

In all honesty, I had screamed too, and the rat hadn't even gotten within ten feet of me. The point was that Mason had pulled a horror movie actress on us and screeched like he was auditioning for the role of the hot, horrible-decision-making, half-naked girl in a bad scary movie. Only he, Gordo, Carter and I had been outside when it happened. If Eli had been there, every person on Ghost Orchid's Facebook page would have known about what happened. Eli had a knack for filming things that ended up going terribly. Like at Rafe's college graduation, when a girl walked off the stage. Sure she could have hurt herself but she didn't, so it was okay to laugh at the video about a dozen—or five dozen—times.

At least, that's what I told myself.

Those blue eyes that I loved in a brotherly way

glared at me. "That mutation was the size of a possum."

"I'm pretty sure it might have been a mouse," I corrected him.

"Potatoe, potato, shut the hell up, Flabby," he huffed. "You would have done the same."

Gordo leaned forward on the couch, resting his elbows on his knees. "Bro, I'm surprised you didn't start crying."

Mason scowled before going on a rant about how much of a girl Gordo was because he got teary-eyed when we'd watched *The Blind Side* a few days ago.

I sat there listening to them go back and forth until Sacha came out of the bunk area a few minutes later. The man slept so much it bordered on being a coma. His face was soft, a little puffy and creased as he made his way through the kitchen, bumping knuckles with Mason and Gordo before he plopped down on my other side. "Morning, Jean-Claude," he yawned, slouching as his legs fell open. One hairy knee relaxed against mine. The shorts he slept in were bunched up high on his thighs.

I tried not to think about the realization I'd come to the night before—the stupid one—but it was a lot harder to do than I expected. The only rationalization I could reach was: Who wouldn't like Sacha? He was handsome, funny, kind and incredibly talented. Wouldn't there be something wrong with me if I didn't like him?

I could deal with a little crush. No big deal. I

couldn't browse the Internet without finding a picture of some attractive guy I would never meet.

And that was the story I was going to go with.

I mean, I could admire him from afar without it meaning anything, right?

"Good morning." I smiled over at him as platonically as possible. Even with a bit of dried drool on the corner of his lips and part of his hair smashed against his scalp, he was a looker after waking up.

Then there were people like me in the morning. Once in my teens, I'd woken up to find the three spawns of Satan hanging out in the living room early in the morning playing video games. My brother had pulled one of our mom's largest crucifixes off the wall and held it in the air at me while he hissed, "*I banish thee!*"

"Morning," Sacha replied with a yawn. He blinked those sleepy crystal-clear gray eyes and long black lashes. "Are you going to the movies with us?" he asked.

"Morning, Mariah." What movies was he talking about? I shook my head. "I didn't know anyone was going to the movies." Awkward.

He lifted a shoulder as he rubbed at an eye with a balled up fist. "I just told you. Come with us. After we grab a shower, Matt—" that was our bus driver's name "—said he'd park at a mall with a movie theater." When I didn't immediately reply, he blew out a long breath of air directly into my face, making me wince. "I'll even let you share whatever you buy with me."

"I have a feeling that even if I don't agree to share my stuff with you, you'd take it anyway." I leaned back and asked in the nicest voice I could muster, "When was the last time you brushed your teeth?"

Sacha cupped a hand over his mouth, making it seem like he was blowing into his palm and breathing it in with a wince. "Your guess sounds about right, and I brushed them last night."

I couldn't help but roll my eyes playfully. "It's time you brushed your teeth again, and you're lucky that I don't have a problem sharing as long as you wash your hands first."

"I think it's time *you* brushed your teeth again—"

I blew into my hand too. "My breath doesn't smell," I argued.

"And I'm very glad to know that you are willing to share." I grinned at him, earning one back in return. "Just for you, I'll brush my teeth now. Happy?"

I nodded. "Very." I wanted to add that a hot guy with morning breath was a tragedy but I didn't. Admitting out loud that I found him attractive would be terrible, embarrassing and pathetic in no particular order. Even though I had a feeling Sacha wouldn't be one of those people who would make a friendship awkward after a declaration of that proportion, I wasn't going to rely on it. Plus, with my luck and his goofy nature, he'd probably make fun of me for it. I sighed in my head and cast a glance at him. "What movie are we watching?"

~

Hours later, after we'd gotten off the bus to shower at yet another travel center, I'd convinced Eli via text message to braid my hair. I hadn't felt like a real girl in what seemed like forever. Being around these guys who had witnessed me go through puberty, braces, the immediate effects of having my wisdom teeth removed, every bad haircut I'd ever had and came to visit me post-surgery when I was high as a kite, drove me to basically not give a single shit about my appearance.

The last time I'd worn make-up other than lipstick and eyeliner had been the first day of tour. I hadn't even bothered putting concealer over my bruise. The last time I wore something other than shorts and sweats had been the same day; wearing shirts without stains on them was the extent of my vanity. Body odor was also a regular worry. I'd been more focused on being comfortable than trying to look cute despite my brother's constant teasing about how I looked haggard. People that came by the merch booth seemed to be okay with me wearing a tank top, having non-stinky breath and a ready smile, so what was the point in trying harder? I'd been making more tips over the last few days than I had before, and I had a feeling it was because of the purple and red coloring along the lower bones of my face.

But each night, I faced girls who had taken time with their appearance, and it made me feel a little down day after day, though I knew there wasn't a point in trying when there was a show. I'd look like a drowned clown by the time we had to get back on the bus regardless of how much or how little make-up I applied.

Laila had always told me that she felt better when she knew she looked nice. In my case, I'd take feeling like a normal, clean girl in a heartbeat. There was nothing that a shower, the dress I'd grabbed from my suitcase and a good braid couldn't give me a kick-start to.

Eli snuck into the back room of the bus with me after agreeing to shower quickly so we could lock the door and get to business.

"You have a lot of split ends," Eli claimed an entire minute after I'd sat on the floor in front of him cross-legged. His fingers parted my hair with no care or gentility, but I knew better than to complain about how rough he was being. It was the usual.

"I'm pretty sure I asked you to braid my hair, not for your expert opinion on whether I need a haircut or not, Vidal Sassoon," I laughed, digging my elbow into the meaty part of his inner thigh.

The bastard yanked on my hair hard while snorting. "I hope you go bald." His large hands brushed through my hair once more before parting it again the way he wanted, not that there was that much hair on one side of my head anyway.

I was not going to whine about the shaved section that made my bone structure look rounder. Nope.

Eli had learned how to braid my hair when we were nine because Mom had broken her hand and couldn't do it for me. What had started as a simple braid down the back of my head had turned into a full-blown interest that led him to learn how to French-braid the hell out of my hair. He'd even nailed a fishtail at some point; when or how he did it, I wasn't sure, and I sure as heck wasn't going to ask either.

The fact was, he was better at it than our mom had ever been. His talent was also one of those things that we kept between the two of us and our parents. Gil and Rafe had never said anything about it so I wasn't even sure they knew. I never gave Eli shit about braiding; it was something he'd learned how to do because he loved me—and I'd begged. I didn't want to taint it with jokes and ruin a good thing.

"I still can't believe you punched Brandon in the throat," he snorted as some of his fingers grazed over the buzzed section above my ear.

I really was quite proud of myself, and I'm pretty sure I preened at Eli's compliment. Then I remembered what Brandon had said and my good mood plummeted. That fucking prick. "Did you hear what he said?"

"Not all of it. I heard bits and pieces when you

were yelling at him, but then you got this crazy-ass look on your face, and it got me wondering why the fuck you were smiling like that." He didn't even pretend to not be nosey. "What'd he say?"

I sighed and reclined against the seat more, the sides of my twin's gigantic thighs pressing against my shoulders. "He pretty much admitted he started talking to that girl he's dating before we split up, and that it'd been a hard decision and he didn't want to hurt my feelings…"

"He cheated on you?" my brother asked slowly, and I couldn't help but smile over the indignation in his tone.

"He said he didn't while we were together, like that matters. Can you believe it? That's why I punched him in the throat. I hadn't even considered he'd been talking to someone else before we split up, E. I felt so stupid—"

His thigh nudged my shoulder. "You are pretty stupid, but he's an idiot, Flabby. You can't be that surprised about it. You wanna be with some guy for the rest of your life that crab walks across the stage and wears tighter pants than you? No. No, you fucking don't."

I started laughing. "Yeah, I know. Shut up."

"I know it's hard to try to find somebody that can live up to me…" he began to say.

"Your mother," I snorted.

Eli chuckled behind me. He messed with my hair for a few minutes before finally speaking up again, his voice lower than normal. "Look, my lease in New York is gonna run out in three months. I'm kinda tired of living there, and I was thinking about moving back to Dallas for a while after this tour ends. We could get a two-bedroom apartment or a house or something, if you want. I'll even let you split rent with me." He nudged me again. "Think about it."

With the amount of crap we talked about each other, to each other, it was easy to underestimate our bond. We were a tag team. We had always been one, and I would bet my life we'd be in our seventies still picking on each other. Just as I opened my mouth to tell him I would definitely think about his offer, someone banged on the door.

"Hey! Can I come in?" Mason's voice bellowed from the other side.

"No!" we both yelled simultaneously.

He didn't immediately respond, like he couldn't fathom why he couldn't. "Why?" he finally asked, sounding confused and disturbed.

"Eli's showing me how he puts a tampon in," I snorted, earning another sharp tug of my hair from my brother.

There was silence on the other side of the door for a minute, allowing Eli to finish my braid. It had always seemed like a miracle to me how gentle those big paws could be when they wanted. I'd seen them beat the crap out of toms, cymbals and faces alike. Hours later, those hands could make the most intricate designs to my shoulder-length hair. No one could say Eli wasn't a multi-dimensional son of a bitch.

"I don't get it… why can't I come in?" Mason's voice finally mumbled through the door again.

I hopped up and threw my arms around my brother, giving him a quick kiss on the cheek while he frantically tried to pull away in disgust. "Thanks, loser. You're going to make my future niece a wonderful mother one day," I told him right before he licked his index fingertip and dipped it into my ear. I made a face and swatted his hand away, afterward getting up to unlock the door.

Mason slipped in, clean-shaven and wet-haired. His alert blue eyes shifted across the small room curiously. I sat down next to Eliza, gently touching the neat strands of hair tucked across my head.

When Mason's eyes landed on me, he frowned and ran a hand through his hair, pushing the damp strands away from his forehead. "You look like a girl."

"I am a girl."

Those same cobalt blue eyes narrowed and then further narrowed as he glanced down the length of my outfit before he flicked his gaze over to Eli. "Are you letting her go out like that?"

"Since when does she listen to me?" he scoffed, throwing an arm over my shoulders. "There's nothing wrong with my Flabby if you don't look too closely at her face."

I laughed. Sure his wording wasn't exactly telling me that I looked nice, but for his standards, it was as good as I would ever get.

"Why don't you ever dress up for me?" Mason asked, taking a seat across from us.

"There's no point; we both know you like your ladies with more facial hair than I have," I snickered.

The imp shrugged and winked at his self-proclaimed soul mate, the man sitting next to me. "True."

The gentle movement of the bus as it slowed to a stop made us shift slightly. There was loud talking from the front before the familiar sounds of the door opening and the guys piling out let me know we'd made it to the mall. Slapping my twin's thigh, I told him I'd see him later before walking out. My idiots and some of the TCC guys had been planning on going to some bar that carried over three hundred different types of beer, and I wasn't in the mood to sit through that experience. Hanging out with Sacha just seemed like a bonus. A very pleasant bonus. A very pleasant, platonic bonus, like spending time with Carter would be.

Right.

I'd barely jumped off the bus's steps, slipping the strap of my purse across my shoulder, when I spotted Sacha and Isaiah outside waiting.

"Is it only us going?" I asked, walking up to them.

Sacha's eyes slanted over in my direction, his

mouth already opening in a certain way that let me know a smart-ass comment was going to be coming out of it in a moment, but nothing actually came out. He looked at me—my face, the bare skin of my chest above the purple cotton of the sundress, and then down the length of my body slowly. It made me self-conscious and I fidgeted. It was second nature to want to pull the front of my dress up but it wasn't like it was low to begin with.

"It's only us," Isaiah's low drawl answered. He looked at me evenly. "I like your hair."

Unfortunately I was one of those people that never knew how to handle a compliment well from people I wasn't close to, or even know what to say afterward. My face got a little warm and I smiled at him. "Thank you."

I smiled at him once more before looking back at Sacha who was busy inspecting my face again. He smiled but it was a distracted, distant sort of look. The entire walk through the parking lot and the mall was surprisingly quiet. Isaiah hadn't really spoken more than two handfuls of words to me in the nearly three weeks we'd been on tour, and Sacha was strangely silent. After buying our movie tickets, I nudged my gray-eyed friend when Isaiah said he was going to the restroom. We got in line at the concession stand.

"Is he usually really quiet around everyone?" I asked, gesturing with my head in Isaiah's retreating direction.

"Isaiah?"

I nodded. "Yes."

Sacha nodded his head, keeping his eyes locked on the menu mounted from the ceiling. "Yeah. He doesn't talk much."

I wasn't much of a talker unless I felt comfortable around someone, and it just so happened that I was surrounded by three of the people that already knew the best and the worst parts of me. If I couldn't be myself around them, who could I be myself around? For some reason, something about Sacha put me at ease and he happened to be an exception.

He didn't say anything else as the line ahead of us shortened, and it was really beginning to weird me out. Why was he being so quiet? It wasn't like I needed to talk all the time, but still. Everything had been fine before I'd showered, so the change in his attitude was pretty confusing.

"Are you okay?" I finally tapped into my imaginary balls to ask, turning just slightly at the shoulders to glance at him.

He frowned, still keeping his gaze on the menu. "Yes, why?"

"You're being really quiet," I said.

Sacha finally looked down at me. He hadn't put on any hair products and his hair was loose and shiny, the longer length falling to the side over the shorter side of his scalp. "My mind is somewhere else," he said apologetically. His light eyes glanced at the neckline of my dress so briefly I almost missed it.

What I didn't miss was his fingers going up to touch the braid draped over my shoulder.

"You look really nice," he commented.

I would have preferred "pretty" but beggars can't be choosers. "Nice" was polite and not at all creepy or aggressive. I smiled at my friend, one of the best-looking friends I'd ever had in my life. "Thanks."

He blinked at me, smiling that distant smile one more time, making me wonder where exactly his mind was. "Want to share a popcorn?"

"Are you asking if I'll get some so you can eat it?" I stared at him suspiciously.

He shrugged the same way he always did. "Yeah, pretty much."

Well, I always did appreciate people who were honest.

"I'll buy a drink if you get the popcorn," he offered.

I snuck another glance at him. He was wearing the same thing he usually had on when he wasn't onstage: running shorts, a T-shirt and his good pair of green-and-black tennis shoes. "Done."

He curled his lips behind his teeth, giving me a hopeful look. "Butter?"

"Butter."

A few minutes later, we settled into our seats in the theater with our concession-stand purchases. He gestured toward the extra-large water bottle he'd bought. "Want some?"

"Sure," I said, already taking it out of the cup

holder. I twisted the lid off, held it up a couple inches above my mouth and was about to pour it when he groaned.

"Drink from the bottle. I don't have cooties."

"You never know," I mumbled, putting the opening to my mouth. He plucked the medium-sized bag of popcorn from my lap while I took a sip.

Handsome, perfect Sacha, with a voice that gave me goosebumps every night, grabbed a handful of popcorn and shoved half the fistful directly into his mouth. "So good," he moaned through an overflowing mouthful.

Isaiah hadn't reappeared since he'd left for the restroom. Sacha had sent him a text message telling him we'd wait for him inside the theater. Nearly at the same time, we both kicked up our legs to rest our feet on the back of the seats in front of us.

My new friend grabbed more popcorn and shoved it into his mouth.

I ate a small amount at a time, too busy watching him ingest handful after handful. It was amazing. It was seriously amazing watching him eat so much so quickly. "Are you planning on eating it all, fatty?"

He gasped in the middle of grabbing more. "You think I'm fat?"

"Yes," I lied, eyeing the flat slope of his stomach like I hadn't seen him shirtless nearly every night. If I were ever honest with myself, I would admit I could draw his six-pack from memory. "Do you only run?" I couldn't remember ever seeing him work out. On the other hand, he was usually always eating.

He mumbled something between a mouthful of popcorn that sounded like "I lift weights too."

"When?"

"Usually during the opening band," he explained. "We have dumbbells and a bench in the back of the trailer." The timing made perfect sense. I rarely saw any of the guys after doors in the venue opened.

"You?"

"Just cardio." I held up my arm and slapped the bottom of my upper arm. "See? No muscle."

He licked his salty lips, looking at me intently. "Where do you live?" he asked out of the blue.

"In Dallas. You?"

"San Francisco."

"That's cool," I thought for a second. "Aren't we stopping there next week?"

The quick, enthusiastic nod he gave me in response made me smile. Excitement radiated through his pores. "Yeah. You can meet my friends."

"Okay." I smiled and nodded, remembering a prior conversation. "What about your family? They don't live there?"

"Not anymore. My mom lives in Australia now; my dad is back in Russia—"

"Are you Russian?" I finally asked. I mean, I'd been wondering where he got his name from and I'm surprised I held off asking for so long.

Sacha nodded. "My parents are. My two older

sisters were born there but the rest of us were born here."

I set my elbow on the armrest and looked at his face. "Huh. That's really neat. What's your last name?"

"Malykhin."

"Spell it."

He did.

"And your sisters?" I asked.

"They're everywhere. One is in Africa, one is in the UK, one in Alaska, and another in Hong Kong." He raised his eyebrows. "I don't get to see them much anymore unless I go visit or we meet up somewhere for the holidays."

"Do you miss them?" I was well aware of the fact I had no right to ask, but I did anyway.

Surprisingly, he answered without even thinking about it. One single shoulder going up in a fraction of a shrug. "A lot, but I'll get to see my mom soon."

"That's nice." I nudged his elbow with mine. "If you ever want a brother, feel free to borrow Eli. You can keep him too."

His lips fluttered with a raspberry before he laughed. "That's very generous of you."

"Just saying. If you're craving being terrorized, made fun of and farted on, he's yours."

Sacha slid me a look out of the corner of his eye. "I already get two of those three."

He did? I tried to think about the way he was with the TCC guys but they all seemed to get along really well, if a little distantly, and they were more mature than GO's morons were. "From who?"

He nudged me again. "You make fun of me on a daily basis… I fear for my safety when I'm around you…"

"Oh, shut your trap!" I started laughing.

"All I need is for you to start farting on me—"

"I would never do that!"

He made a face that made me laugh harder.

"I would never do it on purpose, at least!"

Sacha gave me this huge grin, his straight white teeth on display. "That sounds more like it."

Oh God. I shouldn't think it was funny that he would think I'd fart on him— because I wouldn't— but I did. Especially when he started nudging me with his elbow. I just nudged him right back.

The next thing I knew, we were both elbowing the other, each of us trying to aim for the other person's thigh until he hit his target and I squealed like a pig, making him laugh so loud the people in the rows in front of us turned to see what the ruckus was about.

I smacked his shoulder with my open palm. "You ass."

With another big grin, he grabbed my hand with both of his much larger ones. His fingers were cold. "Do you think I'm mean to you?"

"Yes," I said it but I really had my attention focused on the fact that he was holding my hand between his. Did I try to pull away? No, as stupid as it was.

"I'm not joking. Do you think I am?" he asked, his husky voice lowering in what I could assume was an attempt to be serious.

I smiled at him. "No. Why would you think that? I like the way we play around," I told him because it was the truth. Sure, I played around with Eli and Mason but that was different. Even my ex didn't like to joke around with me a quarter of as much as Sacha did.

"Are you sure? Carter is still mad at me for the whole penalty kick incident." His thumb grazed over the knuckles of my hand gently once and only once. His gaze strayed to my still-bruised jaw.

"Yes. I mean, you're an asshole for kicking the ball at my face but it's fine," I told him, watching his pale eyes drift to my chest quickly. "But you bruise my money-maker again, and I'll kick you in the nuts."

We both laughed at the same time that the lights in the theater began dimming. Isaiah appeared at the bottom of the stairs, walking up with his hands full of treats. I pulled my hand out of Sacha's grasp to grab some popcorn from the bag that at some point had ended up on his lap.

He raised an eyebrow at me when I stuffed my mouth just like he had, but before he could pipe in, I hissed, "If you call me fat, I'll make sure Eli farts on you." The words slipped out of my mouth before I could stop them.

Sacha shrugged before leaning toward me. "If it goes to your ass, I won't say a thing."

I couldn't...

I was...

Pleased. A little too pleased.

CHAPTER TEN

Once upon a time, I had nothing against San Francisco.

I'd been there before a handful of times with Ghost Orchid, and I liked it as much as anyone could possibly like a city that they didn't spend a lot of time in. After the day I'd had, exactly six shows after jabbing my ex in the throat, the city would forever be tarnished by the memory of all the shitty things that happened. I wouldn't go as far as to say that it was the worst day of my life, but it sure as hell wasn't the best.

When I woke up to cramps that rivaled giving birth—at least I imagined so—I hopped out of my bunk as fast as I could.

Only it wasn't fast enough.

My brother of all people had just been getting out of bed at the same time and happened to see the huge red stain I'd been worried about.

"Holy shit! Flabby! What the fuck?!" he barked, pointing and laughing. Literally, he was pointing and laughing at me.

I flicked him off before grabbing my bag from the floor, where we all left our stuff, and darting into the tiny bathroom to take care of business.

Needless to say, he told his two bandmates. It was bad enough to deal with the cramps and back pain, but all that while getting made fun of too? It was like being twelve years old during my first period all over again.

When the jokes just kept coming and coming and coming from my brother, Mason and that twerp named Gordo, and I was *this close* to losing my marbles, I finally went to hide in my bunk.

Hours later, when I slipped on the last step exiting the bus and scraped the hell out of the skin covering my Achilles tendon, I threw a rock at Eliza when he laughed. Only Isaiah and Carter asked if I was fine because they were decent human beings. My brother and friends were damn dipshits.

To top it off, my phone fell out of my pocket and the corner of the screen cracked. I literally raised it up to the sky as if it were some kind of ancient sacrifice to a sun god and scream-grunted like a total psychopath.

I went right to setting up the table for the night after unloading, thankful that Carter was a solid, nice guy who didn't relish terrorizing me.

In a brief moment of guilt, Eli had texted and asked if I wanted to grab something to eat with him since there wasn't any catering available. To be honest, the only reason I agreed to go was because The Cloud Collision's tour manager had given him my buy-out money. Otherwise I would have told him to go suck his nuts and leave me alone. But when I went out to meet him by the bus, I immediately zoned in on my twin.

I stared.

Then I stared some more before mumbling, "I can't deal with you today."

He gave me this dumb look that begged for a smack. "What?"

It should be noted that years ago, Mase and I had thrown away twenty of Eli's stupid, ugly polo shirts that were way too small on him while simultaneously making him look like a giant douche-bag. Because apparently, he wasn't informed that wearing not just one, but two polo shirts at the same time with the collars popped was... just... no. No. I almost shuddered having a flashback of it.

Had he complained about what we'd done? No. He'd bitched. He'd bitched and he'd bitched some more. But Eli was cheap, and he thankfully never went back to buy any more polos to layer.

Until now, apparently.

All two hundred pounds of Barreto stood there proudly with a clean, emerald green polo, which would have been nice and fine... if it didn't have the collar flicked up straight. Ugh. "You likey?" he asked with so much enthusiasm I couldn't find it in me to snort.

I shot a look over at Mason who was standing behind him, staring right at his friend's neck with a funny expression on his face. I think his eye might have been twitching.

"Nice, huh?" Eli asked again for confirmation that only someone who had once worn a trucker hat could give.

Forcing the grimace from my face into a reluctant grin, I nodded. "Sure, E. If the year was still 2002 and you were on the lacrosse team."

"Scissors, we need scissors, Flabs," Mase muttered loudly enough for my brother to hear.

Eli frowned and told us to fuck off before we started walking around the bus toward some hamburger place they'd heard was good. We'd barely made it around the building when I patted my back pocket and realized I'd left my phone.

"Damn it, I left my phone in the bus. Let me go grab it real quick." I didn't even wait for them to agree that they'd stand there for me to get back before I started jogging back to the bus. Knowing them, they'd wait maybe five minutes. If I weren't back within that time, they'd leave me. The fact was, I didn't trust leaving my phone around these guys. Not even the guys in TCC. Though I hadn't spoken to Miles or Julian since the incident with Brandon, I still got along well with the rest of the TCC entourage and wouldn't hold it past them to post dick pictures on my social media pages or something else my mom could see.

I got on the bus to find Gordo on his computer on one of the couches. "What's up?" he asked.

"Nothing. I forgot my phone, and we were on our way to eat. Do you want me to bring you something back?" I asked, already moving through the bus on my way to the middle section.

He shook his head. "I'll grab a bite later." He tipped his chin up and jerked his head to the side, in the direction of the bunk area and the back. "Hold on, Flabs. Sacha's back there with a girl…"

There was a girl back there with Sacha?

What?

There was a girl back there with Sacha?

I…

I felt… I felt my stomach drop to my knees, then continue on a path through the first layer of the Earth's crust and head straight down to its core.

He was back there with a girl.

My heart sputtered, choked and died a little in that split second.

But somehow I found myself nodding, still even-faced at Gordo's warning.

Girl. Back. Sacha.

Sacha, Sacha, Sacha who had just gone to the movies with me and said something about my ass.

Back there with a girl.

Good grief. Why did my chest hurt? Was this

what a heart attack felt like?

Before I could think about it too much, I made the snap decision to still go into the bunk area because if I didn't, Gordo would know something was wrong. Tension throbbed right between my eyebrows at the mystery behind what I could possibly see... or hear...

Fuck!

I nodded at my old friend but managed to hold back the weak smile that would give me away. "Thanks for the warning."

Yeah, I held my breath as I walked into the bunk area. My heart pounded and this knot formed in my throat...

His bunk was above mine. His bunk was above mine.

But he wasn't there.

I heard the voices before I noticed that the door that led to the back room was wide open, and I saw it. Saw *them*.

Sacha was sitting on the bench seat directly in front of the door with his arm over the top of a girl's shoulders. Their temples were touching. And they were whispering to each other.

In the blink of an eye, my chest began to ache again, and even though I didn't want to blame it on the intimacy of the moment I'd walked in on, I knew it was. There's no way to even begin to describe the feeling that flooded my chest before it decided to swim along my spine, shoulders and finally my skull. It was as if I wanted to throw up at the same time a migraine set up shop in my cranium.

I took a step forward closer to my bunk, fighting the nausea in my gut.

"We can't do this here..." he said just barely loud enough for me to hear.

Oh, fucking hell.

My head pounded. My stomach was in a knot. Tears swam in my eyes for all of a split second before I slipped my upper body into my bunk, snatched my phone from the corner I always left it, and came back out, smashing my elbow into the wooden frame that connected all of the beds. Did it hurt like hell? Yeah, but I didn't even have it in me to cuss because I'd made so much noise, and I needed to get the hell off the bus as soon as possible. Two minutes ago, preferably.

What the *hell* was wrong with me?

My heart thumped erratically as I walked by Gordo on the way out; my fists had begun shaking. I recognized the feeling manifesting itself through my body all too well.

I was jealous. Horribly, stupidly, pathetically jealous.

Jealous of the redhead who was sitting side by side with Sacha. With his arm around her. Touching her face with his.

I mean, they could have been friends, but I didn't want to be naïve either. Mason and I were closer than best friends, and we didn't really have physical boundaries with each other, but we never sat together, whispering. Usually we were picking on one another, not cuddling and crap. There was an intimacy to the moment that spoke volumes.

It made me want to cry.

But I wouldn't do it.

Sacha was my friend. I shouldn't have any feelings for him, much less possessive feelings, but I did. They were just buried deep down in the back of my head, obviously, because I'd been swimming in a river called Da Nile.

I liked him. I liked him a lot, apparently, if the awful, shit emotions that were making a snack out of my nervous system were correct. Dumb, dumb, dumb.

I had almost forgotten Eli and Mason might be waiting for me when I made it to the side of the venue building, but they were there, standing around looking at their phones. Before they could see me, I wiped at my eyes with the back of my hand to make sure my body wasn't being a damn traitor and tried to get my facial muscles under control.

This wasn't the time to get upset. Hell, it was never the time to get upset over Sacha spending time with a girl. On the bus. With his arm around her.

I was not going to get upset. I was not going to get upset, damn it.

I'd heard all kinds of stories over the years of band members screwing around with their fans. Hell, Mason had said something about having sex with some girl behind the bus in Las Vegas a few days ago. Every single time I'd gone on tour with Ghost Orchid, all of the monsters would have some kind of one-on-one "interaction" with their fans, even Gordo. That's what single guys did. And some not-so-single guys that doubled as unfaithful pieces of crap.

It was a tale as old as time. Even the least attractive band member got hit on by a fan or audience member once; whether they did something about it was a different thing. There was something about musicians, even semi-popular ones, that made them more attractive to women. I understood that.

Only this time, it felt like a jab to the kidney to see a man I wasn't dating, who wasn't anything more than a friend to me, with someone in the bus.

I felt…

"The hell is wrong with you?" my twin asked with a scrunched-up nose as I walked up to them.

"My leg hurts from where I scraped it," I quickly lied.

Eli blinked. "Dumbass."

And he let it go for a little while.

While we ate, he kept looking at me, asking if I was fine—or in his exact words, "What's up your ass?" I kept telling him my Achilles hurt, that I was cramping, and I wasn't feeling well. Mason frowned the entire meal.

I couldn't help but notice how Eli came to see me during the show that night, which meant he actually came to the stand instead of staying backstage or on the bus the entire time. He didn't ask any more what was wrong, but I knew he could tell something was bothering me. The whole Sacha thing in the bus had left a hole in my chest. I was sad. *Sad*. It was pitiful.

I couldn't even enjoy the show. I shoved my earplugs in and sat with my arms crossed every chance possible. Of course it was the night that the audience was super-chatty and people were mentioning Sacha's name every five seconds because it was his hometown.

At some point, a fan tried to walk off with two CDs that had been sitting as display on the table, and that turned into a debacle with me confronting him, and the security guards having to get involved once Carter called them over. The guy called me a bitch before he got kicked out of the show. So, overall, things could have been going better. A lot better.

I didn't even take a break that night except to go pee and change my pad because I didn't want to deal with anyone.

I thought my night would be over the moment I finished packing up and helping Carter load the dolly.

But fate had other plans and wanted to turn that silver dagger in my gut one last time.

"We're going to eat, Flabs," Eliza told me as soon as I'd gotten on the bus.

I frowned because I was feeling that bitchy. "I'm not hungry."

The look he shot me could have melted wax. "*You*

aren't hungry? Now I know something is wrong. You're never not hungry."

Leave it to Eli to actually pay attention every once in a while. I didn't give him enough credit. My twin knew me. He was a lot smarter and kinder than his rusted, creaky heart gave him credit for. If there were anyone Eli would move Kilimanjaro for, it would be me.

Maybe. If I asked him on the right day at the right moment with a blue moon in the background.

If I lied to him completely and said that nothing was wrong, he would know. He always did and already had, which was why he hadn't stopped asking. So I went with the next best thing: a partial lie. "I feel sick. That's all."

"Hmm." He narrowed his eyes. "Too bad, you're eating. Otherwise, I'm going to be stuck listening to you whine in a couple of hours about how you're starving and that shit is annoying." He glanced at me for another second before pulling me onto the seat next to him, throwing his heavy arm over my shoulders.

I didn't even care that he was sweaty, so I put my head on his shoulder and closed my eyes. Tuning out everyone getting on the bus, I felt it start moving, but I stayed in my spot, appreciating the rare moment in which my brother was both quiet and comforting at the same time. The next thing I knew, the bus was stopping again across the street from some diner. I got out with the rest of Ghost Orchid, the members of TCC following behind, though I wasn't exactly keeping an eye.

A warm hand grasped my shoulder as we walked in. It was Mason, looking at me with concerned aquamarine eyes. "Not feeling good?"

"Not really." I gave him a half-hearted smile.

I didn't want to look behind me, but because I was an idiot, I did. I spotted Sacha in the parking lot with two guys, another girl and the redhead from earlier, before they made their way inside. My stomach sputtered again, and I turned back around to wait for the waitress to join three large tables for all of us to sit.

"Did you see E trip getting offstage?" Mason asked, rooted in his spot next to me.

Under normal circumstances, I would have asked for specific details and been disappointed that I missed my twin embarrassing himself, but it was a testament to the green-eyed bitch in my heart that I could barely smile. "No."

He frowned and yanked on the end of my sweaty ponytail hard enough to make me yelp. "I don't like seeing you like this. Quit it."

"You dick," I groaned, rubbing the spot where my hair was tied back. "I hope your razor yanks a couple pubes out the next time you shave down there," I muttered.

Mason laughed. "There's my bride." He elbowed me with a wink. "And I don't shave."

Oh my God.

Just like that, I told myself to ignore the feeling in stomach and I did, mostly. I snorted, thought about hugging him for a second until I remembered he hadn't showered in a few days, and instead poked at the spot right under his ribs where I knew he was ticklish. Once the tables were ready, I sat down between him and Eli, with Carter, Gordo and Freddy across from us.

I spotted Sacha three seats down on the same side I was on. I may or may not have noticed that he pulled out the chair next to him for the redhead before they took their seats. I ordered my food and tried to focus on the conversation around me—one was about Fruity Pebbles versus Frosted Flakes, and the other discussed woods used as guitar fingerboards. At one point, I noticed Sacha leaning forward over the table looking at me but luckily Eliza moved a split second later, blocking his view.

When I got up to the use the restroom after finishing my meal, I pulled my phone out of my pocket and started poking around at the screen like I was busy sending an important text message so I could focus on that and not the people I was walking by. Once in the bathroom, I used it as slowly as possible, willing away that crappy, unsettling sensation that seemed to jackhammer away at my nerves.

He had a girlfriend, or a girl he was interested in. Was that really so surprising? It shouldn't be.

I wasn't particularly stunning; I rarely put a

whole bunch of effort into my appearance, and we constantly teased each other and talked about bodily functions. That wasn't exactly screaming romance.

Fine. It was fine. Everything was okay; at least it would be.

I ducked out of the bathroom, heading back to the table with a headache. Unlike before, I trained my eyes on the wall ahead of me so that I wouldn't look down when I passed Sacha's seat. Was I being immature? Maybe a little, but I didn't care. My heart was pounding, my head was throbbing, and I felt like a fucking moron.

The warm, firm grasp that landed on my forearm stopped me right when I saw the shaved hair on the side of Sacha's head in my peripheral vision.

"Fight Club," his low voice murmured, tightening his grip on my arm.

It took everything in me to swallow the bile that had mysteriously appeared in my stomach before I glanced at him, as blankly and indifferently as possible. *Friends. We were friends*, I reminded myself. "Hey."

Those pale gray eyes flickered over my face, which I knew was smudged with eyeliner and slightly oily from how much I'd sweated throughout the day. My hair was a side-ponytail mess and there were also ketchup stains on my shirt. So, pretty much, I looked as attractive as possible...

To a blind man.

"Gaby, I want you to meet my friends." Sacha

said, watching me swallow hard. He started pointing at the four people surrounding him. "That's Matt, Seb, Bianca and Liz."

Liz. The redhead.

Reaching deep inside of myself for my inner adult, I pulled my arm loose of Sacha's grasp to look at his "friends" and I waved. "Hi," I greeted them, noticing just how fake the red color in his "friend's" hair was. Who did she think she was? *The Little Mermaid?*

They all greeted me, but it was the final person who made my head hurt worse.

"Hi," Ronald McDonald's illegitimate daughter replied, blinking big, brown eyes in my direction. She had that kind of classic beauty that would give a photographer a boner. And perfect, clear, pale skin.

What a bitch.

"Your hair is so cute," she added.

A big part of me wanted to say something really bitchy like "does it look like I care" or "go fuck yourself." I didn't though. But I really wanted to.

It was my period talking. *Right*.

I just smiled stiffly. "Thanks."

"I wanted you to meet them earlier, but you disappeared on me," Sacha explained with a smile on his face that made my stomach want to revolt.

I nodded at him, but it was so forced I'm sure my extreme level of discomfort had to be apparent.

Awkward.

I coughed and pointed down the table. "I'm

going to finish eating. It was—" I nearly choked on my words because I was a terrible liar, "nice meeting you all."

I didn't even bother waiting for anyone to say anything before I was back in my seat, feeling like a complete fool. I knew how unrealistic it had been for me to say that I'd never have feelings for another man because I didn't want the drama associated with a breakup ever again, but this was ridiculous. I felt betrayed and I had no reason to. I was just a girl Sacha had met and got along with because we were stuck on a bus on a trip together. That was all. My stupid fucking heart sucked; it strained in its cage while I sat there miserably.

I didn't speak to Sacha for a week.

CHAPTER ELEVEN

"What are you doing, little girl?" a voice whispered at the same time a hand clamped down on my arm.

Instead of screaming like most sane people would if they were sitting in the dark watching *Sabrina* with a bottle of wine in hand—I peed myself a little bit. Honest to God. I peed myself. Not much, but enough.

But I'd like to justify what happened by admitting that my subconscious would always recognize the asshole that had apparently crawled across the floor to scare the Jesus out of me.

"Damn it, Mase," I hissed as I pulled my legs to my chest, sitting up straight.

Sure enough, he was lying on the floor with a big grin on his face. "Did I get'cha?" he asked as he brushed his pajama pants off and got to his feet.

"Yeah. I need to go change my underwear now,

thanks." Thankfully, I'd brought my backpack out of the bunk area when I'd gotten up.

I ignored his laughter as I went into the bathroom and changed out of my super-sexy period underwear, putting them into one of the plastic bags we left stashed under the sink in case of emergencies. I noted that my period was, in fact, finally over. I hadn't been sure if my hormones were still out of whack due to it, or if I was just being grumpy because I could be.

I'd still been feeling pretty bitchy all afternoon and all night—okay, all week—but it got worse after I'd run to the trailer in the middle of the opening act's set and zeroed in on Sacha, Julian and Miles being surrounded by five girls wearing shorts that looked more like underwear and cropped tops. Prostitutes.

To be fair I'd tried to stay away from just about everyone except Carter, who was the only calming influence on the tour, over the last seven days. I did it mainly because I knew I was being mopey and moody. There was also the fact that my three baboons knew me too well, and if they put their minds to it, could figure out there was more to my attitude than simply a bad period.

So I'd told them all I was sick.

Which was why I'd been hiding in my bunk for the most part over the course of the week.

Except tonight I hadn't been able to fall asleep. It was the first night of a two-day drive from Winnipeg to Toronto, and I had slept most of the day. I'd laid in bed reading until my eyes hurt, and by that time, the bus had gone silent, leading me to believe everyone had gone to sleep. Quiet as a ninja, I got up, snuck out of the bunk area with my backpack, pulled out the bottle of wine I'd bought that afternoon from the fridge and flipped through the satellite channels on television.

Not even half an hour into the old classic movie and Mase had gotten up.

Hating the idea of going back to bed, I headed back into the living area to find him sitting on the opposite couch I'd been on, sipping wine straight from the bottle as he watched the movie on the same super-low volume I'd left it on. When he heard me close the bathroom door, he looked over and smiled.

"Got some new panties on?"

"Ha ha," I muttered.

Mase simply grinned as he took another drink. His eyes strayed to the screen. I sat in the same spot I'd been in and went back to watching the movie. A few minutes passed before I felt the nudge of glass against my hand. He was holding the bottle out for me to take and I did.

I'd barely taken a sip when he asked, "You finally over it?"

"I'm feeling a little better," I answered, eyeing him, trying to be all cool and indifferent.

He gave me a flat look that immediately made me sit up straight. "Do I have STUPID written on my forehead?"

I blinked. "Is this a trick question or…?"

The jackass didn't even hesitate in the split second between when I finished trailing off and the time it took him to reach across the walkway to pinch my butt cheek. I squealed and tried to pull away but it only made the sting worse.

"Are you over your shit with Sacha?" He finally just went right on out there and asked after letting go of my battered booty.

Umm.

What could I do? I just stared at him. If I didn't admit or deny anything…

"Daddy Mason knows everything." He raised his eyebrows as he sat back against the couch again. "*Everything*," he enunciated.

Oh hell. "What—"

Mason stared at me with those intense blue eyes, and I stopped talking. We both knew it was pointless. Here I was thinking I was being slick by hiding and pretending I had a virus, and he'd known the truth. Which only meant the other two idiots had to know too.

That knowledge was definitely worth the sigh that came out of me as I shrugged, resigned. I scrunched up my nose, wrapping my arms around my bent knees again. "Is it that obvious?"

He shrugged back. "We figured it out the day after San Francisco."

I winced.

"You can't hide shit from us," he said, confirming what I should have already known.

I sighed again. "That's what I was afraid of, damn it." Thinking about it for a second, something occurred to me. "Why didn't Eli say anything?" We both knew he didn't know how or when to shut up. Hell, everyone knew that about him.

"He doesn't want to piss you off."

Yeah, that made me scoff. "Since when?" He usually went out of his way *to* aggravate me.

That had Mase grinning. "Since you left last time, Flabs. Shit, I don't want to piss you off too much either. That whole thing sucked." He paused and gave me what could have been considered a bashful look if it had lasted longer than a second. "How many months did we go before you started talking to us again?"

"A few," I answered almost guiltily. Then again, what did I have to feel guilty about? They'd opened their fat traps and said something that wasn't their business to tell. "I missed you guys too but—"

"I know we fucked up."

We looked at each other in silence. There really wasn't much to say after that. It was the first time any of them had completely acknowledged that they'd done something to hurt my feelings. I'd pretty much woken up one day and decided to forgive them for being assholes. I was tired of being mad, and honestly, I really had missed them.

The next time I saw them at my parent's house

during Thanksgiving, no one brought up what they'd done, and we went on as if that night had never happened. In reality, they'd told the members of the two other bands we'd been touring with that I was going to get breast implants because I had "one small one and one big one," as I remember very clearly. They'd laughed afterward, drunk and high out of their minds, unaware that I'd overheard.

It wasn't even them telling people I was going to get surgery and implants that bothered me. Who cared if they knew? I wasn't ashamed; I'd been ecstatic to finally be able to take this next step. What had reached deep within my soul and made me cry my eyes out in the venue bathroom for ten minutes straight, was that they'd laughed. They'd laughed at something that had bothered me so much for so long. I didn't know of anyone else who had been called "deformed" at the age of thirteen at camp and then laughed at. No one understood what it was like to never be able to wear tank tops unless the neckline was high, or trying to find bras or bathing suits that could be easily manipulated with padding so that my irregularity wouldn't be so noticeable. I never let anyone but my doctor see my chest, *ever*. Not even in a bra. I didn't even let my mom or Rafe see me in a bra. Brandon had been the first person since my plastic surgeon and my gynecologist that saw my breasts since we'd started dating shortly after I'd gotten them worked on.

And these three guys that I loved and that I knew

loved me back, had laughed at my expense in front of other people.

So yeah, I wasn't going to apologize for not speaking to them for a few months. They'd deserved it. Since then, years had passed, and I wasn't about to bring it up more than necessary.

Mase smiled, as if sensing exactly what I was thinking, and patted the seat next to him. "Come here. Come sit next to someone who loves your wino ass."

"I'm not a wino."

He shot me a look. "You were drinking straight from the bottle, sitting in the dark watching one of your favorite movies. You're really going to tell me you're not?"

The fact he knew *Sabrina* was one of my favorite movies didn't escape me, but still. I blinked. "Don't judge me."

"Too late."

That made me laugh. Before I could think twice, I got up and sat next to him, leaning into his shoulder with a resigned sigh. "I'm so stupid."

Did he assure me I wasn't dumb? Of course not. "No shit, Sherlock." He patted my knee. "If it makes you feel any better, I wasn't surprised. After me, he's the best-looking guy on the tour," the modest ass explained. "The guy's a pussy magnet, Flab. You know girls love singers. Gordo has to beat the girls off with a stick and he doesn't even like them. *And* he's an ugly motherfucker. What does that say?"

Ugh.

Of course I already knew all that, but still. He didn't need to just blurt it out like that. There was a hierarchy of attraction in bands regardless of what the members actually looked like: everyone liked the singer even if he looked like he ran a heroin ring; next were the guitar players, the drummers, the bass players and finally the keyboardists. It was like actors that weren't handsome but women liked them anyway because they were famous.

"I haven't seen him mess around with anybody, if that makes you feel any better," he added. "But..."

"Yeah, yeah. I know." But he'd still hung out with that girl. A fact I had been trying to come to terms with for a week.

I told myself what I'd been telling myself since then: he wasn't my boyfriend, he was my friend, and I needed to get over this possessive, jealous crap pronto. I was going to get over it. I would.

With another sigh I peered up at Mason who was still letting me lean into him and smiled reluctantly. "You really knew I was full of shit from the beginning?"

"You've been my best friend my whole life. Of course I know when something's up your ass," he stated.

That had me cracking a real grin. We had been best friends our entire lives; this beautiful, moronic boy-man who once had a gap between his teeth and didn't hit a growth spurt until we were almost sixteen. How many things had we done for each other? More than I could ever count and that alone made my heart swell with affection. Most people didn't have a single best friend, and I didn't just have multiple ones—I even had some that would commit crimes for me. This guy happened to be one of them. Was he perfect? Absolutely not. Neither was I.

But who needed perfect when you had someone loyal, funny, with slight mental problems that knew you inside and out? I didn't. "You know I love you, right?"

He put his hand on my head and ruffled my already messy hair. "Yeah, I know, Flabby."

I smiled at him and he smiled back at me.

Then he messed with my hair some more. "If it makes you feel any better, your boobs are way nicer than that chick's were."

Was it rude? Of course it was, but I laughed anyway, and me laughing only made Mase do it too.

"What would I do without you?"

"Be bored to death," he replied, tugging on my hair.

I crossed my eyes.

"I don't like seeing you bummed, so cut it out. A week is long enough."

If only he'd seen me right after my breakup. Plus, he'd already done who knows what to Brandon's car in retaliation. "See? And Mandy used to say you didn't care about anything."

He frowned. "I forgot about her."

"I just remember her telling me that she was going to kick my ass if I didn't stop text messaging you." Then I'd told her I'd been in Mason's life before her and I'd be in it afterward, just to be a bitch.

He cracked up. "She hated your guts! I forgot about that!" He blew out a breath. "Most of my girlfriends—" for the record, he hadn't had an official girlfriend in at least five years, "haven't liked you, now that I think about it."

Of course they hadn't. Most of them had always thought there was more to our friendship than what there was. It wasn't like I could blame them, but I always tried to be extra respectful and not pinch his butt cheeks out of anger when he was dating someone.

"Remember Teresa Martinez back in junior year? I broke up with her because she said you were annoying."

I blinked, knowing exactly whom he was referring to. She'd been one of his girlfriends that hadn't gotten on my nerves. That fake bitch. While I realized it was dumb to be offended over a comment someone had made ten years ago, I couldn't help but get a little grumpy about it. "She said that to you?"

"Yeah. I couldn't believe it. You're a pain in the ass, not annoying."

I snorted. "Well, she was a slut, I remember that."

He elbowed me with a snicker. "I know. That's why I dated her."

Oh God.

Then he kept on going, as if I wanted to hear all the shitty things his past girlfriends had said about me. Which I didn't. "You remember Crystal Hernandez? Senior year? She called you a bitch. I let her give me a blow job and never called her again."

My hands went over my face as I repressed the urge to laugh. When I finally had myself under control, I cupped my cheeks and shook my head. "What a noble, noble gesture. Seriously. Thank you."

Mason grinned. "Right?"

Dropping my hands, I nodded up at him. There were tears in my eyes, and I didn't even bother blinking them away. "I wouldn't trade you for a million dollars, Mase."

His reply was to beam at me.

"But for ten million, I'd work out some kind of visitation schedule."

～

It was the pain in my neck that woke me up.

There was also the fact that one of my legs was hot, my arm was numb, and I had a headache.

I'd barely opened an eye to figure out what the hell was going on when I realized I wasn't in my bunk. The cushion beneath me was harder than it should have been and there was way too much light. What the hell?

I tried to think back on my last clear memory, and

that was Mase and I on the couch watching infomercials and arguing over whether this bonding glue they were presenting would really work or not. After that I couldn't remember anything. The only answer I had was that it didn't take a genius to figure out that my head hurt from the entire bottle we'd polished off between the two of us.

Once I managed to pry another eyelid open, it was confirmed that I was still on the couch. My skull was using my inner bicep as a pillow and luckily I was facing the back of the cushion instead of outward where everyone could see my face while I was sleeping. It wasn't until I tried to get to my knees that I realized why my leg was so hot. Mase was passed out halfway on top of me, half on his side. He was using my lower back as a pillow, and I think he might have been cupping a butt cheek.

I groaned as I started shaking one of Mason's shoulders blindly, trying not to savor the weird taste in my mouth. "I need to get up," I mumbled, shoving at him until he grumbled and squirmed around. As soon as he shifted, I rolled off the couch and just barely landed softly on my hands and knees before settling onto my butt. I groaned, vowing never to drink so much wine again. That was when I looked up.

Sitting on the opposite couch, staring straight at me with a bowl against his chest, was Sacha.

Of course it was.

I smiled weakly at him and got to my feet with a

mumbled, "Morning."

I looked away before Sacha replied back with a "Morning, Gaby," as I bent over and shook Mason's shoulder some more.

"Go back to your bunk, crackhead," I told my lifelong friend.

Mase groaned and rolled onto his back, opening up one sleepy eye. He waved me off, and I figured I'd done my best. If he ended up with Sharpie on his face, it was his fault.

I staggered to bed, pulled the curtain across and went back to sleep.

~

"Gaby? Are you awake?"

Yeah, I was awake. No, I still didn't really want to talk to him.

I'd been lying down in my bunk for the last hour, head aching, the curtain blocking everything and everyone out while I traded on and off between thinking and reading. I thought about my family that I'd just seen and how they loved me, about Eli who was my partner in crime for life, Laila, Mason and Gordo. I even thought about Brandon briefly. Mainly, I thought about Sacha, how I felt about him and how I needed to get over it. Or at least deal with my crush more effectively.

I'd gotten over a big breakup already and this wasn't even a breakup though to a certain extent, it felt worse. Maybe because there hadn't been a single chance of anything. Or maybe just because I was crazy. More than likely it was just me being crazy and dumb and a sore loser.

Regardless, I needed to get over it.

"Gaby?" the voice whispered again.

I glanced up like I could see through the materials separating Sacha's bunk from mine and felt my lips purse together for a second. In that same moment, I wondered about what he'd want to talk about. I needed a few more minutes for my new mindset to really kick in, so I stayed quiet.

I'd overheard them talking about how we were stopping pretty soon to shower, and I wasn't really in the mood to talk to anyone yet.

Get over it, Gaby. Deal with it. Quit being a little bitch.

"*Best of the Best*?" Sacha whispered once more.

I didn't respond, but I did feel slightly bad.

Was I being an asshole? I'd had guy friends in the past who liked me, and I didn't like in return for one reason or another. But had I been awkward and rude to them? Of course not. Had they been upset with me for not wanting to date them?

No. They hadn't.

In hindsight, I realized that I was being more of a bitch than I needed to. I had gone out of my way to avoid Sacha. When he made some kind of indication that he wanted to talk to me, I'd do something so that he couldn't. I knew I was being immature, but I was so disappointed in myself that I didn't have the heart to want to talk to him.

That wasn't his fault.

All of a sudden, the curtain to my bunk swung open and the next thing I knew, this gigantic body caused an eclipse before rolling onto my bed, closing the velvety material behind him.

And I knew it was a "him" even though my eyes hadn't adjusted. I could recognize Eli's scent in a landfill.

"What are you doing?" I whisper-hissed at him, his head exactly five inches away from mine. His body crowded mine into the back paneling so I was on my side, crammed against the wall.

"Are you awake?" he asked in a normal voice. I still couldn't see his face clearly.

"I am now." I whispered back, conscious that a certain singer might still be in his bunk, listening in.

He poked me in the forehead with his index finger. "Is your period over yet?"

Only he would think about asking me that. I'd swear Eli was the most desensitized man on the planet. There were times when I was younger that I think he seriously believed we were the same person in two different bodies. "Yes. Why?"

"I want to know if you're done being in a shitty mood."

At the mention of my shitty mood, I had a flashback of the scene I'd walked in on and my stomach revolted. I had no right to get so jealous but my brain and body didn't see that point, apparently. I wasn't going to tell him that Mase had told me he knew exactly what had been going on. If Eli hadn't brought it up, I didn't want to either.

"I think so," I answered honestly, poking him in the forehead like he'd done to me. "I hope so."

He made a humming noise in his throat. Neither one of us said anything for a long minute as we faced each other in my bunk, just barely fitting. We just stared until he broke the silence in a low voice. "You aren't planning on going home, right?"

"No." I scrunched up my nose despite the fact he more than likely couldn't see me doing it. "Why would you think that?"

"Because you're not happy."

And there went a point for me feeling like an extra douche. I bopped his nose with my fingertip. "I'm fine, E. Swear. I'm not going anywhere."

I could see the outline of him resting his head on his hand. "I haven't told anybody anything about your boobs, you know."

I hadn't thought once he had. That had been my second condition when I joined the tour, especially after he'd opened his trap the last time I'd been with Ghost Orchid. "Don't say stuff like that out loud. I'm already sure half these guys think we're having some kind of incest thing going on; don't make it worse."

He let out a big laugh that had to have woken anyone still sleeping. "Fuck me, they do, don't they? Mateo asked me a couple days ago if we really were related or if this was just some messed up lie we'd been telling everyone forever."

"Like I'd put up with your crap if you weren't my brother," I snickered. "Ugly."

"Bitch, you were blessed to be born alongside me."

That had me groaning loud. "Oh God. Shut up."

Eli just laughed that laugh that had been my favorite since we were kids. It wasn't obnoxious or mean, it just… was. "We're about to stop. Want me to braid your hair after?"

Like I was going to tell him no.

Then it hit me. How bad had I been that he was actually offering to do it? One more point against me.

"Thanks, loser."

Right before he rolled out of the bunk with one final poke at my forehead, he said, "Your mom is a loser."

Some things never got old: like my brother's crap, and the fact that the sun would rise and shine regardless of what was going on in my life. Or not going on, in this case.

I was done being a mopey bitch. I mentally washed my hands of being this party pooper who had her feelings hurt because some hot guy had a maybe-sort-of-girlfriend. I didn't have a chance. I'd never thought I had one. I was being a possessive sore loser.

It didn't matter. I'd get over it, like I had everything else in the past.

I swear it was like a weight had been lifted off my shoulders once my inner serial killer went on vacation for the next three weeks. I waited until it sounded as if everyone had gotten off the bus for me to get out of my bunk, grab clothes and pay the restrooms a visit. I felt rejuvenated and more like myself than I had in what seemed like too long. Even my head stopped hurting, for the most part.

It must have been pretty apparent I was back to normal because Gordo slapped me on the back when I got on the bus after my shower. "You look like you're feeling better."

"I am." I pinched him in the stomach as proof before continuing on.

I made my way to the bunk area so I could throw my bag on the floor. In the middle of doing so, someone nudged at my lower back. With a glance over my shoulder, I noticed the pale gray eyes first.

"Hey," Sacha said, dropping his hand to his side.

"Hey," I told him, straightening up and shutting the curtain on my bunk. I didn't know what to say or even how to act now that I'd come to terms with the fact that I wasn't just attracted to him physically, that he didn't feel that way toward me, and that I finally wasn't going to let the worst of my emotions dictate my actions.

Yeah. I could handle this. A lesbian could find herself having a crush on Sacha. There was nothing wrong with being attracted to him. Plus, it wasn't like I was looking for a boyfriend either.

I smiled at him, tight, so tight it felt strained as I tried to ease the tension out of my shoulders and the fluttering, nervous muscles of my abdomen.

His hair was wet and there was pink to his cheeks as he looked me over. A backpack hung from one of his hands. "Are you mad at me?" he asked in a lowered voice out of the blue.

I felt a stab of guilt at how I'd blatantly avoided him, because that was exactly what I'd done. Then I thought about him and the redhead on the couch and that gross feeling in my stomach flooded my insides once more. Yeah, the guilt didn't last as long as it should have, but I needed to be an adult and deal with this head-on. It wasn't his fault I had a crush on him, and he'd never been anything but kind to me. In a way, it was like being prejudiced against him for simply being a great person. He couldn't help being likable even if I didn't know how to handle it.

Clearing my throat, I shook my head and kept my focus on his eyes, my features even. "No. Why would I be?" Did that sound as convincing as I hoped?

"You haven't talked to me at all. Every time I look at you, you look away," he stated so matter-of-factly I almost reeled.

And, I felt guilty all over again.

I dug deep for those lying skills I'd used so much as a kid to save Eli's ass and gave Sacha the most honest, remorseful smile possible. "I'm sorry. Everything is fine. I'm not mad at you at all."

Which was true, technically. I wasn't mad at him. I was mad at myself.

"Are you sure? Because you don't get mad very easily, and if I—"

Here he was, blaming himself. Good lord.

I'd never stood a chance, had I?

How could I not like Sacha? I wasn't blind or deaf. He was unbelievably attractive, sweet and just plain goofy. Reminding myself why I liked him wasn't helping the situation any.

Before he could carve a bigger chunk of attraction out of my soul, I shook my head. "You didn't. We're fine. I just wasn't feeling well, and I was..." I hesitated for a split second before I figured "screw it." Sacha said he had older sisters; it wasn't like he didn't know women had periods. "I was on my period."

The fact he didn't even blink at the p-word was impressive. All he did was nod before a small, unsure smile crossed his features. "Sure?"

I nodded.

His expression was only slightly wary. "I'm glad we're okay, then."

This stupid frog had crawled into my throat and all I could manage to do was nod.

Then he reached forward and tapped my elbow with his free hand, the corners of his mouth growing wider. "I've missed talking to you."

Good gracious. I shook my head and in a slightly weird voice, said, "I missed talking to you too."

"It's been pretty boring without you," Sacha added, the sentiment obvious by the creases at the corners of his eyes.

A small smile crossed my face, and I shrugged even as my insides went all wonky. I didn't know why I felt so... hopeless, but I did. I wanted to absorb his words and take them to heart, but a larger part of me didn't want that. What was the point? I filled a void as his friend. Keyword: *friend*.

As much as I wanted to be levelheaded about it and take what I could get, it wasn't easy for me. My mom had always said that I took things to heart, that I felt too much. Once I got my mind set on something, if I couldn't have it, then I didn't want anything else to try and replace it.

Eli happened to yell my name from the living area right then, so I flashed Sacha a smile before making my way toward my twin. When I'd barely passed him, he grabbed ahold of my forearm to stop me.

"I really did miss talking to you."

I nodded at him, not trusting the rusty, unsure words on the tip of my tongue. I needed to change the subject right then. I needed to try and be a better friend. "Let me know the next time you want to go for a run, okay?"

"You got it."

Well, if there was one thing I knew how to be, it was someone's friend. I could do it.

I could.

CHAPTER TWELVE

Carter and I high-fived each other the moment we finished loading up our bins onto the dolly. Tonight had been the last show of the North American tour in Philadelphia, and we were all in a great mood. Ghost Orchid had sold close to five grand in merch, which meant I'd made five hundred dollars. I couldn't believe it.

Something else I couldn't wrap my head around: how much money Carter had possibly made, considering his line was usually twice as long as mine. It must have been enough that my quiet, pensive friend was grinning from ear to ear, and he'd given me three side-hugs in the time we'd torn down our setup.

Part One of the Rhythm & Chord Tour was *over*.

It didn't matter that I'd been tired and restless lately, and over the last few days hornier than a virgin reading erotica since I hadn't had any privacy; I was relieved and excited that this leg of touring was complete. And I had money. I'd spent so little over the last six weeks because we really never did much. If the venue didn't cater, the money I got from buy-outs was more than enough for me to buy lunch and groceries for breakfast and dinner.

We were going to have three days off between tonight and when we left for Australia.

Australia. I was finally going, and I was pretty damn excited.

"Do you want to go shower while I load up?" Carter asked as we passed by the back area where the dressing rooms were.

The venue was one of the few that had showers, and we'd all agreed to get cleaned up before we got on the bus. The Cloud Collision's record label was stationed in Philadelphia and they were throwing an end-of -tour party / delayed CD release celebration at a club for them. I wasn't much of a partygoer, but everyone was going.

"Sure. Hurry and I'll save the shower for you," I told him, and he nodded in agreement.

I grabbed my backpack and ran over to the two separate bathrooms that each had a shower stall inside. Only one of the two doors was closed, so I darted through the empty doorway and stripped, showering and shaving as quickly as possible. I slipped on the dark purple dress I'd bought that afternoon after Eli so eloquently told me that I couldn't go out dressed like a hobo. I put on some make-up, twisted my wet hair over one shoulder, put all my stuff back into my bag, and peeped my head out of the bathroom to find that Carter was sitting on the floor right outside, with Julian and Isaiah standing about five feet away in the middle of a conversation.

"Your turn, bud," I told my newly bald friend.

He grinned at me, the piercing on his bottom lip winking at me as he jumped up, stealthy like a cat, and slid into the bathroom at the same time I slipped out. Julian had apparently still not forgiven me for the Brandon thing so I wasn't surprised when he looked at me with zero emotion. Isaiah on the other hand.... I pulled my dress down even as I smiled at him. The material was riding up my legs so much when I walked that I wondered how slim my chances were that I wouldn't show off my green underwear at some point. The problem had been that I'd only had twenty minutes to shop before I had to head back to the venue, and the choices hadn't been that great: too much cleavage or possible crotch-shots. Look like a hooker or look like a hooker.

I went with the latter.

The fourth person I saw on my way out was my brother, who was already dressed and typing on his phone. He happened to glance up, and glanced back down for a second before he looked up again.

"What the fuck, Flabby? You working the corner tonight, or what?" he cried, pointing at my dress.

"Shut your mouth," I groaned. He did this every single time I wore something that was more than two inches above my knee.

Eli glared at me a second longer before he rolled his eyes and went back to playing with his phone. Just as I started to walk away, he called out after me. "If you make any money tonight, I'm taking a cut!"

I flicked him off and got on the practically empty bus. The sound guy for TCC was inside and so was Miles. Things were still a little awkward between us since the Pickle Dick incident. While we'd only spoken a handful of words since the tour started, he was still giving me funny faces on top of the silence. I understood he was friends with Brandon, but the dumb fuck had thought it would be a good idea to go to a concert where his ex-girlfriend's psychotic brother was playing. Really, he had it coming.

Wanting to avoid the weird looks, I made my way to the back room and planted myself on the long couch with a book I'd stashed in one of the cupboards.

Carter came in a few minutes later dressed in gray skinny jeans and a button-up white shirt that he'd picked up that afternoon too. He smiled at me and sat down in the seat to the right.

"You look nice," I commented, earning a blush from him.

Mason came in next. His eyes were down, and his black pants and shirt were completely unbuttoned to the point I couldn't understand how his clothes were still on. "Hey man, can I borrow—." My longtime friend looked up and stopped talking. He blinked those big, blue eyes at me.

My face flushed when he didn't say anything for too long. "What is it?"

Mason turned to glance at Carter. "Get out and lock the door."

I couldn't help but laugh, kicking my foot out at him. "Quit it."

"Seriously. Flabby," he said, staring at my legs, "when are we getting married?"

My face warmed up again, but all I did was groan in response.

He looked at me for a minute longer before shaking his head and asking Carter if he had an extra belt. I hung out with Carter in the back while the bus made its way to the club. In no time at all, it came to a stop and I could hear everyone in the front getting off. Slipping on the short, black wedge heels I had scored that afternoon as well, I followed after my buddy to see that we were stopped in the fire lane at some place called The Magic Carpet. There was a line of people standing outside; I spotted Eli and Gordo bypassing the line and making their way into the club. Following in their direction, the bouncer just waved Carter and me inside without checking our IDs.

The club wasn't at all what I was expecting. For one thing, bouncy eighties music was playing. Instead of some dark, dingy place that definitely had dry sperm contaminating every nook and cranny, the walls were dark red, the furniture a contemporary black and gray scattered about the edges of the floor. The bar had some neon lights lining the stools, the counter and the shelves where the bottles were placed. Then there was the dance floor, which was the coolest dance floor I had ever seen in my life. The atmosphere was fun and clean.

Carter elbowed me when "Eye of the Tiger" came over the speakers. He made a face and gestured toward the bar with his head. I nodded and followed after him. "What do you want to drink?" he half gestured, half yelled. It'd only been four days since Mase and I drank my bottle of wine, and apparently I'd forgotten my vow to never drink again.

"Long Island Iced Tea," I mouthed back at him.

He nodded right before disappearing into the crush surrounding the bar.

I stood there, tapping my foot and humming along to the loud, ageless song playing through the speakers. Off to one corner were a few of The Cloud Collision's guys already talking to a group of girls sitting at a table. But no Sacha. Not that I was looking. This whole playing it cool and getting over a crush was going okay. If I just sucked it up, smiled and reminded myself there were plenty of other men in the world to have crushes on, it went easily. Sacha and I had even gone for a run in Toronto with a silent, broody Julian, and had lunch the day before in New Jersey. Needless to say, I was proud of myself for trying to be a good friend.

I kept on looking around, putting the Russian out of my head. The two soul mates, Eli and Mase, were nowhere to be found. Carter was back before I knew it, with a small clear glass in one hand, and a larger glass in another, holding it out in my direction.

"Thank you," I mouthed to him.

We stood there for a few minutes, and he walked around with me until we found a small, unoccupied table close the bathrooms. We sat there, sipping on our drinks for a couple of songs before I spotted Eli cutting through the mass of bodies on the LED dance floor and heading straight toward us.

He was holding his hands out in front of him, pretty much dangling his tongue out of his mouth while making the dumbest face I'd ever seen—his normal one. To top it off he was shimmying his shoulders.

I was already laughing by the time he made it to the table, and I slid off the seat, knowing it was pointless to fight with him. Turning to Carter, I held my hand out in his direction. "Come on!" I yelled with a big grin.

He shook his head.

"You sure?" I asked still practically screaming.

He gave me a thumbs-up with a smile.

Carter had already mentioned to me that he had an allergy to dancing, so I wasn't going to force him to do something he didn't want to. I hated when people did that to me. I gave him an "if you say so" shrug and followed Eli's big butt out to the floor.

Eliza started tutting—Egyptian-like dance moves —when we stopped in the middle of the floor with "Walk Like an Egyptian" blaring over the speakers. I mirrored his moves, laughing my ass off the entire time. One song turned into four while we danced in front of each other, our moves getting more and more outrageous as the eighties songs kept coming. The half of a drink I had guzzled probably helped.

I couldn't help but wonder why the hell TCC's record label had brought them to an eighties club, but I didn't care. I loved dancing, but only when I could act like an uninhibited idiot without worrying about everyone judging me. The next thing I knew, Mason booty-bumped me from behind before backing his ass up into my stomach for a few songs.

I pushed Mason out of the way when he started trying to sandwich himself between me and some random brunette on the dance floor. A hand brushed my ass as I wiggled my way through the crowd, and I whacked it away the second it came in contact with me. I'd barely stepped off the floor when I saw Sacha in... oh merciful God. Of all the things in the world he had to wear... He had on suspenders—*suspenders!* —over a shirt that was somewhere between pink and purple, and slim black jeans. He stood a few feet away facing the dance floor, talking to a shorter man with glasses.

TCC's singer smiled the second he realized I spotted him and waved me over. The thought of pretending I hadn't seen him didn't occur to me. We were friends and friends didn't ignore each other, I told myself, even as his eyes swept across my frame as I walked toward him. Yeah, I tugged my dress down.

"Gaby," he breathed into my ear when I stopped next to him. His hand reached out to land on the small of my back, and I had to fight the urge to react.

Good lord, was I that starved for attention I was getting excited over having a hand on the small of my back?

Yes. Yes, I was.

"Hi," the smaller man spat out in a shout.

I waved at the stranger and held out my hand to him. "Hi, I'm Gaby."

"Dennis, beautiful!" He shook my hand for a second too long and smiled, all small, flat white teeth out to say hello.

I'd gone months without a single freaking compliment, but now I dressed like a prostitute and suddenly everyone was appreciative of me. Oh fucking well. I would take what I could get. "It's nice to meet you!" I hollered with a big grin.

"Is this your girlfriend, Malykhin?" Dennis asked. At least that's what I think he asked but all I could do was wonder if I'd heard him correctly or if I was imagining it.

Before I could process the question that had come out of the small man's mouth, Sacha's fingers curled over my hip. "Not yet! I'm going to take her out to dance. I'll see you later, okay?" Sacha yelled at him, leaning forward.

Now, I could have freaked out. I could have. But I didn't. Mostly because I'd done this dance a hundred other times with Mason and Gordo. Whether it was to get them out of some other girl's—or in Gordo's case, guy's—clutches or to get them away from someone they didn't want to talk to, I'd been a wing-man, a scapegoat and a girlfriend without batting an eyelash. So, yeah. I knew my place in that moment. I was helping Sacha escape and I told myself it wasn't a big deal.

Friends. *Friends*. Right. I moved on mentally.

The little man nodded before winking at me.

My friend's hand pressed into my back, leading me toward the dance floor. As soon as we were about ten feet away, he lowered his mouth next to my ear. "I don't know how to dance." His breath washed hot against my skin. "That was our record label owner. He'd been talking to me for the last hour and I couldn't handle it anymore."

"I feel used, Sassy," I teased him, fighting back the disappointment stirring my gut. Scapegoat for the win. All right.

Sacha shook his head, the multi-colored strobe lights illuminating the sides of his short, short hair. "Never. If I pawn you off on him, then it'll be a different story." He tipped his chin down with a sweet grin that went straight to me knees, confirming the fact that I was a weak and pathetic person with no backbone when it came to this singer. "But I wouldn't do that."

"I hope!" I grabbed his wrist, pulling him toward the middle of the crowd where we could be away from anyone in our large group. "You really don't know how to dance?" I had to go up on my tippy toes and he had to lean down for me to speak into his ear.

He confirmed it. "No!"

I shrugged at him. "Who cares! I'm not that good either. Just have fun."

He smiled when the song suddenly switched to "Thriller."

I made a face at him before starting my well-practiced dance moves. My mom had been a huge, huge, huge fan and when we were little, she'd play this record a hundred times, teaching Eli and I the dance moves. I'm pretty sure we could both do the entire song if we wanted, and I wouldn't be surprised if he was off on some random corner of the floor busting a move solo. Sacha stuck his tongue out of the corner of his mouth and mimicked my moves pretty perfectly. I couldn't tell at all that he couldn't dance, but it also helped that we were both laughing uncontrollably throughout the entire song, and then continued through "I'm So Excited" when it came up next.

Sure I looked like a fool, but I didn't care. I wasn't the best dancer in the world, and I probably wouldn't want someone like Julian watching me, but this was

Sacha. My friend who happened to be pretty much perfect in his own goofy way, who had admitted to crapping in a trash bag at one point.

When we started running in place really quickly, he leaned forward, pressing his sweaty forehead against mine. I tried to bat away the funny, warm feeling in my stomach at the contact, I swear, but it was unbelievably difficult. He was too cute and so happy it overwhelmed me. His eyes met mine, all wide and starry like he'd discovered a new constellation. "I don't remember the last time I had so much fun!"

There really wasn't a point in even trying to fight my feelings for this guy, was there?

CHAPTER THIRTEEN

On the first day between tours, everyone with the exception of Sacha was busy nursing some degree of a hangover. He claimed he'd only drunk water all night. Show-off. I'd maxed out after two Long Island Iced Teas and a whiskey sour, but it had been more than enough to make me feel like hell the following morning. Needless to say, I was probably one of the people who felt the best. Gordo had drooped himself over one of my shoulders, and on my other side Carter had a wet towel over his face. The other guys looked like total shit when they weren't busy barfing outside the bus on-and-off all night and early morning. I felt really bad for whoever was stuck collecting carts in the parking lot at the grocery store the bus had stayed overnight.

Once the projectile vomiting and *The Exorcist* reenactments were under control, the bus finally pulled away from the desecrated parking lot. It was a quiet ride to the hotel we were staying at near the airport. Once we pulled into the Wyndham, everyone jumped off and headed into their respective rooms to suffer in private.

My room was next to Eli's and across from Gordo's. I spent the rest of the day vegged out on top of the covers with the air conditioner on full blast, dressed in only my underwear with snacks from the vending machine keeping me fed until the in-house restaurant opened for dinner. I took two long, hot showers without my damn flip-flops on for the first time in what felt like a lifetime. My thighs were sore from all the ridiculous dancing the night before. More than half of it had been with Sacha, who laughed and smiled through it all awkwardly with me.

I did in fact learn firsthand that he was way worse at dancing than I was. But he was so silly and enthusiastic that it more than made up for his big, goofy feet and sharp hips.

The other half of the night I'd spent dancing with my brother, reading crazy text messages that Carter's pissed-off girlfriend was sending him because she couldn't believe he'd gone to a club without her, and watching Gordo strike out with guy after guy at the bar.

Close to noon the following morning, the phone next to my bed rang.

"Umm... hello?"

"Gaby?" Sacha's voice carried over the receiver.

"Oh, hey." I'd been wondering who the hell would be calling my room instead of my cell.

He let out a long sigh of relief. "Thank fuck. I think I called everyone but you."

I snorted because I knew he didn't have my cell phone number. From their camp, only Carter had it. We text-messaged each other throughout the night if it was too loud to talk in person.

"What are you doing?" he asked.

I kicked the covers off my legs and groaned. "Being a bum. What are you doing?"

"I just took a crap, and now I'm bored out of my mind. Want to go play some soccer?" He said it all in one breath, like taking a shit was the same as watching TV or something. When I didn't respond, Sacha immediately threw out, "No death match crap again, just a regular game."

"I will if you promise not to mess up my face... wait. How are we getting there?"

Sacha made a flat, huffing noise. "I rented a car. Unless you want to walk, I'll follow you in the car," he chuckled.

What the hell else was I supposed to do? Watch more television? "Sure."

"Meet me in the lobby in fifteen," he ordered.

We hung up, and I got dressed for the first time in twenty-four hours. I sent Eli a text to let him know that I was leaving and headed to the lobby to meet up with Sassy. He was waiting there, in his black shorts and white T-shirt with Mateo and Isaiah alongside him.

"Morning," he said before Mateo echoed his greeting.

"Hey, guys," I told them, stopping in front of them.

Sacha shot me a smile. "Ready to go?"

I nodded and we headed out to the parking lot. There was a small red Kia parked in the lot. Mateo jumped into the front seat while Isaiah and I rode in the back.

"Are you ready for Australia?" Isaiah asked me quietly soon after buckling up.

"I hope so, I'm really excited. I keep checking to make sure my passport hasn't walked out of my bag on its own."

He gave me a hint of a smile. "It's my favorite place to tour, you'll see. "

"I like Australia," Sacha piped up from the driver seat.

"I like Europe," Mateo added.

Sacha made a farting noise with his mouth, his attention focused on the road. "Everybody knows you just like going to the Red Light District."

"The Red, *Red* Light District?" I slowly asked like there was another Red Light District in the world.

Mateo had the decency to give me a sheepish smile over his shoulder. "Yeah."

"Interesting," I drew out the word, trying to imagine Mateo walking up and down the street, picking up hookers. He was average height, average build, dark-haired and dark eyed. Julian definitely looked like more of the type of pick up a prostitute, but what did I know?

Mateo began babbling about how there were more than just hookers in Amsterdam, but I kind of zoned him out a little. We pulled in next to a park soon afterward and jumped out of the car. I snatched the sunblock from Sacha when he was done with it and slathered on more than I probably needed. We paired into two teams. Mateo slapped Sacha on the shoulder in his way of claiming him, leaving Isaiah and I paired up together.

We ran and ran and ran.

Up and down the field over and over again, chasing each other around. Just like the first time we'd played, the game started off pretty clean. We kept a respectable distance between each other and only focused on our feet to steal the ball. But after a few close goals, Sacha's hip checked mine and it was game-fucking-on.

"You little cheater," he laughed when I poked him in the ribs to distract him.

We played on and off for close to two hours until I had to lie on the grass from how hard I was panting. Sacha snaked his hand out for me to take and hoisted me up onto my feet. We got back into the car, having decided to stop for food on the way back. As soon as we settled in, he passed me his iPhone between the seats.

"Put in your number," he demanded.

We were leaving the country in two days, and I didn't see the point in giving him my number when he wasn't going to be able to use it, but I kept my mouth shut. I'd just finished typing in my name and number when his phone started ringing. "Liz" appeared on the screen, making my stomach churn at the memory of Ronalda and Sacha sitting on the couch together.

Ugh.

"Your friend is calling," I muttered, handing him back his phone while trying not to make a face. Or at least a face Isaiah could see from his spot next to me.

Sacha glanced at the screen once he took the phone out of my hand, paused for a moment, and finally put it to his face to answer.

"Hey...I just got done playing soccer... With Mat, Isaiah and Gaby... Yeah, she played... No, I guess she doesn't worry about her bikini line... Having a tan line isn't the end of the world, Jesus... No... No... We're leaving in two days... I haven't changed my mind... Liz... Liz... We already talked about this... Look, we're going to eat. I'll call you when I get back... Because!"

Yeah, I was totally watching his face in the mirror. I had no shame. Sure I was trying not to make it noticeable, but my ear was out and listening to every word.

Later on, I could remind myself why my stomach hurt and deal with being in a bad mood, but in that instant, I was listening.

Sacha blew out a loud breath, his eyes darting to the ceiling for a split second before continuing his call. "You need to think about what I told you. I'm not going to change my mind... Now isn't the time to talk about it... I told you in the bus—we've already gone over this. Okay?... I know... Okay... Bye."

Well, then. That was awkward.

Isaiah gave me a long side-glance before he cleared his throat. "She still giving you shit?"

Sacha nodded stiffly. I could see his hands flexing on the steering wheel. "She's just—," he grunted at the end in what I could only assume to be frustration.

Was it wrong that I sat there chuckling internally to myself? Nah. Well, maybe a little. I should have been sad that my friend was upset, but I wasn't.

"Women," Sacha huffed, turning really quickly to look at me with an impish grin.

I leaned forward and flicked his cheek in response.

∾

"What are my chances of dying of heatstroke?"

"You have a better chance of dying if I trip you on the way down."

I shot Sacha a dirty look as we walked down the stairs to our seats. It was the second day of our mini-break between tours, and the lucky bastard had gotten free tickets to a Philadelphia Alliance game. They were a soccer team for the Men's American League. One of TCC's fans had messaged him and offered tickets following a post he'd made on the band's Twitter account about our soccer game the day before. The four tickets he'd received were split between us, Julian and Mateo. Isaiah had bowed out with other plans. The big shocker of the day had been Julian, who finally wasn't acting as if I had herpes. He'd actually smiled at me when I met up with them in the lobby.

"These are awesome," I said when we found the lower level row where our seats were located.

Julian wiggled his way in first; I followed behind with Sacha next and finally Mateo. The game was set to start in five minutes, and I really needed some water. The bright, blistering sun was almost painful. I'd put sunblock on the day before but I hadn't reapplied it, and I'd gotten slightly burnt. My only relief was that the sun would be setting in about an hour. When a vendor started walking up and down the aisle immediately after we'd sat down, I shot up and tried to catch her attention.

"You guys want one?" I asked them.

Sacha and Julian nodded, and I shuffled to stand in front of Sacha so I could grab the three bottles and pay for them. Did I stop in front of him on purpose? No.

I was a damn liar. I sure as hell had. I was wearing my best pair of khaki shorts, and while I hadn't grown into great breasts, I did have a decent butt, so sue me. Slinking back into my seat, I caught Sassy wiggling in his seat as he reached for the wallet in his back pocket.

I scowled over, tapping his arm. "Don't worry about it."

He frowned slightly before nodding. "Thanks."

Julian who hadn't spoken to me in weeks, leaned over my seat. "Thanks, Gaby."

I nodded at him and settled in, gulping down half my bottle in one sip. "Do you ever go to games back home?" I asked them.

"No, San Jose is the closest city with a team, and we're usually gone every summer anyway. You?"

"Same here. Houston is a few hours away. I've gone with my best friend a few times; her cousin actually plays for the women's team there and sometimes gives her tickets," I explained. "We've paid to go see the men's team a few times. Laila likes to check out the guys."

Sacha raised a brow, though his attention was focused on the field. "And you don't?"

"Well, I don't exactly leave my binoculars at home."

He laughed and turned toward me. I struggled not to make a stupid face at his closeness. He smelled like clean, sweet man. "You're something else, you know that?"

I tried to take his words for how he really meant them and managed to raise the corners of my mouth just a little.

He smiled and leaned back, but his eyes were different as he did it. Those pale gray irises were bright, alert and a bit guarded. That was weird.

The game started immediately after that, and the screaming in the stands ensued. The first half was insane; there were a couple of close goals and everyone would go berserk when the opposing team got too close to the Alliance goal. When two minutes were left on the clock in the first half, a Philadelphia striker scored a goal and the stands went to hell. I wasn't even an Alliance fan, but I jumped up with everyone else and double high-fived everyone nearby. When I turned to Sacha, he slapped both his hands against mine before pulling me in for a hot, tight hug that lasted exactly three awesome, friendly seconds.

During halftime Sacha and Miles got up to go buy things from the concession stand, leaving Julian and I together.

"Sorry about the Brandon thing," the man next to me said unexpectedly, shifting in his seat to look at me.

Tearing my eyes away from the dancers parading across the field at the end of their halftime routine, I gave him a hesitant smile and shrugged. "It's okay. I'm sorry Eli and I both lost our minds."

"We've been friends for a long time, you know. We toured together a few years ago when I filled in for his guitar player." He pursed his lips together. "I should have known you were his Gaby, but I wasn't thinking…"

I could remember Brandon mentioning to me when we first started dating how he'd replaced members in his ensemble before I came around, so Julian's explanation made perfect sense.

"It's okay. Consider yourself lucky it was only temporary."

His snicker was so loud it caught me off guard. "Oh fuck, they suck, right?"

I nodded like I'd win an award for telling the truth about the human hemorrhoid's band.

"I don't have it in me to tell him his music blows now," Julian said with another snicker.

That had me throwing my head back to laugh. "I never did either. He thought I wore earplugs because I didn't want to damage my ears."

Julian joined me, chuckling. "You're a cool girl, Gaby. I'm sorry for being an asshole."

I'd just gotten over being an asshole to his bandmate, so I couldn't really be a hypocrite and not accept his apology. "Don't worry about it."

He reached his hand out and I couldn't help but smile at him in return as I shook his hand. "You really punched him in the throat?" he asked with amusement written all over his tone.

My face got a little red. "Yeah."

Something cold pressed against the back of my neck and I yelped. Sacha held a bottle out, a furrow to his eyebrows as he looked down at me. "I brought you some water."

"Thank you, Sassy," I told him, taking the bottle. He had another one in his hand and a small-sized popcorn tucked under his arm.

Julian let go of my hand before he spoke. "You didn't bring me one?"

Sacha snorted as he took his seat. "Fuck, no."

My gray-eyed friend settled the container of popcorn right smack in the middle of his lap. I didn't even think twice before dipping my hand into the bucket and grabbing as much as I could. Sacha smirked at me before taking his own handful and cramming all of it into his mouth.

"Are you having fun?" he asked.

I nodded. "I sure am. Are you?"

"Yeah." He smiled. "I am."

The game started up again and things got intense. It was one close goal after another, run, run, run, and a mess of screaming insanity. During a lull in the game, the two huge screens on opposite ends of the stadium lit up with footage on the field before the camera panned out and KISS CAM came up in huge pink, glittery letters on the screen. I smiled to myself when I saw it because I'd always gotten a kick out of the Kiss Cam at any sporting event I went to. The older couples were my favorites.

But when the screen zoomed in and focused on two people in the audience, it wasn't an old couple.

It was Julian and me.

My face flamed up like the guy in *Fantastic Four*

had gotten ahold of it. I looked in the direction where I figured the camera was and started laughing, shaking my hands and head in denial. The camera moved up and down in refusal of my gestures.

Yeah, my face turned even redder.

"Ah shit," Julian laughed right next to me.

I turned to look at him out of the corner of my eye and groaned when I saw the angle on the screen move up and down again while people in the crowd cheered us on. We looked at each other with dumb expressions on our faces, and I let the burn of embarrassment filter down to my chest.

"Gaby," I heard Sacha behind me, but I couldn't turn around. The camera was still on me. On Julian and I. I was frozen in place.

The crowd roared as the camera zoomed in again, a pink heart circling Julian's face and mine.

The guitar player in the shot next to me shrugged those big shoulders with a wide, careless grin on his face. "Fuck it?"

"Gaby," Sacha repeated my name, but I continued fighting the urge to turn around, I really did. The last thing I needed was to turn in his direction and make the camera focus on him and I for us to kiss. That kind of humiliation wasn't something I wanted to sign up for.

"Fuck it," I said to Julian with a rough, embarrassed laugh as my face got unbelievably hot.

He smiled and I smiled back at him nervously. Julian grabbed me by both ears, tugged my face closer to his and kissed both my cheeks twice as I burst out in what could only be described as giggles. The laughter in the stands was undeniable.

I choked a little and forced a cheesy grin onto my face as my heart kicked into a quick gallop at the unexpected and unwanted attention. It could have been a lot worse, right? They could have zoomed in on the object of my unrequited attraction to the left. I was still grinning as I patted Julian's shoulder for being a good sport, but I wasn't smiling for long.

When I turned to face Sacha immediately afterward…

He wasn't smiling. He wasn't smiling at all.

CHAPTER FOURTEEN

"Sit next to me on the plane."

I was in the middle of toeing off my shoes to place them on the plastic trays at the security checkpoint when Sacha nudged me with his elbow. All of the rest of my stuff was already on the long metal table heading to the x-ray. A few feet ahead, Gordo was getting screened. One side of my cheek came up when I caught Sassy's gray eyes. He'd been acting so weird since the day before at the soccer game, I wasn't sure what was going on with him.

But, I'd take him the way he was being right then, normal and playful.

"You want me to?" I asked just to be sure.

He nodded, smiling that huge grin that took up his face while simultaneously making me think of unicorns, before he glanced down to undo his belt. I swear I tried not to look in the general direction of his crotch, but I failed. Miserably. Maybe I should look at someone else's crotch? You know, to even it out so that I wasn't just eyeing his.

"I have movies on my laptop," he tried to bribe me, as if that was necessary.

I peeked down the line to see that Gordo was far enough away so that he couldn't overhear us. Glancing back at the perfect specimen of a man, I made a face. "What movies?" Like that really freaking mattered. I'd probably watch *Barney* with him if he wanted.

"You don't have any faith in my taste?" he scoffed.

"Eh."

"Next!" the TSA employee called out.

I groaned and went on to pass through the screening machine. A few seconds later, the woman waved me forward. Sacha went next. I waited to collect my things and kept an eye on him as he stood on the other side of the metal detector, talking to the employee there before being directed to someone else down the line.

Sacha pulled out two small black bags from his backpack to show the TSA worker. He presented the man a few small boxes with colorful lettering on them and presented a piece of paper. I was putting on my shoes while Sacha nodded at whatever the guy was telling him, stuffing his things one more time into his backpack.

"Ma'am, can you move down?" one of the airport

employees asked me as soon as I had all my things together.

I moved out of the way and went to stand off to the side. Sacha walked up to me just a minute or two later, still shuffling things around in his bag when he stopped.

"They find your stash of dildos?" I chuckled.

"Nah, just my anal beads," he laughed, pulling out a box that said something about lancets. When I furrowed my eyebrows in confusion, he shoved the box down his bag again. "They like to check everything sometimes," he explained, but I was still confused.

"Lancets?" I asked him, thinking of what they could be for, and then it hit me. I remembered my aunt Dora used to carry around boxes of lancets in her car in case of some freak emergency that she ran out. "You're diabetic?" The way I asked made it seem like it was some deep, dark secret he was sharing. Then again, I guess I sort of felt like an idiot. We'd been sharing a bus for an entire leg of a tour. How hadn't I known he had diabetes?

"Yeah." He finished zipping his bag before glancing up. "I never told you?"

Sacha hadn't told me a lot of stuff because we seemed to just joke around the majority of the time. We talked about some things like our families and our likes and dislikes, but he was still a stranger to me in certain ways. That seemed abundantly clear now.

"No." I tried to think if he'd done anything to give it away, but I couldn't. He was picky about what he ate most of the time and he didn't drink, but that wasn't unprecedented or unheard of.

He touched my arm to lead me in the direction of our gate. "I always test myself in the back room; that's probably why you haven't seen me check my glucose."

That wasn't surprising. He woke up after I did and went to bed after me. "Do you have to take insulin?" I asked because if he did, I'd be the worst friend in the world. How the hell do I miss these things? We'd spent a month together, not counting the week I was being a PMSing bitch and ignored him.

He shook his head. "Nah, I have Type 2. I've had it since I was a kid, so I've learned how to control it without medicine."

I remembered how my aunt would get sick pretty often. She'd have days where she felt like crap, but I knew she had to take insulin. "So…I won't have to stab you with a needle?"

Sacha bumped his shoulder to mine as we kept going to our gate. "Nope. Sorry, Princess."

"Damn it," I sighed in disappointment, earning me a chuckle in response. "You brought enough of everything, though?"

He bumped me again. "I did, don't worry."

"Does it run in your family?"

"Yeah. My grandma, my mom, my oldest sister

and I are all diabetic." He hit my hand with the back of his. "I'm gonna use the bathroom; meet you at the gate?"

"All right." He shot me a little smile before turning to go toward the restroom. I stood there and watched his butt for possibly ten seconds. He was wearing sweat pants—like most of us were in preparation of our two-day travel itinerary—and his just happened to magnify his butt perfectly. Ha-lle-lu-jah.

Stop. *Stop it, Gaby.*

The clearing of a throat had me turning in a different direction. My brother and Mason were walking toward me, both of them smirking like they knew something I didn't. Damn it.

"What?" I asked after joining the two of them.

"I saw you." Eli waggled his eyebrows.

I tried to control my face so that I wouldn't give myself away completely, but then again, this was my brother. Not just my brother, my damn twin. We pretty much had ESP. But... "I don't know what you're talking about."

"Oh no? You weren't just standing there checking out his ass?"

I blinked and I scoffed but couldn't hide the stupid grin on my face. *Busted.* "No. I just thought he had a stain on his pants."

Even Mason snickered as Eli pushed at my shoulder. "What? Kissing Julian wasn't enough?"

"What?" I croaked out, knowing I hadn't told him

about what happened because I hadn't spoken to him since before the game. Once we'd gotten back to the hotel, I'd gone straight to my room.

"Yeah, you were all over TCC's fan page. Somebody posted a picture of y'all on the Jumbotron at the game yesterday." He laughed from deep in his big barrel chest.

The blood drained from my face. If being on the Jumbotron period wasn't bad enough, being on The Cloud Collision's media page was so much worse. They weren't exactly a new band. "Seriously?" I choked.

Familiar green eyes glittered at me in amusement. "Oh yeah. Their fan totally posted that shit for all four hundred thousand of their followers to see."

The idea of so many people seeing and judging me... no thanks. Once, a couple years ago, Eli posted a picture of him and me on their Ghost Orchid page. Needless to say, the comments had flattered and insulted me at the same time. Since then, I'd tried to stay away from having my face plastered on the Internet for everyone to see. Some people were cut out for criticism from strangers. I wasn't. "He just kissed my cheek, Jesus Christ. He didn't stick his tongue down my throat," I argued.

Eli made kissing noises as he pursed his lips together like the baboon he was. "Flabby and Julian, sitting in a tree—"

"Shut your mouth," I groaned, knowing he was just trying to be a pain in the ass. While Julian was attractive, I felt nothing toward him except friendship or something close to it.

It was Mason who threw an arm over my shoulder, leaning almost too much weight onto me considering he was almost a foot taller. "You should look at the pictures."

I narrowed my eyes at him. "Why?"

He squeezed my shoulder. "Just do it."

"But why?" I asked again, knowing he didn't have it in him to be cryptic longer than a second.

The breath he blew out of his mouth told me I was right. "*Somebody* didn't look exactly happy."

My eyebrows went up on their own, remembering the exact face he was referring to. Sacha *had* looked disturbed, maybe even angry, and that was a surprise. In a month and a half, I hadn't seen him more than marginally frustrated. He was incredibly even-tempered and almost always had a smile on his face. With last night being the exception.

But Mase was right.

When I'd turned around after the Kiss Cam and seen the expression on Sacha's face, I'd frozen and taken a second to absorb it. In the blink of an eye, he'd wiped the look off and smiled tightly. He'd kept smiling tightly the rest of the game. From that moment, all the way up to him getting in line behind me to go through security minutes before, he'd acted a little strangely.

I didn't let myself think about it. What was the point? Maybe he thought I was a floozy for letting his friend kiss my cheeks. As soon as the thought entered my brain, I pushed it away. That wasn't like him. It was dumb.

"Who knows what he was thinking. It doesn't really matter," I said to him with a shrug.

My friend squeezed my shoulder in return as we made it to the gate and went to a vacant seating section where we plopped down.

I glanced at my ticket before slipping it into my backpack's zipper. "Is one of you sitting next to me on the flight?"

"Why?" Eli asked.

"Because…"

He leaned back and eyed me. "Let me guess, you're going to sit someplace else?"

When I nodded, Eliza started howling and thrust his hand out in Mason's direction. "You owe me twenty, bitch."

"Damn it, Gaby," Mase grunted, already reaching into his pocket for his wallet.

"You assholes bet?"

They both nodded in agreement, exchanging money. "Duh."

"You failed me, Flabs. Come on. I thought for fucking sure you'd tap into those marbles you call balls and not ditch us," Mase huffed.

For one second I felt a little guilty for wanting to go sit with Sacha despite how reckless for my heart it was, but then I remembered. "Oh, right. Like that time you guys left me at that party to go mess around with those girls, and I had to walk home with Gordo in the middle of the night?"

Yeah, that had them shutting up.

"I hope you both get Ebola," I added with a laugh. It really wasn't that surprising that they'd made bets or that one of them was upset they'd lost. I used to make bets with Eli over the most random stuff. Like how Mom react to certain things. With our mom there were certain levels of anger: she'd rub her forehead if she was only a little mad, next she'd start slamming drawers, then she'd scream our full names out, or finally, if she was really mad—and this was only with Eli—she'd start crying, asking God out loud what she had done to deserve to get treated "like this."

Sacha appeared a second later, sitting down in the empty seat next to mine and began talking to my brother about some band they really liked that had released an album that day. An hour passed by quickly. The next thing I knew, we were waiting in line to board the plane, and Sassy was asking Miles if he'd mind sitting with Eli and Gordo on the plane so I could take his seat. Miles was extremely laid-back, and he didn't seem to care about the change in seating arrangements.

Once onboard, the plane was the biggest one I'd ever seen. There were three sections with four seats in the middle and three seats on each other side. I just followed Sacha as he slipped into a window seat in the middle of the aircraft with me taking the middle. Carter waved before sitting with Mateo and Julian on the opposite side of the plane. I saw everyone else scatter into different rows.

A lady came and sat in the seat next to mine, telling Sacha and I hi.

Folding my hands into my lap, I turned my head to look at my seat buddy, who had his attention focused on me. "Is there anything else I should know about before the plane takes off?"

One smoky-colored eye went a little squinty. "Like what?"

"Oh, I don't know. Do you get nauseous on flights? Is little baby Sassy scared of flying and you're going to need me to hold your hand or something?" I asked.

That beautiful mouth with its plumper bottom lip, pursed. He blinked. "Do you emasculate every man in your life?"

"Just the ones I like."

He cracked a grin before reaching over to tug on the seat belt across my thighs. "All right, then."

I opened to say something but before I could, the prerecorded flight attendant came over the speakers with emergency procedural information. She went on and on.

"I'm probably going to pass out soon," he warned me when the speech was over. He was already settling the little pillow into the space between his head and the paneling.

I nodded in agreement. I'd gotten up early to go

buy last-minute things with Carter that morning and we'd walked around a lot. A nap was in demand. "If I snore, wake me up, okay?"

"No promises." He smiled.

Sacha began telling me about how loud Julian could snore, and then I told him about how my dad used to keep us up all night because he sounded like a dirt bike. The plane took off at some point and sure enough, my eyelids started to droop in no time. The little pillow the airline had provided was smashed behind my head, and I remember giving Sacha a sleepy smile.

I passed out.

Who knows how long later, my legs started to feel a little weird and uncomfortable, so I opened my eyes to find that I wasn't sitting up. My upper body was draped over Sacha's lap; the only thing keeping me from being face-to-crotch with his human *kolbasa* was the pillow. My fingers were wedged underneath one of his thighs and something warm was resting on my neck. I wiggled one hand out to feel that his fingers were cupping my throat. He wasn't moving, which meant he was probably asleep too.

I wasn't going to overanalyze it. I would have done the same with my baboons. I closed my eyes and went back to sleep.

~

"Would you like anything else, sir?"

I had to slap a hand over my mouth to keep from laughing. The flight attendant was bent at the waist and leaning over the lady in the seat next to mine. Hell, I could have poked her forehead if I wanted to. But she didn't care about us; I don't even think she really saw the other passenger or me sitting there.

Her focus: Sacha.

Sacha, who had just woken up three minutes before and had a little bit of drool on the corners of his mouth while one cheek was pink and lined from the position he'd been in. His eyes were still heavy with sleep. After a four-hour nap, I'd woken up with a stiff back, neck and hips, and then shook his arm to get him up when I spotted the flight attendant coming down the aisle with a cart.

"No, thank you," he answered her with a slightly awkward smile on his face.

The woman, more than likely in her early or mid-thirties, stayed in that position a second longer than necessary before lowering her voice to sound... sultry. Yeah, she definitely sounded sultry. I didn't even think it was possible to sound so sexy. "Are you sure? Anything else at all?"

I squeaked right before Sacha pinched my leg. "No thanks."

"Okay," she replied before sauntering off to the next row with her cart.

"Holy shit!" I tried to muffle my laugh, whispering because I knew she was right behind us.

Sacha shot me a look out of the corner of his eye

before picking up his cup of water to sip from. "Don't say anything," he groaned.

"Sassy, that lady totally wanted to scramble your eggs."

I heard him choke and cough before pinching the bridge of his nose with a gasp. "Jesus Christ, Gaby," he hissed as he tried to get himself under control. I made it look like I was cracking eggs in midair and then stirring them. He reached out to push my hands down with a groan.

"You think I'm joking, but I'm gonna barter your nuts for some snacks later when I get hungry. We still have two hours left on this flight." We were stopping in San Francisco to connect with our second flight to Sydney, and then one more to Perth. Thankfully, the first layover was only an hour long.

Sacha's shoulders started shaking as he laughed, his hand slapping an imaginary Band-Aid over his mouth. "I'll share my snacks with you. Just don't trade my virtue for food."

That had me throwing my head back. "Your virtue? Ha!"

"Gaby Barreto, are you trying to tell me that you think I've tarnished my reputation?" He was trying so hard not to smile, but this guy probably smiled in his sleep—it was an impossible feat.

Putting my hand on top of his wrist, I made an incredulous face. "Do you remember the Pickle Dick incident? I'm pretty sure you," I leaned closer to him because the lady on my other side was awake, "said you liked p-u-s-s-y. I'm sure your virginity's been long gone, kid."

The apples of his cheeks turned pink as he smiled. "Yeah, I did say that," he chuckled. "And I haven't been a virgin for a while, but I have four sisters and too many fans that like me but don't even know me. You probably wouldn't believe me if I told you how many people I've been with."

I didn't really want to ask when exactly he lost his virginity or what his tally was because it made me feel incredibly strange deep in my chest. Superhuman jealousy flared within my organs, which was stupid. "That's nice," I told him because it was. Most men nowadays slept with women whose names they couldn't remember the next day. My friends and loved ones included.

"You, Princess?" he asked with a raised eyebrow, something flickering in his light colored eyes.

I narrowed mine in return. "Me what?"

"Is your virtue intact?"

I laughed. I swear, it wasn't like I wanted to laugh at that specific question because I knew it made me look like a total whore—which I wasn't, for the record—but still. He laughed too, right before I forced myself to sober up my expression and get as serious as possible. "Yes."

His eyes went wide and it looked like his jaw became unhinged. "No shit?"

"No, jackass." I leaned forward to dig my elbow into the meat of his muscular thigh. Sacha was slim but he had a pretty serious build. "I haven't been around the block. I've only had one serious boyfriend —," there was no point in mentioning Brandon's name and especially not my high school boyfriend's name, "and if you can't feel it, then it didn't happen right?"

Sacha snorted with a smile; huge, bright, so magnificent it made me think of the moon. "That's right, but I don't know what kind of guys you've been hanging out with if you can't feel it…"

I scrunched my nose, lifting a shoulder.

That magnetic smile morphed into something wicked before he leaned toward me. "You should definitely feel something."

I swallowed.

A slice of a shiver shot up my spine and I fought the flare of gooey feeling in my throat. "Yeah, probably," I practically panted.

He smiled at me, and I smiled back, my organs all out of whack.

Sacha reached up, licked his thumb and then dabbed at the corner of my mouth. "There. You had a little dry saliva going on there."

Yeah, I sat there like a completely dummy. My mouth was more than likely gaping. If anyone else had done that to me, I would have whacked his or her hand away. That was a fact that didn't escape me. Neither did the fact that I considered what he'd done to be sweet. Too sweet.

But one thing was certain when I started to think

him wiping my drool off was intimate…

I needed a vibrator. Pronto.

∾

"None of you found it in your hearts to tell me it was fucking winter here?" I hissed at the three monsters standing there comfortably with hoodies on.

They stared at me with wide eyes as I bounced around the sidewalk with my arms crossed over my chest. It was fifty-ish degrees in Perth, and I'd been expecting it to be, oh, maybe eighty or eighty-five. Instead we were stuck outside baggage claim waiting for the promoter of the Australian tour to come pick us up, and I was freezing my imaginary balls off. I was from Texas. We had two seasons: fifty weeks of summer and two weeks of something between a semi-brutal winter and a crappy spring. If it were less than seventy degrees, you would never see me without a jacket on.

My lower back was bothering me after that last ridiculously long flight, and I never wanted to sit again. Well at least for a few hours. With only my cropped sweatpants and an old Ghost Orchid T-shirt on, I wasn't prepared for the wind. Apparently, everyone else had known what was in store. They were all in zip-ups or pullovers except me.

"Come here, I'll keep you warm," Mason heckled from his spot a few feet away.

I rolled my eyes and snickered. The members of

The Cloud Collision were slowly trickling out of Customs and baggage claim since they'd lined up last with their work visas. I'd been fine coming in as a tourist on vacation.

"I'm sure one of us has an extra jacket you can borrow," Gordo said.

Not offering to let me borrow his.

Frowning, I walked around behind my brother and pressed myself, arms still crossed, against his back to block some of the wind. "So what's the plan?"

"What plan?" Eliza asked.

"Are we getting another bus or what?" I screeched when a particularly cold blast of wind hit us from behind.

Eliza laughed. "That's why I like you, Flabs. You're always up for whatever without worrying about the details."

"And that's probably why I always get in trouble with you," I snickered against his shoulder. It was true. Growing up, Eli would say "Let's go" and I'd go without questioning where. My trust in him had always been astronomical. Sure we'd get into trouble for being out of the house too long or doing things we shouldn't have been doing—this was namely just Eliza—but it had usually always been worth it.

He looked at me over his shoulder. "We're staying in hotels and the promoter is driving us around."

I nodded against him. It wasn't like I really cared if we were on a bus again or not, but the idea of sleeping on a real bed regularly sounded amazing.

"Do I get my own room?"

"You're sharing one with me," Mason claimed.

"In that case, I'm sleeping in the hallway."

Eli snorted. "Dude, I wouldn't want to share a room with you either after that stunt you pulled—"

"I was sleeping," Mase groaned.

My brother didn't even wait for me to ask what Mason had done before he started talking. "I woke up one night when we were sharing a room a year ago, and this motherfucker was jacking off five feet away. I kept yelling, but he wouldn't wake up until I threw the phonebook at him. He's the reason why we don't share rooms anymore. I'll pay for it out of my own pocket so I don't have to see that disgusting shit ever again."

"I was asleep," Mason echoed his earlier explanation.

Eli made a disgusted sound. "Whatever you say, man. Everybody is getting their own room anyway. I'm hoping to get some Aussie puss—"

"Please stop talking, I don't want to know," I cried, pressing my forehead in the crack between his upper arm and ribs.

"What don't you want to know?" Sacha's voice asked from behind me.

Turning my head to look at him, I saw he was already wearing a bright red hoodie. I grimaced in his direction. "Eli wants to get laid, and I don't want to know about it."

He smiled. Miles and Carter were trailing behind

him, pulling along their own suitcases. "I don't blame you." His eyes swept over me huddling into my brother. A frown came over his mouth. "Where's your jacket?"

"I didn't bring one," I said, wrinkling my face. "No one told me it was cold here."

Sacha didn't even hesitate, unzipping his hoodie, dropping his backpack to the floor and pulling free from the sleeves. "Here," he said, holding it out in my direction. "I don't want you getting sick." The right side of his mouth lifted in a soft smile.

Bless this wonderful, sweet, thoughtful man.

"Thank you!" I slipped that sucker on faster than I put on my bra after a shower in a cold room. The inside was already warm from his body heat and it had that distinct clean scent that I associated with him. It was two sizes too big, but I couldn't have cared any less.

He nodded at me, crossing his arms over his chest. The dark, thick tattooed bands on his arm popped against the simple white of his shirt and the gray of his sweat pants. He was way too good-looking for his own good, and I think that the fact he was so casual about it, so indifferent to his shockingly striking face, added to his appeal.

"You aren't cold?" I asked, being a perv and eyeing his nipples to see if they had perked up.

"Nah. This isn't that cold."

"Excuse me." I mocked him, rolling my eyes playfully. "But seriously, thank you. You're a real gentleman."

He just stood there, not warning me of the hard arm that wrapped around my neck a second later, squeezing down on my windpipe. "Go to sleep, Gaby," Eli's voice chuckled in my ear, reminding me of when we were younger and he would practice his wrestling moves. He used to practice the "sleeper hold" on me all the time in hopes he could make me pass out. I tried tipping my mouth down to bite his arm before he pulled away, giving my earlobe a yank in the process.

The honk of a vehicle made us all turn around. A big, white van pulled up alongside the curb with a trailer hitched to it; a young guy jumped out, immediately going toward Sacha. He introduced himself as Vince, the promoter for the Australian tour, and wrangled us into the van with all of our crap. I ended up sitting between Carter and Gordo on the ride to our hotel.

Australia reminded me of what most Americans pictured Texas to be. Texas wasn't cattle and cowboys, like Perth, Australia, wasn't kangaroos and koalas on every corner.

Vince told all of us where we could eat nearby, what places to stay away from, and other stuff I was too distracted to listen to. We pulled into a decent-looking hotel, and Julian pulled my suitcase out of the back for me. The promoter got us all our room keys, and I found that our rooms were on different floors. Half of us were on the first floor while the other half were on the second floor.

On the way to drop off our luggage, I realized I was on the same floor as Mason, Gordo, Julian and Carter.

"You sure you don't want to share a room?" Mason asked as we both stood at our respective hotel room doors, sliding our keycards through.

Propping the door open with my foot, I nodded. "Positive." Idiot.

"If you change your mind…"

"I'll go sleep with Gordo."

His mouth flattened and he blinked those beautiful blue eyes at me. "I can wait until our wedding night if you want."

I pulled my suitcase into my hotel room and blew him a kiss when only my head was hanging out of the doorway. "You are so thoughtful. Thank you for understanding."

I let the heavy door slam shut behind me. The hotel room was clean and small, and I sure as heck wasn't going to complain. Unzipping my suitcase, I pulled out clothes and took a nice, long shower to wash off the millions of germs I'd picked up on the three flights to Perth. I'd barely pulled on my favorite jack-o-lantern leggings when someone began banging on the door.

"Who is it?" I yelled, tugging a black tank top on.

"Sacha, *Bloodsport*."

CHAPTER FIFTEEN

Sacha?

I eyed myself in the mirror and shrugged. "Coming!" I called out, hustling toward the door as I wrapped a towel around my wet hair.

The lock had barely been flipped when Sacha asked from the other side, "You hungry?"

Pulling the door wide, I smiled at the fresh-faced, wet-haired man leaning against the door with his hands in his pockets. "I'm always hungry."

The words had barely come out of my mouth when Carter and Julian walked by. "Come eat with us, Gaby." That was my fellow merch salesman inviting me out.

I almost asked where they were planning on going, but really? It wasn't like it mattered. "Are you guys leaving right now?"

Sacha nodded but his attention was focused

lower. On my pants. And he was grinning.

"Okay, give me two minutes to change," I said already taking a step back and pulling the towel off my head.

He lifted his gaze, the corners of his eyes crinkling in amusement. "Why? You look adorable."

My cheeks went warm, but I groaned, pushed the compliment out of my head and took another step into my room, holding the door with my hand. "Yeah, yeah. These pants aren't warm anyway. All I need is one minute, I promise." I dashed inside, stripped off my leggings, threw the towel over a chair and put on a clean pair of jeans. Slipping Sacha's hoodie on and my shoes, I grabbed my purse and room key. I opened the door and found my friend where I'd left him. Down the hall by the elevators, some of the other guys were waiting around.

"Ready?" Sacha asked, dragging the hood part of his jacket over my too-damp hair.

"Ready." It was right then that I noticed he was only wearing a long-sleeved shirt since I had his jacket on. Guilt poured through my veins. What if he got sick? He was the most particular singer I'd ever met; he was always trying to take care of himself and his voice. Hell, his warm-up routine alone before each show took an hour. "Do you want your hoodie? I don't mind staying, especially if someone brings me food back."

He took my elbow, his fingers so long they

wrapped around it with length to spare. "Keep it until you get one. You don't need to be getting sick, Princess."

"Are you sure?" I asked, looking up at him and eyeing his own not-so-dry hair. "No one cares if I lose my voice, but I might get stabbed if you lost yours."

Sacha looked down at me and sort of frowned. "I'm positive. I'll be fine." He blinked. "Have you always been this short?"

That had me groaning. "Yes, Captain Obvious."

"Are you sure?" He reached over and patted the top of my head through his jacket. "You're so cute. I can put you in a carrier—"

I hit him in the arm with a cough. "*Stop*. God, stop it."

Sacha laughed, squeezing the elbow he was still holding. "I'm joking." He dodged my next hit just barely. "But really, how tall are you? Five feet?"

Tipping my head back, I glared at him. "I should have pawned you off on that flight attendant when I had the chance…"

≈

"Flabs, let me get a bite of that," Mason said, his hand already extended across the table as he wiggled his fingers.

I didn't even bother responding before passing my burger over in mid-chew. The Australian promoter had pointed out a restaurant on our drive to the hotel that was within walking distance. We'd all met up in the lobby and made the three-block trip like we were training for a marathon. Needless to say, the last time we'd eaten had been on the flight hours ago and everyone was starving.

Without bothering to ask for permission as usual, Eli took the opportunity to grab my glass and take a big gulp of water just as Gordo, who was sitting on my other side, snagged a few fries off my plate. In the seat across from my brother and next to Mase, Sacha raised his eyebrows as he watched Mason hand me back my food.

I smiled, taking another bite. "I'd offer you some…"

He snickered. "Yeah, thanks. It looks like everyone else is eating half your food anyway."

I shrugged, popping a fry into my mouth. "It's why they tell you not to feed stray animals—"

My brother pinched the back of my arm hard.

"Oww, E, you ass," I cried, rubbing the spot where he'd gotten me.

From the other side, Gordo pinched my other arm.

"Damn it, Gordo," I hissed.

Down the long table, some of the guys were turning around in their seats to look at something, but I was too busy trying to pinch Gordo in revenge to notice what it was.

I'd just got him back when I overheard one of

them say, "Look at those monsters."

It was Miles whose voice that I recognized that answered. "How big do you think those things are?"

There were murmurs as replies that I couldn't hear clearly, but I wasn't an idiot. I knew exactly what they were talking about. Which was why my spine went a little rigid without conscious prompting. I tried not to listen.

Then they started laughing, and I swear it was like reliving that moment two years ago when I'd overheard my loved ones talking to our tour mates about boobs—specifically mine.

"I'd motorboat them—"

"Motorboat? I'd love to—"

I scratched at my eyebrow and blew out a breath, telling myself to ignore the conversation. They weren't doing it around me, technically. They weren't talking to me. It also wasn't like guys didn't talk about women like that all the time either, because they did. Not to be a hypocrite, I'd willingly admit I ogled half-naked hot guys from time to time.

"They look fake. Don't they look fake?" someone whose voice I couldn't pinpoint asked, and that had me really sitting there uptight.

Eli nudged my hand with his, meeting my eyes. He had this weird little tilt to his lips, and I knew he was well aware of what was bothering me. He nudged me again.

"Every girl I've ever met with fake—"

I started shaking my leg beneath the table, telling

myself to keep my mouth shut. *Not your business, Gaby.*

"—slut—"

I dropped my fork on the table, at the same time my face got hot. Really, really hot. Even my ears heated up enough that they began to ache a little.

When I was a kid, I grew up watching an actress on television with huge breasts and equally magnificent blonde hair, become a sex icon. While, on the other hand, magazines portrayed women with small chests, slim frames and narrow hips as a standard of beauty. But I was short, had wavy dark hair, a little chubby and had my poor, irregular-sized chest. I didn't fall anywhere close to either of those body types.

I'd had an A-cup and a C-cup for almost ten years, from my final growth spurt at fourteen to my surgery at twenty-three. No one could ever understand what it was like for me to deal with that or the lengths I went to hide it. I only wore shirts made out of certain materials. Never anything even remotely low-cut despite how much I would have loved to if only because I knew I couldn't. None of my tops had ever been tight.

I wore T-shirts over my one-piece suits because there was special, waterproof padding on my 'small side.' Picking out my prom dress had been a nightmare. Bra shopping gave me severe anxiety. Wanting to mess around with my boyfriend in the back seat of his car in high school had been an awkward experience of telling him not to touch my chest when he'd obviously really wanted to, and I'd really wanted him to as well.

There were so many times I cried because of how I detested my body.

It wasn't as if I wanted much. All I wanted was to be normal. I'd hated what I'd been born with and wondered *why me*. Why did I have to grow up to be shaped like that? I'd fucking *hated* it with every fiber of my being.

So what was I supposed to do? Was I going to live like that the rest of my life? Sure, I could have, but it was such a debilitating fear that someone would notice the imperfection that I would never be comfortable in my skin. As much as I didn't want it to bother me, it did.

I didn't want guys staring at my breasts. I didn't want to do porn or make money off my body. All I wanted was to feel better about myself. To get an even tan. To wear a bikini for the first time in my life because I didn't have to worry about padding coming out. I wanted to be with a guy and not worry about what they would think, or who they would tell if they found out one of my breasts was so much bigger than the other. I wanted to be confident with myself.

So I made it happen.

No one had tried to talk me out of it. No one shamed me into feeling like having implants made me a bad person or a floozy. My loved ones had been behind my decision from the beginning.

I saved up as much money as I could while on tour with Ghost Orchid to pay for the best cosmetic surgeon in Texas, and it had been worth every single penny. I would go through the initial soreness, pain and fear all over again. The first bikini I bought four months afterward had probably been the most conservative bathing suit on the planet, but I'd cried anyway when I put it on for the first time.

Who was anyone to make me feel bad about what I had done? And while every woman had her own reasons for doing what she wanted to do with her body, I was a firm believer that people needed to mind their own business. If you weren't hurting anyone and weren't asking for handouts, no one had a right to open their traps.

Just as soon as I opened my mouth to tell the TCC guys I had implants and that they should shut the hell up, two people beat me to it. Two totally unexpected people.

My brother.

And Sacha.

They spoke at the same time, making it was hard to figure out what exactly was said, but it sounded like a mix of "Would you shut the fuck up?"

I blinked. Then I blinked some more, totally caught off-guard by the ugly, unyielding tone in both of their voices. A knot formed in my throat, and I swear, for one long minute I just sat there absorbing the fact that they'd said something. Finally, quickly, the moment clicked and I remembered what was going on.

"Why?" That might have been Mateo asking.

It was Sacha that leaned across the table to glare at his bandmate, a no-nonsense expression on his face that made the corners of his mouth go tight. "Because you sound like ignorant assholes. My mom had surgery done. Are you calling her a slut?"

The silence that came over the table was deafening.

And so, so, so fucking awkward. Holy shit.

But it was the anger and loyalty radiating off the TCC singer and how it made me feel that shocked me the most. Did he know he was standing up for me? Of course not, but I took the victory to heart anyway, like he was my champion too.

I tipped my head to glance in Eli's direction only to find him already looking at me. He gave me a wide-eyed and more than slightly impressed look that said, "what was that?"

I told him with my eyes, "I have no idea."

His gaze said, "that was bad-ass."

Mine replied, "I know."

No one said much for the rest of dinner. Whether it was because we were all tired, too busy eating or if someone was feeling crabby because of how Sacha had reacted, I had no clue. I fell into the first two categories; I was also busy thinking about what he'd said about his mom. The curiosity was killing me, even though I knew full well it wasn't any of my business whether it was true or not. Everyone finished eating and we all lined up to pay for our meals individually, with me paying for Eli's when he happened to disappear. I waited by the doors for Sacha.

One of the last few people to pay, he was busy stuffing Aussie currency into his wallet when I said "Boo."

He smiled faintly as he stuffed his wallet into the pocket of his jeans.

"What's wrong?" I asked.

Sacha rolled his eyes and raised a shoulder. "Nothing that matters." He reached up to tug the hood over my head again. "I'm glad you're at least talking to me."

I smiled at him, hoping the pleasure and pride I was feeling over what he'd done radiated onto my face. "I think you're pretty wonderful right now."

He had a funny expression on his face. "Yeah?"

"Yeah." I bumped my shoulder with his. "That was really nice of you, you know. Saying something to them," I explained just in case he didn't know what I was referring to.

Sacha glanced at me out of the corner of his eye, getting to the door first to hold it open before waving me forward. "Let's go before everyone else finishes paying. I don't want to deal them right now."

Nodding, I went into the cool night with him following behind.

We walked in silence for a little bit before he

suddenly said, "They're real assholes sometimes."

I shrugged my shoulders so that I wouldn't outright say, *yeah they are.* "Well, you've known them for a long time and you're together constantly. It happens."

He nodded, his attention on the sidewalk as we made our way toward the hotel a few blocks down. "You know from experience?"

Another flashback of the incident so many years back flashed through my brain, and I had to fight the urge to snort. "You have no idea how mad those three have made me. I can feel a headache coming on just thinking about it."

Sacha let out a soft little snicker.

Sensing he was still frustrated, I kept going. "Once, I went five months without talking to any of them. Before that I'd never gone more than a week without seeing them since kindergarten."

"What happened?" he asked, and why wouldn't he? If he'd mentioned the same thing to me, I would have asked too because I'm nosey.

"Well…" Damn it, what the hell could I say? I wasn't exactly ready then—or possibly ever—to tell him about my boobs. I'd told Brandon about my operation the night I decided that I was ready to sleep with him for the first time. The three idiots knew because we'd been friends forever. There were no secrets between us. I'd been talking about getting the surgery done for years, but they knew mainly because it was them: my twin and the two guys who were pretty much skin tags I couldn't get rid of.

But Sacha wasn't a lifelong friend, and we weren't about to strip down or make him my third boyfriend, so he was only going to get a small part of the story.

"They all got pretty drunk one night a few years ago and said some really mean stuff about me behind my back to the other guys on the tour." I blew out a breath and bit the inside of my cheek. "I didn't take it too well."

He visibly winced. "Is that why you stopped touring with them?" he asked, obviously remembering our conversation from a month back.

I nodded. "They really hurt my feelings."

"And that's why you don't like being around your brother when he's been drinking?"

Damn, he was perceptive. "Bingo."

"But you forgave them."

"Of course. Besides my friend Laila that you met, they're my best friends. Eli's my twin. I'm kind of obligated to forgive him for all the stupid shit he's ever done, but I told him before coming on this tour that I wasn't going to do it unless he promised he wouldn't drink around me like that again. It's fine now. They'll always get on my nerves and drive me a little nuts. It's normal. I'm sure you know that."

Sacha made a little humming noise in the back of his throat. "I go months without seeing them when we're not on tour. Mat and Isaiah are roommates. Julian lives a couple blocks away from where they do, so they see each other often. I start to miss them sometimes when it's been a while, but after a few weeks on tour, I remember why I don't hang out with them when we're home."

He shook his head with an exasperated sigh. "There's only so much you can take, being around the same people all the time."

Well. Okay. That hurt a little.

I nodded, lowering my gaze to the ground. "Yeah, I get it," I replied as the burn of what he'd said sizzled along my skin. I mean, he'd asked me to sit with him on the flight to Australia, hadn't he? And he'd invited me to the soccer game, right? It wasn't like I'd been chasing him around. No one had ever accused me of being terribly clingy or needy before.

But still. His words stung. A lot.

"Ah shit." He sighed. "Gaby."

"Huh?" I crouched to fiddle with my shoelace, trying to blink the rejection coursing through me away. Really, I hadn't been trying to be a leech.

"Hey." His voice was soft.

"Hmm?" I untied my shoelace and retied it, oblivious to the fact he was lowering himself to ground in front of me until his knees bumped mine. I could smell the spicy, clean scent of his shampoo and body wash. Why did I do this to myself? Why couldn't I be attracted to someone that saw me as more than a friend?

More than anything, what I wanted in that instant

was to not care that he'd just said he was tired of being around the same people all the time.

People like me.

I wished I could just walk off, give him the space he wanted, and not have it hurt my feelings. Because if it was Mason saying he was tired of having me around, I'd tell him to screw off and eat shit. Then an hour later, he'd probably give me a hug and ask me when we were going to have kids together.

But it was different with Sacha. Of course it was different with him, and that sucked.

"Hey."

His knees kissed mine and I told myself to shake it off. To not let it bother me. I shouldn't let his words matter.

"Gaby, baby," he said in that same soft voice that was so different from the one he used onstage every night to sing to his fans. Those big palms curved over my shoulders unexpectedly, and I made sure to keep my chin down. "I didn't mean you."

Fighting the urge to clear my throat, I nodded and forced myself to glance up, a tight smile framing my mouth. "I know," I said, but the words sounded as forced as they felt.

The smile that came over him said he knew exactly how full of shit I was. Those harsh features that made his face so attractive, softened instantly. "Hey, I'm serious. I put my foot in my mouth. I didn't mean you."

"I know." My chest... my chest felt weird. "Have

you seen Eli?" I blurted out, anxious to get away.

"*Fight Club,*" he sighed. "Don't look at me like that and make up some shit about your brother. He left when everyone got in line to pay anyway."

"I'm fine," I insisted. "I know what you meant, Sacha."

"Sacha?" His thumbs drummed over my collarbones as he tipped his head down. "Now I know I really fucked up."

"I'm fine. Really." He shook his head, his expression an agitated one, and I forced a smile on my face. "Come on. Make sure no one kidnaps me on the walk back," I said.

"You look like I just kicked you in your invisible nuts, and I feel like shit for saying something so stupid." He slid his hands down my shoulders to my upper arms and finally to grip my hands, which were on my knees. He wrapped them in his before standing up, pulling me to my feet. He slid his hold until he had his fingers around my wrists, giving them a light squeeze. "I'm sorry. I didn't mean you. Pinky swear." He squeezed again. His tone was gentle and low. "I would never mean you, honey. "

I didn't say anything, settling for a nod, and he sighed again. His thumb stroked over the sensitive skin on the inside of my wrist, over a long vein that stretched on forever. Then he released me. "Let's go."

Keeping my eyes on the cement directly in front of each of my steps, I called myself an idiot for letting his words bother me and also for letting him know that they did. Stupid. Stupid, stupid, stupid. Why was I being so dumb about this? About him?

We had only walked a few feet in silence before he suddenly stopped. "How could you think I'd get tired of you? I'm the one always following you around. And—you're so fucking cute, I can't stand it half the time."

Yeah, I was so distracted I didn't see the curb.

I busted my fucking ass and almost ate concrete.

My knees thought they were competing in the figure skating national championships for first place, and my hands tried to win second.

Sacha shouted something, but I was too busy laughing at what happened—and telling myself to ignore the fact that he'd called me cute—to hear exactly what came out of his mouth. There were tears in my eyes as his hands went to arms to help me. Rolling onto my butt and then plopping it on the curb so that I wouldn't get hit by a car—because that would be my luck—my chest shook.

"Are you okay?" he asked even as he sat next to me and flipped my palms up to take a look at them. "Oh, Princess," Sacha hissed as the side of his thigh pressed against mine. Red scrapes with the barest hint of pooling blood marked the meaty parts of my hands.

"I'm okay," I said on a shaky laugh as I peeked at the hands he was still holding in his. It was my knees that really stung. Pulling my leg close to my chest, I squinted and took in the two tears on my jeans between my shins and knees.

Honestly, I could have cried from the holes alone, damn it.

"Oh my God, these were my favorite," I moaned.

"What happened?"

"My jeans are torn."

Still holding my hands, his light gray eyes met mine. His mouth twitched. "You just fell on your face —"

"Not on my face—"

"—I thought you might have broken a wrist, and you're worried about your jeans?"

Well, when he said it like that, it made me sound like an idiot. I coughed. "Yes, but I'm not hurt and these were my favorite pair," I explained.

Sacha blew out a breath as he closed his eyes and shook his head.

I closed my fingers over his and snorted, taking in his features since he looked like he was praying for patience or something close to it. I guess he wasn't lying about being worried. I nudged him, ignoring the pain coming from my knees and palms. "It was pretty funny though, wasn't it?" I used the same words he'd chosen when he'd kicked the ball at my face.

He didn't reply for so long that I thought he really had been too worried to think that me missing the curb and falling to my hands and knees was hilarious.

Then he finally glanced up and the entire side of his mouth was screwed up high in the cutest expression I'd ever seen, and he shrugged one muscular shoulder. There was also a chance his eyes glittered. "It was pretty damn funny."

CHAPTER SIXTEEN

"Get it off!" Julian howled, shimmying his back in front of Sacha.

Sacha was too busy being doubled over laughing his ass off to give half a shit about the fact that his friend had gotten crapped on by a bird.

For the second time in less than an hour.

We were at King's Park in Perth, the largest inner-city park in the world, the day after we'd arrived in the Land Down Under. Sacha, Julian, my brother, Isaiah and I had all caught a ride to the beautiful location late that morning. What had started with me banging on my brother's door so he could accompany me somewhere, ended up becoming an extended invitation to the other guys during breakfast.

"Quit laughing and somebody wipe it off!" Julian was practically screeching as he made his stop in front of me, hoping I'd be his savior.

I wanted to help Julian with his issue. Really. I did. The problem was that I couldn't stop cracking up either.

"Gaby! Please! Get it off!"

It seriously took everything inside of me to get it together. I finally cleaned the gooey spot with the last napkin I'd tucked into my pocket earlier, but it took longer than it normally would have. A second later another bird swarmed overhead and made him start cursing in annoyance and probably fear. It was bad enough to get pooped on once, but twice? And in front of Eli and Sacha? There was no way Julian was ever going to be able to live it down.

"I feel like I should take a shit on you too now. What exactly am I missing out on, you know?" Eli cackled, slapping the poor guy on the back before immediately yanking his hand away and checking it with a grimace.

The same bird swooped dangerously over our heads, and I started crying, not imagining the look of pure horror on Julian's face all over again.

"You better run before they come after you again," Sacha teased him through a gulp of air. He stole a glance in my direction, and then lost it once more; this loud, belly-aching laugh that fueled my own.

I'm not sure how it happened, but Sacha and I were suddenly leaning on each other, forehead to shoulder despite the near foot in height difference.

Warm breath on warm neck as we cracked up at Julian's expense. I'm pretty sure he gave us the finger before stomping off to the exit that was on the other side of the park.

Eli and Isaiah followed after him, taunting him with threats about a bird coming for him.

When my chest finally started craving a lungful of breath, I pulled away and plopped down on the nearest bench to wipe my tears off and collect myself. "Would you laugh at me that much if I got crapped on?" I asked him.

He looked at me straight-faced, but it wasn't serious at all, I could tell by the amusement in his eyes. "What do you think?" When I smirked at him, he winked and laughed. "I'd probably laugh harder, Princess, and take a picture to keep with me forever."

It was a little pathetic how much I enjoyed his teasing. On the other hand if the roles were reversed and it was him that got a special delivery? There's no doubt in my mind I would have documented it. "Touché. If it was you, I'd frame it and put it in front of my toilet, so every time I'm in there, I can enjoy it."

"I don't know how I feel about you looking at me while you're—," he made a face, "using the bathroom."

I gave him a shrug, which only made him shake his head, and thrust out a hand in my direction.

"Let's go catch up to them," Sacha said, wiggling those long, slim fingers in front of me.

"All right," I only just barely didn't whine. Before

the whole shitting incident, we'd all agreed to take a break and eat something at the café, but from the looks of it, that didn't seem to be the plan.

We'd been walking around for hours, and I'd brought the wrong shoes. On top of that, my knee was still killing me from falling on it the night before when Sacha had said… well, what he'd said. I wasn't letting myself think about it too much. Mase was always saying stuff without really meaning any of it; Sacha's comments didn't have to be any different.

He raised an eyebrow and moved his fingers faster. "Come on. I'll give you a piggyback ride back, you cripple," he offered.

Piggyback ride? Yes. Piggyback ride on Sacha's back? Double, triple, infinity yes. I slapped my fingers out and took his hand without a second thought, letting him pull me up.

"Hop on before I leave you to the birds," he threatened.

"Yes, sir," I told him while I jumped as high as possible. He grabbed the backs of my thighs and hoisted me up a little more while I wrapped my arms around his neck. "Let's go, my chariot. I've cleaned up enough shit for the day."

He laughed and slapped me high on my thigh before beginning our walk down the path. We were both quiet for all of a minute or two before Sacha turned his head a little so that his cheek was right next to mine. "I like the way you smell. What is that, oranges?"

"Yes. I took a shower this morning," I reminded him while trying not to be shameless and inch my face closer to his.

"Was today your once-a-week shower?" he deadpanned.

I sighed. "Twice this week, Sassy. Consider yourself lucky."

Sacha stopped walking. "Should I call Guinness? Tell them about your new record?"

I let go with one hand and bopped him on the nose. "Jackass."

~

"He doesn't know," I told him.

Sacha made a face. "He knows."

I couldn't help but snort as we looked at my brother flopping around the floor like an a little kid on too much candy, talking to Gordo about who knows what. We'd been sitting behind my merch table for about half an hour counting T-shirts and talking about the worst injuries we'd ever had after I had shown him the huge bruise below my kneecap from the night before. The fact that Carter was sitting behind TCC's table, doing the same thing by himself, wasn't lost on me, but I promised myself I'd help him out later once my assistant was gone.

"He knows he has blood, but he doesn't know what type," I clarified. "If he ever ended up needing a blood transfusion and he couldn't call my mom, my sister or me, he'd end up dying when they gave him a different type."

"Nah, he knows. He has to."

Eli threw a drumstick in the air, and then tried to catch it by pulling the waistband of his pants out to catch it... with his ass crack. "No way."

Sacha and I turned to look at each other and we each made a weird face.

"I bet you twenty bucks he can't even name the different types," I told him with a snort while watching my brother try his trick again.

He slapped my back gently and nodded. "Deal." Sacha brushed off his

pants, winked at me and yelled across the venue, "Eli!"

Eliza turned to look at him before extending his arms out of his sides. "What's up?"

"Help me win twenty bucks—"

I hit his arm. "You damn cheater." Of course Eli would put in some effort to try and remember if he thought I'd lose money.

"—I can't remember what blood types there are. Do you know?"

My brother frowned. "Blood types?"

I snickered and smacked Sacha in the side with the back of my hand.

"Yeah. There's OB, right? What else?"

OB? What the hell? On the other hand, a wrong suggestion was fair enough, it wasn't exactly cheating.

Eli coughed. "Uh, A? Positive? B *uhhummum...*"

"What was that?" I asked him, trying my best to hold back a laugh.

"A minus, aaaahhummmhhhmmhmm," he garbled again, saying the something really loudly and then trailing off in volume as soon as he kept making noises. I couldn't help but laugh, which only made Eli frown again before shooting me the finger. "I don't know! What do I look like? Some kind of blood professional?"

Blood professional? I slapped a hand over my mouth and ducked down so he wouldn't see me laughing at his stupidity.

"What did I tell you? He's so smart when he wants to be, but when he doesn't..." I told my gray-eyed friend through my giggling. "If you ask him what day our Mom's birthday is, he'll tell you April thirty-first."

Sacha smiled. "But there's only thirty days in April."

I waggled my eyebrows. "Exactly. I have to text him to remind him of every birthday in our family." I thought about it for a second. "If we weren't born on the same day, he wouldn't know what day my birthday was. That's for sure."

"What day is your birthday?" he asked.

"December second. Yours?"

"August thirteenth."

"I'll have to make sure to remember and send you a One Direction birthday card or something." I smiled at him.

He blinked. "You're too generous."

I shrugged, still smiling. "What about you? Do you know your family's birthdays?"

"I know everyone's. If I forgot, my sisters would probably skin my nuts." He paused and thought about it. "Well, Dena, my eldest, would. The rest would put a personal ad on Craigslist for a one-night stand, men only, and put my number as the contact," he laughed.

"That's a good one." I laughed too. "I'll have to remember that in case you ever piss me off."

He mocked a gasp. "Me? Piss you off? Whatever do you mean?"

"Shut your mouth." I elbowed him in the rib. "It's bound to happen one day. You'll catch me on my period again or something."

Sacha stuck his tongue out at the corner of his mouth. "I survived eighteen years with my sisters, and you're a lot nicer and prettier than they are. We'll be fine."

My cheeks went hot, and yet again, I told myself not to take what he was saying seriously. He was nice. Unbelievably nice. Nice people said sweet things to others because that was something they did. I wasn't going to be an idiot and misinterpret it. "Yeah, sure, Sassy." I blinked at him, trying to school my cheeks so that they weren't traitorous blushing bastards. "I'll let you pay me my twenty dollars later, you don't have to sweet-talk me."

∾

Later that night, while TCC was performing, Eli trailed to the merch area to sign some autographs.

"Flabby?" he yelled into my ear while I was helping a fan, with one eye on Sacha in his prim and proper clothing as he moved across the stage.

"What do you want?"

A finger slicked across my bottom lip. "You need a bib," Eliza laughed.

I snickered, shooting him a dirty look. "Leave me alone. You don't see me raining on your parade when you're flirting with girls."

He started to say something else, but Sacha started talking into the microphone about some guy in the audience wearing a Christmas hat and how Christmas was his favorite holiday. "But it's not my favorite day in the year," he said with a smile at the crowd.

Eli leaned into me. "It's steak and BJ day."

I leaned away from him, smirking. "That's your favorite holiday," I told him, earning an excited nod in response.

The opening rift of one of their songs swept through the venue as Sacha stood on one of the floor speakers and pressed the microphone against his lips. "December 2nd!" he screamed into it before the loud crash of the drums signaled the rest of the song.

What in the hell was happening?

"My birthday? Is he gay?" Eli asked me with a

confused look on his face.

I punched him in the stomach just for being an idiot.

CHAPTER SEVENTEEN

It was the *bang, bang, bang* on the door that scared the shit out of me.

The fact that it was two o'clock in the morning only added to *what-the-hell-is-happening* panic that burned through my thoughts.

We'd gotten back to the hotel an hour ago. It was long enough for me to shower and begin to wind down from the hectic sold-out show in Perth. The fact that half the dates in Australia were sold out was both exciting and daunting.

Mostly exciting. Australians had the sexiest accents I'd ever heard. Whoo.

"Who is it?" I called out a little hesitantly, wishing I had a knife or a bat or at least a rock I could chuck nearby. Then again, every room around mine had one of the guys on the tour in it. If I yelled loud enough someone would come, right?

Eh. I could use a lamp if push came to shove.

Someone—or something?—scratched at the door lightly.

Jesus Christ. "Seriously, who is it?"

There was more scratching.

Damn it! "Eli, I swear to God—"

A loud laugh pierced through the door. "It's me."

Me.

Sassy.

I groaned and grumbled climbing off the bed. "Damn it, Sacha. Are you trying to give me a heart attack?"

"Yes."

Yeah, I rolled my eyes, but I'd be lying if I said I wasn't greedily sucking up the attention, especially after what he'd said during The Cloud Collision's set. His favorite day was my birthday? That wasn't him calling me cute or saying something else along those lines. So what the hell did it mean? *What the hell did it mean, damn it?*

It wasn't like I could talk to any of the monsters, or even Carter, about it. It also wasn't as if I could hop onto Skype and get Laila's input because of the time difference. This wasn't an e-mail-worthy conversation; it required a face-to-face conversation.

I had no one.

So...

I wasn't going to bring it up and possibly make our friendship awkward until I could figure out how I was supposed to handle what he'd said and might have meant.

"One sec, Sassy pants," I said in the middle of turning the deadbolt. I'd barely cracked the door when his smiling face greeted me. "Hi."

"Princess," he said with a long blink of his cool-colored eyes as he pushed the door open and slid inside.

He toed off his shoes the instant after he'd kicked the door closed. Before I'd even locked it, he was climbing onto my bed and reclining against the headboard. My mind said, "Danger!" But my ovaries screamed, "Naked! Now!"

Instead I did what any friend would have done: I jumped onto the bed as if him showing up to my room in the middle of the night was no big deal, and sat cross-legged next to where he took a seat.

Fresh-faced and damp-haired, he pushed his black locks straight back before rubbing at one of the shaved sides of his head. "I thought you'd be asleep by now."

"I was still trying to wind down." Plus, he'd banged on the door so loud that it would have woken me up even if I'd been passed out, but I kept that to myself. "What are you doing up?"

"Couldn't sleep, and I'm not in the mood to get any writing done tonight."

I raised my eyebrows. "Writing your next album?"

He nodded. "This tour is for the last record we have with our label and our contract runs out in exactly a year; we want to release another album the day after it's over. I wanted to go ahead and get started on the songs now."

"You're self-releasing it?"

"Yeah. I'm pretty certain we're going to have to sue our label for back royalties they owe us afterward." He winced.

I made a face that he mirrored.

"It'll be fine," he assured me.

"I'm sure it will."

He nodded, rubbing at the side of his head again as his eyes strayed to the chunk of my head that had met a death with Carter's clippers weeks back. Sacha tipped his chin up. "Are you planning on shaving it again?"

"No. I'm lucky if I get two haircuts in a year; keeping up with it is too much trouble. I'll just look dumb until it grows back in. And it's probably way too cool of a haircut for me anyway."

"You're cool." He smiled. "Most of the time."

I sort of choked but still laughed. "Oh, thanks for such an awesome compliment."

"It's what I'm here for."

I rolled my eyes playfully, settling my back against the headboard. "Sometimes I feel like I've known you my entire life, and other times, I ask myself what the hell I was thinking trying to be your friend."

The grin that took over his mouth astounded me. "I've thought the same about you. What would my life be like if you hadn't kicked me in the ass?"

I crossed my eyes and groaned, earning a bright laugh from the guy next to me.

"I've never met anyone I've felt so comfortable with so quickly," he said like it was nothing.

Why did he have to be so sweet? I pushed that question into the back of my brain and beamed at him, appreciating what he was saying. "I'm picky with my friends, you know."

"So I should feel honored that I'm your best friend?" he asked, raising a dark eyebrow while a goofy, crooked grin covered his lips.

I couldn't help but snort. "We're best friends?"

He sat up a little then, nodding with that same ridiculous smile on his face. "At least."

Wanting to focus on his words but being too scared, I waggled my brows at him. "How old am I?" I asked, knowing he had no idea.

"Twenty… three?" he asked, twitching an eye.

"You're fired. I'm twenty-six." I groaned, flicking his thigh in return. "What's my favorite color?"

He made another face. "Blue?"

"How did you know?"

"You're always wearing blue," he boasted with a wink. "What do you think my favorite color is?"

I stared at him right in the eyes. "Pink, duh."

He blinked those long fanning black lashes once and only once. "Do you have any idea how easy it is to love you?"

There was no way to respond to that. Plus, he

was joking. I mean, he was joking, right? Instead of taking the risk of saying something I'd regret later, I reached forward and attempted to flick him in the forehead, but he caught my hand. I tried to yank it back, but almost punched myself in the face instead. I scowled.

"What's your favorite thing to listen to?" I asked, figuring that since we were on a roll getting to know each other a bit more, I might as well take advantage.

"You know, I don't have anything specific I like," he answered, pursing his lips. What a typical musician answer. "I like and hate everything. I can listen to anything as long as it's good. What about you? Kidz Bop?"

I threw my head back and laughed. "Oh yeah, I'm so glad you told me about how catchy it was."

Sacha smiled and made a gentle, amused noise in his throat that sounded faintly like a snort as he fluttered those thick, long eyelashes in my direction. "I'll send you the rest of my collection when I get home," he teased me. When I grinned at him, his expression softened and his eyes flickered down to my hands. "You haven't been with anyone since you and Brandon broke up?" he asked abruptly.

The question sort of threw me for a loop since I wasn't expecting it at all. But that void that I felt for my ex was numbed and so insignificant I couldn't bother to remember anything about him that used to mean something to me. "No," I told him simply. "I thought my heart was broken for about a little bit.

Then I was too pissed and depressed with life to bother with anything besides school for a while. Now, I'm just minding my own business, enjoying the tour, taking advantage of being the captain of my destiny for a little bit."

And having a huge, massive crush on you that defies all sense, I thought.

He nodded thoughtfully. "No regrets, then?"

"None." That was the truth. "Everything happens for a reason, and I know that things wouldn't have worked out between us in the long run anyway, you know what I mean?"

"Yeah," he replied in a soft voice. "My last girlfriend, Liz—you met her in San Francisco, remember?" How could I forget? I nodded and threw up in my mouth at the same time but luckily his attention was on his hands instead of the faces I was making. "She broke up with me because she hated me being gone all the time. She wanted me to choose her over my music, but," those pale gray eyes looked into mine, "I don't know. It didn't seem like the right thing to do. I didn't want to do it. She knew before we started dating what I did for a living; it wasn't a surprise. I haven't wanted to date anyone since her, because I don't want to get stuck in that type of relationship again, I guess."

The idea that someone, specifically Ronalda, would ask Sacha to quit on his dream and his incredible talent to fight off her loneliness, made my heart churn. His gift didn't deserve to fade away, and those selfish reasons made me burn. "I think someone who really loves you wouldn't ask you to give up what you love, what you were meant to do," I told him in such an even voice it shocked me.

He smiled at me and nodded. "I think the same thing, Princess."

≈

"I'll meet you in twenty," Sacha whispered into my ear as we were getting off the van after a very late dinner in Geelong.

It was a mutual decision that both of us would shower before he came over to my room every night, even though I would have gladly let him shower in my room. With me.

Not that I would ever make the offer out loud but there was nothing wrong with simply thinking about it. That night in Perth, where he'd stayed until close to five in the morning, had just been the beginning. What followed were five consecutive nights of sitting in my room with a handsome, showered and delicious-smelling man.

Unfortunately and unsurprisingly, it was pretty innocent. We sat on the bed and talked a lot, watched television and ragged on each other for our likes and dislikes. When I told him that I'd seen *My Girl* about a million times, he'd rolled his eyes so far back I was worried those pretty irises would stay there. When he told me he'd seen all of the *Transformers* movies in person at least six times, and even sat in line for twenty-four hours to catch the first showing of one, I stared at him blankly.

The thing that killed me the most about our friendship was that the more I learned about Sacha, the more I liked him. I liked that he volunteered at a pet shelter, that he knew how to play four different instruments, and that he had a pet turtle named Mercury that Julian's brother babysat when he was on tour. I thought it was amazing that he worked at a studio as a session pianist and back-up singer when he was home. The bastard was sweet and thoughtful, and he laughed at my jokes and my embarrassing stories.

This huge, blinding forest fire of happiness filled my chest when I was around him. While it should have been a beautiful thing that I liked him as much as I did, it wasn't. I had no idea where things stood between us. We were definitely friends; that was blatantly obvious. I loved spending time with him because he had this way about him that always put me in a good mood but...

I wasn't sure whether there was actually something *more*. Our joking could be considered flirting. He spent more time with me than he did with anyone else by multiples. When we were at the venues and he wasn't busy, he'd began coming to visit the merch table even if he had to wear a hoodie to avoid getting mobbed by fans.

This, us, was so complicated.

I didn't want to assume anything, so I didn't. After all, he'd mentioned Ronalda as his ex, but I couldn't help but remember that conversation that I'd overheard. Then there was his comment when we'd been in the car back in Philadelphia about how he'd told her something about it not being the right time to talk about whatever. Was there something else that could possibly be going on? I had no fucking idea, and I sure as hell wasn't going to ask.

Pushing those thoughts out of my head, I skipped to my room and showered as quickly as possible so I could be ready for my nightly visitor. Was it a little desperate? Maybe. But I didn't care. It wasn't like anyone saw me.

The knock on my door came just a couple minutes after I finished smothering lotion all over my skin. "What's the password?" I asked walking toward the door.

"Gaby is the princess of the universe."

I snorted. My hands paused on the deadbolt as I smiled to myself. "Anddddd...?" I asked, just to be a pest. Like what he said wasn't enough.

There was a pause. "I have cookies."

"Bingo!" I unlocked the bolt and didn't even bother ushering Sacha in. He did his usual routine, kicking off shoes, peeling off his hoodie and plopping onto his side of the bed.

He tossed over a packet of cookies he had more than likely bought at the vending machine. "Save me half of one," he requested sweetly, wiggling his butt onto the mattress to try and get comfortable.

I nodded at him, already tearing the package open before jumping on the other side of the bed. I had to crawl with the cookies in my mouth over to a spot right by his chest, where I crossed my legs. He looked over and patted a spot slightly closer to him. "Come keep me warm."

He could have put a jacket on, but I didn't remind him of that.

The small part of my brain that still hadn't recognized he was my friend and only my friend, wanted to say that if he wanted to, he could crawl under the sheets, but only someone with an IQ of 20 would say that to him.

I also could have messed with the thermostat in the room but… nope.

In hindsight, what I should have done was turn down the air even more so I could give him a reason to cuddle. I didn't do that either though.

What I did was scoot closer to him. So close he reached out to palm my knee. I stared at his hand and kept my mouth closed despite knowing how stupid it was.

Sacha flipped through channels with one hand at the same time the other one patted my kneecap while I ate the sweet vanilla cookies he'd brought. I was more focused on his long fingers rubbing my legging-covered legs than the movie he'd put on.

"Do you have any Chapstick?" he asked me a second later.

I moved my head in the direction of my backpack, which was sitting on the floor right next to him. "Top pocket," I answered in as lady-like a way as I could without spitting crumbs all over the place.

He nodded, reaching over the edge of the bed to grab my backpack and planted it on his lap to search through it. The top pocket was unzipped and he reached in, looked at whatever he was holding and made a face. "What's this?" he asked, holding something out.

I coughed all over him. Literally. Crumbs went all over his shirt and sweats but I couldn't find it in me to give a single shit when I recognized what he held.

My little bullet, which looked like a lip balm tube made of metal, was sitting in his palm. I'd bought it while we were still in Darwin the day after we left Perth, on an outing with Carter when we had nothing to do at the venue for hours. I'd ditched him at the music store while I ran to the shop next door and bought my new friend.

"I'm sorry!" I gasped, trying to wipe at his chest. There were tiny pieces of cookie all over his heather-gray shirt. I snatched the small vibrator out of his hand, slipped it under my thigh and then started brushing his clothes off.

He laughed and shrugged, picking pieces off too, popping the larger ones into his mouth. "Was that what I think it is?" he asked in a low, amused voice.

"Lipstick? Yes," I lied, keeping my eyes on his T-shirt while I finished picking off the remaining pieces.

Sacha nudged my knee. "Liar."

"You're a liar," I muttered.

"I am?" he asked me in that same voice he'd used with his last question.

I slowly dragged my eyes up to his gray irises.

"Yeah." My skin got itchy all of a sudden. "Your passport says that you're a male but you're really a female."

"Gaby," he groaned, trying to disguise his laugh. "You're giving my manhood a complex."

Thank the lord I didn't have any more cookies in my mouth at his use of the word manhood.

Looking up at him, I saw that his eyes were trained on the leg that I'd shoved the bullet under. Then he looked at me and I swear his lids looked heavy.

Three hours later, when I started swaying with sleep, he pulled back my bed sheets. "I'm leaving. Lock the door after me before you fall asleep," he whispered, and then he kissed me on the tip of my nose.

Yeah, I suddenly wasn't so sleepy after that.

～

"What's the password?"

"Gaby's birthday should be a national holiday."

I grinned like an idiot, and fortunately, I was in my room alone so he couldn't see my facial expression. It had to be bordering on ugly from how hard my cheeks strained in such a short amount of time. "Andddd?" I asked, in what had become our game.

He laughed from the other side of the door. "I bought you a book."

My grin widened exponentially while I unlocked the door to let him in. He'd barely made it in before he was kicking the door closed and putting a hand on each of my cheeks. I hadn't seen him all day.

When Eliza woke me up that morning for breakfast by drumming his fists on the door in beat to a Ghost Orchid song, my first thought had been: *I feel like hell.* My body hurt, I had a raging fever and I just felt like overall crap. Eli took me to the doctor, where I was told there was a virus going around that I could have caught from anyone. I ended up staying in my room with my brother for the majority of the day until he caught a cab to the venue in the evening.

"I don't think you should be in here. I don't want to get you sick," I warned.

He rolled his eyes, not moving his palms off my face. "I don't get sick. I'll be fine. Are you still feeling like shit?" he asked me softly.

I nodded, staring straight into his bright eyes. "Yeah."

He leaned forward and examined my face. "I've been worried about you all day. Mason didn't tell us you were sick until we were halfway to the venue. I just thought you and Eli went to go do something on your own."

"You missed out on a doctor's visit and the strangest-tasting soup I've ever eaten," I smiled at little at him.

Sacha gave me that lopsided grin I liked. "Party animal." His hands brushed down my neck to rest on my shoulders. "Want me to go get you something?"

I shook my head and gestured toward the bags on the nightstand. "*Rosemary's Baby* brought me a sandwich and juice when you guys got here, but thank you."

I don't know why every time I thanked him, he smiled. Always. He reached behind him for a second, his elbow wobbled in the air, before handing me a book. "The lady at the bookstore said that since you're a history nerd, you'd probably enjoy it," he said, setting the paperback into my outstretched hand.

Memoirs of a Geisha was the title.

I threw my arms around him and hugged him weaker than I normally would have, slightly smirking at him calling me a history nerd. I did like my historical fiction, especially since I hadn't had time to read much while I was in school. "Thank you."

Sacha wrapped his arms around the middle of my back and squeezed me to him tightly enough to make up for my lacking strength. "You're welcome."

"You're the nicest man I've ever met. I don't care what anyone says about you."

He chuckled lightly, rubbing my back. We pulled apart after a minute, and then he was taking off his shoes and lying on the side of the bed I hadn't contaminated yet. "So you have a virus, huh?" he asked, flopping his long arms open across the mattress.

"A big, stinking virus," I told him, sticking out my tongue. "I should be better the day after tomorrow supposedly."

He made a face while I put my present on top of my backpack. "That sucks," he replied, watching me. A slow smile crept across his cheeks. "Poor little sick baby."

Snorting pathetically, I took a sip out of the bottle of water I had on the nightstand before flopping on the bed next to him. I sprawled out on the queen-sized mattress, which didn't say much because I wasn't exactly a supermodel-like height. "Suck it."

"Suck what?" he laughed.

"My invisible nuts," I snickered, turning my head just a little to face him.

He was sitting up on the bed while I was laying down flat. "I forget about those things." The hand closest to me reached over to grasp my forearm. "I see this girl who's usually pretty fucking gorgeous and the last thing I expect is for her to have a pair under her clothes," he chuckled.

I soaked up his compliment for all of a split second. "Wait a second. What you mean by 'usually?'"

"You're sick," he explained with amusement tinting his voice, ignoring my question about the nickname.

"So you're telling me I look like shit?" I finally laughed despite the sharp pain in my throat, not at all insulted by what he was implying. There was no way I didn't look the way I felt: like a big, old pile of poo.

His palm stroked my arm. "You don't exactly look your best, Princess, but you're still pretty," he offered me.

I smacked his hand off and laughed, attempting to roll away from him.

Sacha laughed louder, slipping an arm under my body and pulling me over. Part of the way onto him. "Quit fishing for compliments. You're still pretty." He crushed me to his bouncing, entertained chest. His other arm finished the circle around me, my breasts pressed against his ribs, the side of my head meeting his pec.

"All I hear is blah, blah, blah," I laughed into the soft material of his red hoodie, ignoring the sirens going off in my head and the way my heart so suddenly pounded in my chest at his proximity. This wasn't what friends did. This was absolutely not what friends did. But I sure as hell wasn't moving or saying something to ruin the moment.

He squeezed me to him tighter. "You're a pain in the ass."

"Like you're one to talk."

"Shouldn't you be sleeping or something? Isn't that what people do when they're sick?"

I nodded against him. "Yeah, but there's this annoying guy that likes to hang out in my room and keep me up every night."

"What an asshole," he hissed, shaking his head as he said it.

"I know, right?" I laughed.

Sacha tilted his head down so that his lips were so close to my forehead I could feel their heat. "Want me to leave?"

As if there was another possible answer. "No."

He didn't say anything, but I felt him start wiggling his way down the bed. "I'll wait until you start to fall asleep, then."

"Okay."

We sat there quietly with the television so low it just sounded like a whisper in the background, until, "Hush, little baby, don't say a word—"

"What are you doing?" I started laughing hoarsely.

"I'm singing you a lullaby to put you to sleep," he said.

I shifted just a little in his arms, tucking myself into his warmth and ignoring the voice in my head that said friends really didn't do this kind of stuff. "Okay, continue."

His chest moved with silent laughter. "Sacha's gonna buy you a mockingbird—" I snorted, trying to cover it. His chest shook more but it didn't break his song's stride. If anything his sweet, beautiful voice got a little louder. "And if that mockingbird won't sing, Sacha's gonna buy you a diamond ring."

CHAPTER EIGHTEEN

"Flabby, why don't you dress like that?" Mason asked.

We'd been sitting in this karaoke bar for all of fifteen minutes. Half of the guys at the table had been staring at the same two girls for fourteen out of fifteen of those minutes. The other half of them were busy chugging down as much beer as they possibly could as quickly as possible. Today was Julian's birthday, and the guy apparently had a healthy, amorous relationship with karaoke. Go figure.

I didn't even bother looking in the direction of the two women because I'd checked them out ten minutes ago. In skirts that showed more ass than my underwear do, and with shirts that plunged so deep I'm surprised nipples weren't laser beaming all over the place, I was completely uninterested. If I wanted to look at boobs, I'd look at Lucy and Ethel in the mirror.

"Like a prostitute?" I asked him, taking a sip of water.

Mason leaned into me from his spot on my right and nodded. "Ye-ah," he pretty much hissed it out with way too much enthusiasm.

Sacha who was two seats down, next to Carter, who was on my left, was looking at me with a grin on his face. The fact that he was one of the few not checking out the two half-dressed girls hadn't escaped me. It was his grin that fueled my fire of ridiculousness. "You know I quit the biz a long time ago."

The guys closest to us started laughing, and Mason pulled on the end of my ponytail before grabbing where the hair band was and using my loose hair as a whip. "I'm glad you didn't grow up to be a slut," he said with all the seriousness that was Mason Meyers.

Cocking my head to look at my longtime friend, I karate chopped him gently in the throat, making him gag. "I couldn't. You stole that role from me."

"Asshole," he laughed, yanking on my hair one more time.

Eli walked back to the table in that instant, carrying a large glass bowl between his paws. When we were debating what to do for Julian's birthday celebration and karaoke had been the one and only thing the new twenty-eight-year-old wanted, we'd agreed that each person would write down a song that we wanted to see performed. It had to be a popular, Top 40s type at some point in recent history. The problem was that there were some of us—*moi* included—that weren't musically inclined, so the consensus had been that we could pair up if we wanted to. Anyone who wanted to go multiple times could.

"Choose your doom, bitches," Eli called out, placing the bowl in the middle of the two tables we had pushed together.

In no time at all, we filled the bowl with pieces of paper with song titles on them. Carter, my partner from the moment the duets had been made a possibility, gestured with his head for me to go pick out our choice. We'd agree to get it over with first. Each person or team—there was only one other duet that consisted of two of the TCC lackeys— would choose a slip when their turn was up, to keep the choices a surprise.

"Let's see what we," I started to tell Carter as I opened up the slip to see Justin Bieber's "Baby" written on there. "Damn it, Eli!"

My twin grinned. "How do you know I chose it?"

"Mom," I groaned. It was the song he'd saved as his personal ringtone on our Mom's phone when he called her. Fucking idiot. Something about him being her baby. Like I wasn't technically the baby in the family. If that wasn't enough, I could recognize his chicken-scratch handwriting from a mile away.

He threw his head back and laughed. "Oh, yeah."

Carter made a face and sighed. "I guess it could be worse."

I couldn't even disagree with him. It could be. He got up to join me with sagging shoulders, and Julian threw his hand out to knuckle-bump us on the way to the stage. The karaoke stage was one of the biggest I'd ever seen, but I didn't let it intimidate me. The guy working to the side of the stage asked us what song we wanted to sing and when we told him, he smirked but nodded, handed over two microphones and waved us up. My brother had already spoken to him about our large group, and we'd agreed to switch on and off with the other people at the bar.

"FLABBY!" my brother bellowed from the table.

I could see them all laughing their asses off when the music started up and the lyrics appeared on the screen behind us. I glanced at Carter and slapped him on the back. "Remind me never to do this again unless I've been drinking," I told him, pulling the mic away from my face.

He grinned and nodded. "Remind me never to do this again, period."

That was an even better idea. Swallowing hard, I pointed at the birthday boy in the audience and said, "Happy Birthday, Julian!"

Then we started.

I sang the lead and Carter sang the chorus. We were only about a quarter through the song when I was laughing too hard to actually sing along. The rest of our performance was just an awkward mess of us mumbling, and the guys catcalling.

"I wanna be your baby, Carter boo!" That was Eliza.

"Be mine, Gaby!" Mason cackled.

When it was finally over, we bowed and ran off the stage. A few people I didn't know threw out their hands for high-fives as we made our way back to the table. The guys all began whistling as we got closer to the table, and I went to sit down in Carter's old seat to be next to Sacha.

"How bad was it?" I asked him. My face was so hot I was sure I was blushing all over.

He was grinning from ear to ear. "You weren't bad at all, but I wouldn't plan on releasing a solo album anytime soon," he laughed. "Or ever."

"Jerk." I poked him in the side and smiled. The same thought I'd been fighting with for the last few days rolled through my head. Did Sacha really like me? My deductive reasoning said that chances were high, but I was still too scared to be the one to say something. To say anything.

Mason went up a few minutes later when no one else approached the stage and sang along to "I Kissed A Girl", which was atrocious but funny enough to make me cry. But it was when my brother went up to sing to "My Heart Will Go On" and instead decided to start stripping halfway through that it got ridiculous.

"Take it off!" Julian had yelled.

Eli began peeling up his shirt, which made me

scream, "Put it back on! Put it back on!"

I don't think it was intentional for that song, but it was then that I felt Sacha put his arm around the back of my seat. I turned to look at him over my shoulder and gave him a little, shy smile. We stayed like that through Julian and then Miles's performances, until Sassy decided it was his turn.

Something warm pressed against my bare shoulder as he drew his head back, and I knew, *I knew* he'd kissed me there. Holy shit. A moment later, he pulled a slip of paper out of the bowl and marched up to the stage, shaking his head the entire time. It was when the opening beat to "Since U Been Gone" started that I almost peed myself. It was the song I'd chosen.

To no one's surprise, and thankfully for our ears, Sacha hit the high notes without a problem. He curtsied to the audience of people who were busy clapping and yelling in appreciation of the fact he wasn't tone deaf. When he got back to the table, he resumed his position in the seat with his arm around the back of my chair but closer than he'd been before. He leaned forward mirroring my posture. I didn't dare move. It was dark enough so that no one could see him press his lips against the same spot he'd kissed before.

I shivered and didn't say a word. But I did edge closer to him.

We stayed like that quietly until it was his turn to go again after Gordo's rendition of a Red Hot Chili

Peppers song. Julian's choice of "Tubthumping" had Sacha and my brother rushing the stage and joining him about a minute in.

There were still a couple more papers in the bowl by the time he was done.

"I think you should start a Chumbawamba tribute band," I told him when he sat down next to me.

He slid his arm over the back of my chair once more, smooth like silk. "I'll do it after I finish my Vanilla Ice gigs."

"Oooh, that would've been a good one to put in the bowl. I'd like to see your little butt up there trying to rap "Ice, Ice, Baby,"" I snickered.

His eyes narrowed. "You think I have a little ass?"

I was on dangerous ground and I knew it. But screw it. I'd never know unless I tried, right? What did I have to lose besides my dignity? "No. I think you have a great ass."

Those pale eyes went slightly wide, but he said nothing. He simply looked at me. And then he leaned forward and pressed those warm, full lips against that spot on my jaw that ended at my ear. His mouth lingered there, lips on skin, hot on smooth.

His phone lit up. It had been sitting on top of the table the entire time, and I glanced down in a daze from the most intimate kiss I'd ever gotten. What distracted me wasn't at all that he'd gotten a text message from his mom, but the fact that the background was a picture of me he'd taken at breakfast a few days ago when I had shoved two pieces of napkin up my nostrils because I had a runny nose.

There wasn't a trace of embarrassment or fear in his eyes when our eyes met.

～

"So what's going on with you and your boyfriend?" Eli asked me right before he shoved a forkful of eggs into his mouth during breakfast the next morning.

I made a face in the direction of my plate before shooting a glance upward to find Gordo's eyes on me, a smirk on his face.

"Mason?" I asked, going back to my food.

Eli made a gagging noise, elbowing me hard in the ribs. "I'm not gonna go into details on how disturbing it is that I say 'your boyfriend' and you automatically think of fucking Mase."

"He's always calling me his wife, or telling people I don't know that we're getting married," I replied, elbowing him back as hard as he got me. It was partially the truth… but mostly, I didn't want to talk about the man who had been kissing my shoulder hours ago.

"I love Mase, but it'll be a sunny day in my asshole before you and him get together," he mumbled.

I snorted, biting into my biscuit. "Who the heck else would you be talking about?" I asked, but I knew. Oh, I knew damn well he was referring to

Sacha.

Freaking Gordo snickered from across the table before putting his hands up in surrender when I glared at him. "I didn't say anything."

"Sacha, Flabby. *Sacha*. Your boyfriend. Your snuggle bug." Eliza finally answered.

Suddenly the half-eaten biscuit on my plate needed to be eaten immediately. I shoved the entire piece into my mouth to avoid the conversation my brother was trying to edge into. I'd had talks about boys with Eli in the past, and they never ended—or started—well. "There's nothing going on between us. We're just friends."

Because we were.

Eli made a noise that sounded like "hmmph" deep in his throat. It was incredulous and disbelieving. Then he asked the question to prove it, his attention back on his band mate. "Gordo, do you think I'm blind?"

Gordo shook his head.

"Gaby, do you think I'm blind?" he asked.

"Not blind, just dumb." I smiled.

He shot me a frown. A moment later, he threw his arm over my shoulders and started shoving his plate away with his free hand. "Flabby Gaby, that kid is in love with you."

In love.

With me?

I leaned forward and tried to sniff his breath. "Are you still drunk?"

But my brother kept talking before I could keep going. "Anyone with eyes and ears knows that guy thinks you shit out Lucky Charms."

Gordo and I burst out laughing.

"Is that a good thing?" I asked him.

Eliza shoved my face away with his palm, ignoring my commentary again. "And I think that you love him, too."

The noise that came out of my mouth sounded like a hybrid "moo" and squawk at the same time. "I —," I slammed my mouth shut before opening it again with a sputter. "What? We haven't even—we haven't even—"

That didn't help the situation any because Eli threw his head back and laughed from deep within his throat. That huge, bellowing laugh that could cause an earthquake. "Gaby, remember when you swore you were in love with Reiner Kulti? But you'd never met him? If he would've shown up at our door, you would've sold your soul to the devil to be with him."

I nodded because it was the fucking truth. If that happened now, I'd kick the retired soccer icon to the curb, but ten years ago? I would have totally been a teen mom.

"You know that day you were sick?" Gordo asked me in his quiet voice from across the table. When I nodded he continued, "He looked miserable the entire day. He kept asking once every hour if we'd checked on you. If anyone had made sure you had something to eat. Blah, blah, blah."

The words settled onto my skin, my pores absorbing them slowly.

"And he's always talking about you. 'Gaby said this, Gaby said that.'"

Eli shook his head in disgust. "What killed me was that a few days ago, this girl—"

"That girl!" Gordo exclaimed, knowing exactly whatever girl my brother was referring to.

"This girl," Eli settled his hands in front of his chest, leaving enough space so that two melons could fit. "This girl that looked like a Victoria's Secret supermodel came up to him, and she was pretty much raping him with her eyes from the get-go. She's telling him what hotel she's in, what room number is hers, and he's just in his own fucking world. *In his own fucking world*. Like he wasn't paying any fucking attention. When she left, all the TCC guys were like 'Dude, hit that!' What did he do? He shrugged." My brother shook his head like he couldn't believe the words coming out of his own mouth. "You don't shrug when somebody that hot comes onto you."

Gordo nodded in understanding.

But my brother wasn't done yet. "So Julian tells him, 'Sacha, she's so fucking hot. Do it.' And this guy," he snickered, shaking his head. I couldn't tell whether it was in disappointment or amusement. "He tells him, 'She is hot, but she's not my type.'"

"That girl was everybody's type," Gordo added.

"Even I would have thought about going to her hotel room. *You* would have messed around with her, Flabby."

I opened my mouth to make a comment about Gordo being attracted to a woman for the first time in his life, but Eli apparently needed to keep going. "And I knew it! I fucking knew it right then, and everyone else knew it right then. This motherfucker is in love, but then he seals the deal when he said, 'I'm not interested.'"

Gordo looked like he was in church as he threw his hands in the air. "Every human being would have been interested."

"So, my point is, Flabby. That guy more than likes you," he finally finished. "Quit being dumb and worried and all shy and shit because we all know you're really not, and get on it. "

I was reeling. My heart felt like it could beat through softened butter. I remembered, I remembered all too well his mouth on my shoulder. On my jaw. Oh God.

"I guess that means, I gotta start saving, huh?" Eliza asked me with a squeeze to the shoulder.

"For what?" I croaked, still thinking more about what he'd said.

"Your wedding, estupid. I'll pay for your motherfucking wedding if you're going to marry Sacha one day." He held up his glass of orange juice in Gordo's direction for a toast. "I like that guy."

CHAPTER NINETEEN

———————

I'd almost forgotten that Sacha's mom was supposed to drop by to see her baby boy.

Two days before the end of the Australian leg of the tour, I was completely caught off-guard by the stunning, intense woman who came into the venue while I was helping Julian put together his drum set.

Mrs. Malykhin—if her last name was still that since she and Sacha's dad were divorced, from what I gathered—was a delicately boned woman with the same color hair as her son. Tall and slim, her carriage was erect. Seriously, if there was someone that looked like an ideal queen it would have been her.

She also seemed to speak the way I imagined royalty would. I could hear her from across the venue as they headed in our direction.

" —had the nerve to say my early phrases were underpowered. *Underpowered*. Me. Can you believe the nerve...?"

Sacha answered with something I couldn't hear clearly, but he did reach over and put his hand on her shoulder as the beginning of a smile curved over his mouth.

The "ugh" that came from my side had me turning my head to glance at Julian who was busy setting up his kick drum while I did his cymbals for the first time. As a late birthday present, I'd offered to help him set up from time to time. His attention was on the same people, except his nose was scrunched. When he realized I'd caught his expression he poked at the inside of his cheek with his tongue, his face unapologetic. "His mom is..." he trailed off with a whisper, "a snob."

"Really?" I whispered back.

"Yeah." He glanced back over at his band mate and visitor. "You'll see.""

"You're scaring me."

"She's a famous opera singer," he quickly explained. "In her mind, Sach is throwing away this amazing talent she gave him and it's all our fault, and she lets us know that each time she shows up."

I grimaced and Julian nodded.

He paused before adding quickly, "Don't call her Mrs. Malykhin."

Before I could thank him for the warning, the husky female voice called out. "Hello, Julian."

The TCC member plastered a smile on his face as he walked around the part of the drum set he'd been working on. "Hi, Miss Viktoriya." He gave me a meaningful side-glance that I took to be a sign. "It's been a long time."

Taller close-up than she looked from across the venue, she had to be at least five-ten and definitely didn't look old enough to have her youngest child be almost thirty, much less have five kids. The elegant woman held out a slim hand in Julian's direction. He took it and kissed it.

Literally. He kissed her hand. I'd never seen that happen in person, and I suddenly wondered why.

My eyes shot over to Sacha who was standing a few feet behind his mother. He smiled at me, opening his mouth at the same time. "Mom, I want you to meet someone," he said as he closed the distance between him and me.

Miss Viktoriya turned her entire body to face me. The similarities between mother and son were striking. They had the same cheekbones, the same transparent gray to their irises, and the same kind of extraordinary beauty. All that attention and confidence was now on me, and I lost the fight to not fidget.

But wonderful Sacha must have sensed or seen my anxiety because he cut in. "Mom, this is Gaby. Gaby, this is my mom."

Damn it. He'd called her by what he knew her as but that didn't give me a clue whether to call her Miss Viktoriya too or not.

I smiled tightly at the woman and held out my

hand in her direction, making it clear—at least I hoped—that I wasn't going to be kissing her hand like Julian had done, no matter how famous she was. "Hi, it's nice to meet you."

Even as she took my palm in hers in a handshake that was absolutely not limp-fish in any way, shape or form, she eyed me up and down discreetly. "It's a pleasure to meet you as well. I've heard so much about you."

So much about me? What the hell was up with that?

I knew I wasn't exactly at my best, but I'd opted to wear jeans instead of sweats and a formfitting kids' sweater I'd picked up in Brisbane that had a koala on it with *Australia* written in rainbow letters. Eli had been nice enough to braid my hair after I'd promised to give him Tylenol in return for his headache, like I wouldn't have given it to him regardless.

I glanced expectantly at Sacha who was just standing two feet away by then with a pleased expression on his face, smiling this grand, beaming thing that made my chest shimmer on the inside. We hadn't gotten a chance to talk since the whole kiss-on-the-neck thing the night before. I'd fallen asleep on the ride home and barely made it to my room intact.

"We're going to eat. Do you want to come with us?" he asked me.

"I can't, I promised Carter I'd help him count

merch."

He nodded but it was his mom that spoke up. "That's too bad. Maybe next time," she said but I couldn't tell if she was being sarcastic or if she really meant it.

"Sach!" Miles started yelling at him from the back door to the venue.

He frowned and said something about being right back while his mom stayed where she was, her attention on me. The second Sacha was far enough away from us, she took a step forward. Her entire demeanor turned serious and tense.

"Is this all you do?" she asked coolly.

"Do you mean sell merchandise?" I made sure to draw the question out so that I could understand what she clearly meant. Apparently Sacha had told her enough about me so that she'd know I sold merch. I eyed Julian but he was busy pretending to mess with his equipment. Coward.

"Yes."

"Right now it is. I just graduated. I'm not sure what I'm doing."

Miss Viktoriya hummed, giving me another thorough inspection. "From high school?"

"From college."

Her ridiculously long eyelashes lowered just a fraction. "What did you study?"

Yeah, I didn't care for her tone at all, and I felt my own eyes narrowing in her direction. "History."

The tip of her nose rose a quarter of an inch.

"What are you planning on doing with that?"

Why did I feel like I was going through the weirdest, most judgmental job interview ever? Well, if she thought I was going to cower, she had another thing coming. "I have no idea."

"I see," she said but it wasn't exactly in an "I think you're an idiot" tone, more like... curious. Actually interested. On the other hand, maybe I was imagining it.

Glancing to the side quickly, I spotted Sacha making his way back toward us. Apparently so did she because the next thing I knew, Miss Viktoriya, reigning queen of perfectly powered opera performances, took a step forward and whispered, "My boy has always known what he wants, and he dives into things head first without hesitation. Break his heart, and I will ruin your life."

She left me with those words.

"What did she say to you?" Julian finally spoke up once the opera singer was gone.

I blinked at him, still figuring out what the hell she'd meant. "I think she just threatened me."

He didn't look remotely surprised; he simply tipped his chin down. "Makes sense."

∾

That night, when he knocked on my door and I asked him for the password, he said, "Gaby should get a gold medal for being alive."

I laughed because I wasn't sure whether that was a good thing or not, like most things that came out of his mouth. "Anddd?"

"I have a present for you," he said following a chuckle.

"Seriously, Sassy, you don't always have to bring something," I told him, opening the door with a smile on my face.

He grinned as he shuffled in, kicking off his shoes as he pushed a yellow bag in my direction. "I saw it when I went to dinner with my mom," he explained before I'd even opened the bag.

"You're spoiling me," I looked up at him briefly before pulling out a small white shirt with a baby kangaroo on it, the words *Call Me Joey* written in lime-green bubble letters. I laughed and threw my arms around Sacha a split second later, aiming for his waist. "Thank you, Sassy."

Sacha squeezed me back, wrapping his arms over the tops of my shoulders. "You're very welcome."

We stayed like that for a moment, then two moments, five moments, eight moments. One of his arms loosened around me before I felt him smooth a hand down my wet hair. "You know you don't have to buy me anything ever," I said. "I'd let you in even if the only thing you brought was bad breath."

He laughed while rubbing that free hand smoothly over the small of my back. "I know."

"Okay."

His hand slipped an inch up the back of my shirt,

fingertips brushing my bare skin at the same time his mouth dipped down to my temple. "I like that you don't expect me to buy you things, that's why I do it."

Something tugged at my brain, making me think of Ronalda and how Sacha would pull her chair out for her, and how she wanted him to sacrifice so much for her. Maybe he did things like that because she demanded it? I pushed the thought away, not wanting to think of her when it was me in this moment with this beautiful man.

"Thank you, anyway." I told him dumbly, breathlessly.

Sacha pulled away just an inch before tipping my head back. He gave me a sly, seductive smile. "You're the easiest person in the world to please," he breathed, kissing my cheek softly.

The fact that he was kissing my cheek and I was standing there handling it as if it wasn't a big deal was something I was going to replay later on when the moment was broken and I wasn't living in it any longer.

"Is that a good thing?"

His smile morphed again, into one that made me think of a secret. "It's a great thing."

CHAPTER TWENTY

Sacha poked me in the side. "Stay awake."

I didn't even bother covering my yawn as I eyed him sleepily, the television a steady hum in the background. The last time I'd looked at the clock, it showed that it was after three in the morning. Eli had woken me up early to explain that our flights had been cancelled and that we'd be leaving the following afternoon instead.

I wasn't sure why he hadn't just told me at a normal hour in the day instead of at the crack of dawn, but then again, I didn't know why my brother did half of the things that he did.

My gray-eyed, self-proclaimed best friend was lying on my bed, shoulders pressed against the headboard while I sat cross-legged next to him, nodding off. "I'm sleepy, but you can stay," I told him with a yawn again.

"Come here," he murmured, patting the empty space between our bodies.

What do you do when a man like Sacha Malykhin wants you to lie down next to him? You do it. Preferably naked, but I was too tired to even think anything more suggestive than that. So I settled for a tired smile and untangled my legs to scoot into the designated spot. I stretched out next to him while he moved to lie flat against the bed, extending his right arm out for me to lie on top of. He curled his arm as soon as I settled in, pulling me over so until I had my head on his chest.

I may have draped my arm over his stomach as nonchalantly as possible.

"You're warm," I mumbled against his black T-shirt. I yawned again and blinked, trying my best to stay awake and enjoy our closeness. "I never told you," I yawned. "You look just like your mom."

"You think so?"

I nodded into him. I hadn't told him what his mom had said. I didn't see the point. Then there was also the fact that I wasn't sure what the hell she meant by ruining my life, so... I was going to let it go and blame it on her being a diva. "Girlish features and everything."

His chest rumbled under my head. "You always know what to say to make me feel like a million bucks."

"You can thank me for my friendship later."

He laughed again. "I'll remember to do that." It

was his turn to yawn. "Sit with me tomorrow?"

"As long as you—," I let out another long yawn, "let me sleep on your legs, and I'll let you nap on mine."

"Deal."

I pressed my forehead closer to his smooth jaw.

Sacha squeezed me to him with a sigh. "Go to sleep, Princess," he said in his quiet voice.

"Okay," I mumbled.

Sacha stroked my arm with his fingers, once, twice, three times. "*Frère Jacques, frère Jacques, dormez-vous? Dormez-vous? Sonnez les matines, sonnez les matines, ding ding dong, ding ding dong,*" he sang softly.

I smiled against him, tilting my head up, up, up. "Goodnight, Sassy."

He stroked my arm once more before I felt him shift beneath me, my head tucking deeper into his chest. The moment was sleepy, and warm, and sweet, and it was perfect. He pressed his lips against mine gently just for a moment, and then he kissed my nose.

He'd kissed me.

Even in my nearly delirious state, I recognized that sinking feeling deep

in my chest. No eclipse could overshadow the fact that I was absolutely in love with this guy, and it was the easiest and simplest thing in the world.

$\approx$

"You look comfy," Sacha drawled with a smile. He was sitting on the bench in front of the one I was on, with his bright red hoodie sleeves pushed up to his elbows. God, he was so cute.

I glanced down at the two men sleeping on me. My brother had his head on my lap, drooling, while Mason had his head on my shoulder, also drooling. Despite the fact that it was two in the afternoon, the pair were apparently exhausted over whatever craziness they'd experienced the night before. All I understood from their rambling babblings was something about a strip club, New Zealand girls and a banana.

I didn't want to know anything more. I could live without becoming scarred for life.

So now they were passed out on top of me, soaking my hoodie and jeans with their saliva, but I didn't have the heart to push them off. The drive to the airport was a little less than an hour, and they were busy taking full advantage of it.

"I've been more comfortable," I smiled at him, thinking about when I'd woken up that morning.

Sacha had been wiggling under me, trying to ease me onto the bed as gently as possible. He'd pressed a kiss on my cheek, told me he had an interview and that he'd see me later, then he blew hot morning breath on my face and left. Only I would think that was charming.

His phone started ringing for the fourth time since we'd gotten into the van, and he sighed. Again.

It wasn't my business to ask whom he was avoiding but... the curiosity was fucking killing me. Isaiah, who was sitting next to him, grunted in frustration.

"Answer the phone, man. I'm sick of hearing it ring," he complained softly.

I could see Sacha roll his eyes before pulling out his phone and shifting his position to face forward. I immediately got a little wary of his action. There'd been a handful of times that his parents or his sisters had called while we were together, and he'd answered their calls without a second thought. He didn't care if I heard what was said but his hesitation at answering that call right then, told me there was something he was trying to avoid.

I trusted him. A lot. He hadn't given me a reason to doubt that he cared for me or that he was honest. On the other hand, we had only known each other a little over two months. It had taken Brandon three years to fuck up.

"Flabby," Eliza groaned as his hand started patting around my knee before landing on his face. He wiped at his lips and then touched the spot of drool he'd left on my pants. "Ahh fuck."

As much as I wanted to eavesdrop on the conversation that Sassy was having in front of me, my brother had decided to start yapping right then. What a useless ass.

"Is that drool?" he mumbled.

"No, it's Kool-Aid, dumbass," I snickered, brushing my hand over the short ends of his hair that had just barely began to curl after more than a month.

Eli smiled against my leg, making a noise that sounded like a low, sleepy chuckle. "Drink it later, then." He blinked twice before closing his eyes and going back to sleep.

Gross.

The faint conversation from the seat in front of ours made me stop breathing so I could listen better. What's funny was that everyone else awake in the van had lowered their voices when Sacha started talking. It had only taken me a few weeks to learn that these guys were worse at gossiping than teenage girls. Even though they tried to play off their interest, they ate up anything that caught their attention.

Like the time Isaiah got propositioned by a fan, who offered him five hundred dollars to sleep with her.

Or the time that a fan had asked my brother, Gordo and Miles if he could lick their shoes.

Then there was the time that Mason—

There were a lot of things that had happened that the guys had been all too excited to talk about.

Obviously, there was something about this conversation that caught their attention.

"I already told you... Lizzy, I'm not changing my mind..." Sacha spoke into the receiver. *Lizzy? The fuck?* Before I could ponder it much longer, he kept going. "No, there's no one else. I don't want to get back together because it's my choice. Just like you decided you didn't want to be together, I don't want to pick up where we left off..." I felt like I was being stabbed as he talked. "I care about you. You know that. You mean a lot to me, but that doesn't mean I want to be with you. I'm done explaining this to you over and over again."

I could see his reflection in the glass. His eyes were closed and his forehead was pressed against the cool window. My heart was beating frantically even though I know it shouldn't be. Nothing that Sacha was saying was technically wrong. Technically. It was his choice that he didn't want to get back together with his ex. He did care about her. I mean, they'd been together for a while.

But—

But—

But—

I felt sick. Sacha cared about me too. I knew he did. Every vessel in my blood knew it. But maybe that's why he hadn't put more of a move on me? Because he didn't want to be tied down to anyone? A simple kiss wasn't a promise ring or anything. It didn't have to mean anything romantic. And... there was a difference between loving someone and being in love with someone. I knew that.

My realization and acceptance from the night before was strangling. I was in love with a man who maybe loved me according to others, but maybe didn't love me the way that I wanted. Maybe he didn't want a relationship. I had men in my life that loved me in a platonic way. What was one more? And why did I feel betrayed that he still cared about Ariel Number Two? Sacha was a nice guy. Hell, he was the nicest guy I had ever met. It was probably just in his system to care for people, but...

I reached over Eli's big body to grab the backpack he had on his lap, and fished out his expensive studio earphones, plugging them into my phone as quickly as I could as I zoned out the man on the phone. Flicking through the albums I had saved in my library, I chose the one at the top of the list and raised the volume as loud as tolerable.

Closing my eyes, I let my head drop back to the seat and put a hand on each of the guys beside me.

CHAPTER TWENTY-ONE

I slept my way to Dubai, and somehow managed to make it to London without speaking more than twenty words to Sacha. Most importantly, I didn't fall asleep on his legs and he didn't nap on mine. When we caught our connecting flight, it turned out that he was sharing a seat with a stranger so I sat with my brother and Gordo instead. Gordo—who had heard the same conversation I had—didn't say a word. It was the red Starburst he gave me later on that really showed his sympathy.

When we finally landed in London, the promoter for the tour drove us in a Sprinter van to a hotel where we'd be staying for the night. A new tour bus would be picking us up the next day.

I made an effort to stand and sit away from my gray-eyed friend. My mood was pretty rotten, and I felt pretty groggy from the jetlag. As excited as I'd been about going to Europe, I didn't feel like doing a freaking thing on our first day off. Everyone was so relieved to be on land again, and I definitely wasn't going to be the party pooper in the bunch bringing everybody else down.

If my good mood were a raft named Gaby, it seemed like it was on the verge of sinking.

Eli had waved me off when I got settled in my room and said he'd be back for me later, regardless of whether I wanted to go somewhere or not. He knew something was bothering me, but he was smart enough to know not to ask about it until later. Even though he'd inherited the Barreto temper from our mom, bits and pieces of it were still etched into my chromosomes. He was well aware of what to expect when I was in a slump.

What I didn't take into consideration was that Sacha had gotten to know me as well.

When a knock sounded on my door a couple of hours after we'd been dropped off, I didn't bother asking who was there because I'd assumed it was Eliza. Only it wasn't.

"You didn't ask for the password," Sacha said with a frown when the door was opened.

I shrugged and held it wider for him to come in. "I thought you were Eli," I answered him simply.

"Oh." Sacha eyed me critically as he stepped into the tiny room. He'd showered since the last time I'd seen him, dressed in jeans and a white V-neck. He dropped his long body onto my bed, propping himself up with his elbows. "What are we doing today?"

Closing the door, I turned to look at him while attempting to ease the thunder going on in my heart. "I was planning on staying in."

"I thought you wanted to walk around?" He raised a dark eyebrow.

Another shrug. "Maybe tomorrow, I'm tired. I'm sure someone else can go out with you."

Sacha just blinked at me. "I want to go with you."

No, no, no, no, no. I smiled at him. "I'm sure you'll have just as much fun with someone else."

He stared at me for so long in silence I wasn't sure he was ever going to respond until he finally did. His question cool and controlled. "What's wrong?"

"Nothing."

"Gaby."

I gave him the weakest smile in existence. "I'm just pooped and groggy, and my head really hurts."

He blinked again. "When did it start hurting?"

My shoulders went up. "Earlier, before the first flight." *Right after I heard you tell another woman you cared about her.*

He grumbled rolling up to sit on his bottom. He rubbed his hands up and down his pant legs. The look on his face was enough of a warning. "Tell me what's wrong. You're being weird."

"I'm fine," I pleaded. "I just want to be alone right now."

Those pale eyes twitched in disbelief and possibly hurt. "Don't do this to me again."

"What?" I asked him even though I already knew what he was trying to hint at.

"You're pushing me away. I don't like it."

"Sacha, I'm not—" Damn it.

He grimaced. "See, you never call me Sacha." He pushed off the edge of the bed to stand. "Tell me what's wrong."

I shook my head and averted my eyes to the ceiling. Sure I'd teared up for a split second, but I'd swiped at them and that was it. "It's nothing," I muttered.

"You're lying," he replied.

I was, and I hated it. I wasn't a liar. Maybe sometimes I left things out by omission, but I didn't enjoy doing it. I was terrible at it. But what would I tell him? The truth? *Hey Sassy, I realized I was in love with you last night, and then you told your ex that you care about her but that there isn't anyone else in the picture.* Right. That sounded like the worst idea ever.

When he gripped my wrist with his warm fingers, I sucked in a breath. "Gaby baby."

Eli had told me once a very long time ago that you weren't living unless you took risks. The thing he never mentioned was that risks were scary. I didn't deal with rejection well. But what was four more weeks? It'd be easier for me to ignore him for that time than it would be for me to lie and pretend that I was fine when I wasn't.

"Tell me, Princess," he said with a squeeze to my wrist.

I'd never really considered myself very brave before. Usually I found my strength from my brother, who didn't care enough what people thought to worry about consequences, or Laila, who wasn't fazed of most things. My trust in others was usually the reassurance I needed to do things that made me nervous. I knew that they would never do anything to kill me.

All I had was four more weeks left.

I sighed and looked everywhere except at him. "I looked into something more than I should have and now I just feel stupid. That's all."

"What was it?" he asked in a voice barely above a whisper.

Balls. I had invisible balls and I could do this. "I thought that someone liked me, but I realized that maybe it wasn't the same kind of attraction that I was hoping for," I told him slowly, meeting his eyes in the greatest act of bravery I'd ever accomplished singlehandedly.

His beautiful face swept into a clouded, dark expression. "Who?" His question was asked slowly.

Jesus F. Christ. I swallowed hard. "Who what?"

"Who doesn't like you?"

Oh brother. "You're a nice guy, Sassy. I know that. Everyone knows that. Hell, I think Eli has a crush on you." I smiled at him just a little, reminding myself that it wasn't his fault he was so likable. "It's not in your nature to be a complete dick, and that's okay. I get it. I like that about you a lot, but you don't have to pretend. At least don't pretend with me."

Sacha's eyebrows furrowed before he scowled at me, confusion marring the planes of his features. "What are you talking about?"

"Oh my God," I moaned and went to take a step back but he held my wrist tight.

Men. Idiot, idiot men.

I must have stared at him long and hard enough that it finally hit him. His hand went up to that favorite part of his skull he was always rubbing, and he scoffed in disbelief at the same time. "You think I don't like you?"

And I wanted to die. "I think you like me in a different way than I like you, if you insist on knowing." *Kill me. Kill me now.*

"What?" he hissed, taking a step forward. "Why would you think that?"

My eyes went to the ceiling again. I didn't want to have this conversation. Every fiber of my being was revolting against me. "Everyone in the van heard your phone conversation, Sassy. *No one special. You care about your ex-girlfriend but you don't want to get back together with her.*" I tugged my arm back uselessly. "I get it. It's fine."

But it wasn't.

Sacha let out a long breath. "You heard what I told Liz, and you think that what I said changes anything?" He took another step toward me. "You really think that I don't like you?"

When I didn't say anything in response, he tapped at the corner of his mouth with the tip of his tongue. "Gaby, I can tell you that I hate you. I can tell you that I think you're the worst person I've ever met. The ugliest girl on the planet. I can tell everyone in the audience tomorrow that I'm gay, but do you think that changes a single thing?

"You make me happier than anyone else ever has, and if you knew how many people I've met, you'd understand what that means. I know you don't know Liz, but that was the only way I knew I could get to her. If I'd told her that I thought you were the best thing on the planet, it would've made her relentless. She doesn't know what 'no' means. And it's no one's business but mine how I feel about you," he said quickly.

As much as his words warmed me, they weren't what I wanted. They weren't a fleck of a confirmation. They were an explanation that made complete sense to me, but that didn't ease my worry enough. "I get it. I think you're great too," I told him with a sigh. "But that's not—"

"Is the sun the biggest object in space?" he asked me in an even, determined voice.

I had to think about that one for all of a split second before I shook my head, confused at what he was asking. "No."

"How do you explain to the sun that there are stars far away that dwarf it?" He lowered his face to mine. "I've liked you from the moment I met you." He blinked, his eyebrows knitting together in surprise. "Damn, Gaby. I'm fucking crazy about you."

Say what?

His eyes bore right into mine, drinking in the confusion that I'm sure was apparent in them. "Don't look at me like that."

"You're—you—" I—what—

His fingers pinched my earlobes. "You haven't been single for long. I didn't want to rush you into anything, and I wasn't about to let you out of my life even after the tour ends," he explained in a low, even cadence. His voice was hypnotic and I was hooked. A small, frustrated smile covered his mouth. "You're an idiot if you think that you're no one special to me. You're the most special." His lips hovered over mine. "The most."

Dead. I was dead and this was the afterlife.

He slowly pulled me forward. His hand cupped my cheek; his soft lips were filled with purpose when they covered mine so tenderly I couldn't think to breathe. Sacha's mouth opened slowly, coaxing mine to do the same. Just as gradually, he angled his lips to kiss me as deeply as possible. He tasted faintly like mint.

Two hands cradled my face suddenly as he held us in one piece, like he was worried I'd try to pull away. He moaned deep in his throat when I kissed him back with the same intensity he kissed me. One of his palms drifted to the back of my neck, gripping it strongly while his other arm wrapped around my waist and brought my lower body flush against his. Every lean muscle of his upper body pressed against mine, bunching and flexing with the force of his actions.

Then he pulled away a fraction of an inch to give my cheek a wet, open-mouth kiss. "Do you need me to spell it out for you?"

I shivered and nodded, tilting my head more openly toward him. "I think so."

CHAPTER TWENTY-TWO

"You hurt my feelings," I told Sacha in a low voice after those awesomely wonderful first kisses.

I'd briefly thought about not telling him how much his words had bothered me, but I decided against it. I'd already jumped in with both feet by admitting that I liked him, and that it was him that made me feel stupid. At this point my dignity was around the block and it wasn't going to return anytime soon.

"Gaby," he sighed, reaching forward to wrap his long fingers around my wrist. Tugging me toward him, he patted the open space between his extended legs. It didn't take a genius to understand that he wanted me to sit between them, but I couldn't. At least not yet. Instead I sat a couple of inches away from his closest thigh. "That's the last thing I'd want to do."

I nodded. Something deep in my gut told me he was speaking the truth. "It's okay."

Turning his entire body toward me, one foot on the floor, his other leg bent and resting on the mattress, his hands landed on my shoulders and slowly inched their way down my arms. His smooth palms curved over my biceps and elbows. "It's not okay. I should have settled things when I saw her," Sacha replied. He leaned forward, wrapping his arms around me in a loose, comforting hug as one of his kneecaps pressed against mine. "I've been nuts about you. I guess I just assumed you knew."

"Oh." Knew? How? Okay, maybe the signs had been there but I hadn't let myself get too attached to them.

"Gaby," he whispered, bringing one hand up to drape the end of my ponytail over my shoulder. "I don't know what I'm doing with you half the time." Sacha snickered almost lazily. "I like you so much it makes me stupid."

I couldn't help but snort, pulling back and glancing up at him. "I think you were already in that boat long before I came along, Sassy."

He chuckled softly, leaning forward a moment later to kiss my cheek. It might have made me snuck in a surprised breath. "See? Not liking you is like fighting gravity."

This fucking guy was going to be the death of me.

"Lots of people don't like me, like Miles," I scoffed. "Everyone else just puts up with me because of Eli, probably."

Lips planted themselves high on my cheek twice and each time I had to battle the urge to crawl into his lap and ask for more. "You don't see things clearly." His nose made the trip down until he was nuzzling my throat. "You're special to a lot of people, but especially to me."

I looked at him, seeing those smoke-colored eyes much closer than I was used to. I wasn't fishing for compliments, or reassurance in the love that people like my brother and Mason had for me. I knew that they cared. Their love was easy and unconditional.

Whether this thing between us was just a whole lot of "like" or love—that I wasn't sure about. I'd grown up sharing things my entire life. There had never been a "mine" option with my siblings, everything belonged to the community, but with Sacha… there wasn't that option. There could never be that option.

"It's over, though?" I asked him, looking down at the bed. "Between you and Ron—I mean, Liz?"

Another slow kiss landed on my throat as he kept eye contact with me through his lashes, lingering the heat of a thousand fires. "I swear."

"I can smell your bullshit a mile away," I warned him, trying my best to focus on what I was saying and not how he was making me feel with all those kisses.

Sacha laughed low. "Oh, I know, Princess. I don't expect any less, but I promise. There's nothing there and there hasn't been for a long time. Even when there was, it was nothing close to this." He touched my ear. "You know you can trust me."

The hell of it was, I knew I could.

"We're fine then?" he asked with hesitation stamping his tone. "Better than before?"

I nodded and blinked at him, needing and wanting to make sure that we were on the same page. "Just to make sure... you have feelings for me too, right?"

Those light colored eyes rolled before he pressed his forehead against mine, his nose touching my own. I could sense his breath on my mouth as he whispered, "So many feelings you have no idea."

Well, shit. What came out of my mouth was probably the dumbest, most understated reply that I could have possibly come up with: "Okay."

"Okay?" he asked. I could feel his grin, though I couldn't see it from how close we were.

"Yes. Okay." I felt like I could breath for the first time in hours or longer. Did that mean I knew what was going on? No. I guess I'd missed the guidelines on when people were officially dating and when they weren't since my past experiences were nothing to compare against. Brandon had simply called me his girlfriend one day when introducing me to people and that had been that. My boyfriend in high school had *asked* me to be his girlfriend. How the hell were you supposed to know?

A loud knock on my door snapped us out of our

bubble. I groaned and jumped up to check the peephole. My brother stood on the other side with his arms crossed over his chest before I let him in.

"We're going on one of those double-decker tours. Put some shoes on," he said quickly, before narrowing his eyes. "And some make-up. Definitely put some make-up on."

Asshole.

I stood there with my mouth open a second, which made him frown and then peek over my shoulder to spot Sacha sitting on my bed. A slow grimace covered Eliza's face before he shuddered.

"Oh fuck, I'm going to be sick," he groaned before gagging.

I laughed and socked him in the stomach. "Shut up. We're fully clothed, you idiot."

Eli smiled quickly and winked at Sacha, only confirming the man-crush I felt he had on him. "Come on, Sach. You can translate what those tour guides are saying."

"They're speaking English," I told my brother, feeling one of my eyes begin to twitch.

"But they have accents, Flabby, hello."

I looked over my shoulder to find Sacha shaking his head, so I snickered. "Luckily for you, E, Sacha speaks stupid, so he can translate."

∾

"And you wonder why you don't have any friends."

Sacha shot me a look as he raked both hands through his hair. He'd just finished telling me that I was out of my fucking mind for wanting to get on the ride. Those pale eyes peered up again, taking in the Ferris wheel-type thing that was currently scaring the shit out of him. He blinked and swallowed hard. "I can't do it," he stated.

"You're really that scared?" I asked, crossing my arms over my chest.

Eli and Gordo were standing close by, my brother busy gesturing and leering at a group of women to our right. Knowing him, he was planning on which girl he would hit on first. The poor, poor soul. Thankfully, no one was witnessing the freak-out that I thought Sacha was about to have. He glanced at me again before looking at the London Eye warily.

"You're scared of heights?"

Sacha swallowed. "I can handle normal heights; getting on a ladder or on a counter, but *that* is too tall. Way too tall," he let out in one breath, watching the huge contraption.

I turned around to look at the looming attraction. It was pretty damn tall. Even though I wasn't scared of heights, it was intimidating. Eliza had been the one to suggest that we get on after our double-decker tour bus adventure. I was more than glad that we'd gotten through it without my brother insulting someone with the dumb shit that came out of his mouth. Gordo had been the one who got stuck sitting next to him, while Sacha and I crowded together on a seat. Now that I thought about it, it was me that had hung off the edge of the bus taking in the sights while he sat up straight and took everything in that I know he'd seen before.

It wasn't his first time visiting London, and it wasn't my brother's either, but I liked that they both went out of their ways to do things that they knew I hadn't done. Things that they wouldn't have done if I hadn't been around. I couldn't imagine Eli or Gordo riding along on a tourist bus for fun. Hell, I was surprised Eliza wasn't hitting up a pub instead, but I wasn't about to bring it up.

"If you really don't want to get on, we don't have to," I told him, smiling just a little at his fear.

He groaned and looked up at the contraption behind me again, teeth grinding. "But you already got our tickets—"

"Oh lord, Sassy, I'd rather stay down here with you than have you flipping out up there," I poked him in his stomach, enjoying how normal everything felt after the conversation we'd had in my hotel room. "It's fine. Don't worry about it. I'm scared of the dark, so don't judge me."

He raised an eyebrow at me, giving me the tiniest hint of a smile. "The dark?"

"Yep," I told him. "I have a nightlight in my room."

He laughed, taking a step forward. "For some reason, I'm not surprised." His hands reached up to land on my shoulders, squeezing them lightly and I let the flutters of attraction fly through my belly. "You know there's nothing to be scared of, right?"

I shrugged and looked behind me. "Have you seen scary movies? There's plenty of stuff to be scared of. Freddy Krueger, Michael Myers, *Chucky*. I didn't want to shower alone for about a month after I watched *It*. No thanks."

Sacha smiled that big grin that made my chest flutter. This was all new and sudden, but at the same time, not really. This had been coming, hadn't it? Even Eli wasn't teasing me or making faces. That had to be a sign. This—him—was easy. Effortless. It just felt right.

It probably should have been strange that less than a few hours ago, I didn't even want to speak to him, but it wasn't. He liked me. I liked him. And Ronalda was out of my Happy Meal.

What more could I want, besides a naked Sacha?

"If they come after you, I'm there," he chuckled.

I laughed, thinking of how my baboons would leave me to die if it came down to it. "Unless we have to climb up the side of a building."

"In that case, it was nice knowing you," he snickered.

Oh dear God. I loved it. I really loved it.

"Disgusting and Gross, ready to go?" Eli asked.

Taking a step back, I turned my head to see my brother and Gordo standing there, smirking. I rolled my eyes. "I don't think we're getting on."

He gave me an incredulous look. We'd been

riding roller coasters together from before I was even tall enough to ride, so he knew there was a legitimate reason I wasn't getting on. "Why the hell not?"

Sacha made a noise in his throat, and I knew he was getting ready to say something. But I didn't want to do that to him. To tell Eli Barreto you had a weakness was the equivalent of bleeding within a mile of a shark.

"I need to go number two," I blurted out before thinking and immediately cringed. Of all the things I could have said…

Sacha snorted.

My twin nodded without batting an eyelash. "Got it." Of course he would. If there was anything in the world he took seriously, it was taking a shit.

A few minutes later, he and Gordo trotted off toward the entrance to the Eye. Sacha groaned for a minute before leading me after them. "Come on. If I pass out, at least break my fall."

My chest tightened again at his small act of braveness. For me. Because he knew I wanted to get on. "I swear I won't tell anyone if you faint."

"You're too kind," he smirked with wide eyes, looking up at the attraction again.

As soon as Eli spotted us in line, he threw his arms out to the sides and asked in a voice that was way too loud, "I thought you needed to take a shit?"

CHAPTER TWENTY-THREE

"Flabby, I'd love a massage," Mason blatantly suggested, bumping his shoulder against mine.

I bumped his back. We were sitting in our new bus: a fancy double decker that made our U.S. bus seem tiny. The first floor had the kitchen and living space, while the upstairs had the bunk area. At that moment, Mase and I were sitting on one of the couches eating fish and chips that my brother had scrounged up somewhere before the show ended.

It had been a great first day. The first two legs of the Rhythm & Chord tour had been amazing, taking us all over the U.S. and Australia, but London had been beyond perfect. The crowd was different. The energy was different. And I was enjoying the hell out of the fans with their accents.

"Mason," I bit into a fry. "I'd love to not have a period, but we don't always get what we want."

He barked out a laugh, dipping his fish into my vinegar. "Well, I'd love it if you didn't have a period either, you damn psychopath." Mason winked at me before pulling on the end of my ponytail.

I snorted. "I'd love it if you took a shower."

"I did!" he gasped, knowing he was full of shit.

"Yesterday," I laughed.

Mase just smiled this sideways, teasing grin as he finished off his food. He stole a small piece of fish from my plate, and then tried to distract me from his thieving ways by throwing an arm over my shoulder and leaning into my side. "So, Flabby, are you and that kid finally together?"

"What kid?" I asked him in a low, secretive voice.

"Sacha," he whispered back.

We were pretty much alone on the first floor with the exception of Miles and Julian who were on the other end of the bus. Everyone else was on the second floor doing God knows what. There really wasn't a point in him trying to be secretive, but I thought it was amusing anyway. The bastard tried to be quiet at the wrong times.

"He's older than you are," I noted before adding, "and I don't know, why?"

His dark blue eyes narrowed. "Because I need to know whether to tell him what'll happen if he does anything stupid," he said matter-of-factly.

I had to tuck my lips in to keep from smiling at his form of a threat. "Really?"

Mason nodded, tightening his hold around me.

"Flabby, you know I don't have any sisters—"

"Thank God," I let out one tiny snort, imagining a female Mason.

He sniffed. "But if we aren't getting married—"

I snorted.

"Then I need to make sure some douchebag isn't going to break your heart," he said before wincing. "Again."

I couldn't help but roll my eyes at his addition. "Thanks for the reminder, asswipe."

Mason simply smiled and shrugged. "I got him back for you, don't you worry there." The reminder of what had gone down in San Antonio just made me grin. They had been so quiet about what exactly happened that required Brandon to get three new tires, that I still had no clue. Why he hadn't gone for all four was beyond me, but knowing Mason, there was a reason.

That didn't mean it was necessarily a good reason, but whatever.

"Did you tell him about Laverne and Shirley already?"

Yeah, I had to pinch the bridge of my nose after that question. "You mean Lucy and Ethel," I clarified. "No, I haven't told him. I don't know how."

"Don't ask me, Flabs. I say surprise the shit out of him." He did his best *Striptease* reenactment by pretending to rip his shirt wide. "What is he going to do? Barf? Say *oh no?* Pssh. No way."

"Oh, Mase," I smiled at him, "what would I do

without you?"

He shrugged, all loose muscles and languid smiles. "Dream about me."

"Ha!" I leaned toward him and pressed a kiss to his cheek. "In my nightmares."

Mason snickered and squeezed me one more time before dropping his arm with a sigh. "Speaking of nightmares, your brother and your honey bun are coming over; I think we made him jealous."

I rolled my eyes and got up to throw away both of our plates. Sure enough, Eliza and Sacha were right behind me in no time. But my gray-eyed friend, who had told the sold-out audience that night how much he liked brunettes, didn't seem flustered at all. The last thing I'd want to deal with was someone jealous over the likes of Mason. My Mason, who was like a hot adopted brother that escaped from a mental facility.

Once the other two joined us, we hung out for a couple of hours playing Spoons while they told me places we should try to go while the tour was in England. I wasn't really tired, but I went to bed at the same time as Eliza anyway, leaving Mason and Sacha in the living area watching television.

At some point once I'd dozed off, I woke up sensing pressure on my hand before I saw light coming through a crack in my curtains. Squinting, my eyes adjusted enough for me to be able to see it was Sacha touching me. His bunk was located directly above mine once more.

"You okay?" I whispered.

Those long fingers I admired on a regular basis stroked my jaw. "Yeah. I didn't mean to wake you. Go back to sleep." He didn't give me a chance to ask what his intention had been. He ducked his head into my bunk, kissed my cheek, squeezed my shoulder and shut the curtain.

Yeah, I couldn't go back to sleep after that. It wasn't until at least ten minutes later that I started wondering why I hadn't invited him to lay with me.

The next night, after an awesome show in Glasgow, I was already in bed when the curtain got pulled back. I knew who the intruder was before my eyes finished adjusting.

"I can't sleep," Sassy Pants whispered.

I yawned, thought for a second about how I could possibly answer, and then waved him in. He thought about it for as long as I did: one single second. There wasn't too much room in my tiny little bed but I didn't care, and apparently, when he climbed in immediately afterward, he didn't care either. It wasn't the first time he'd slept next to me so whatever. The idea that this was moving fast, when in the past I'd waited more than four months before sharing a bed with my ex, didn't occur to me. This was Sacha. My friend and more, and nothing felt like this—us—did.

I had to shuffle until my back was against the wall behind me while he wiggled in, closing the curtain behind him.

"Sing me a lullaby." He slid his arm around me effortlessly and pulled me to him, lining us up so we were face to face.

My laugh was weak and sleepy as I kissed his soapy-smelling, clean cheek. "Rock a bye, baby," I started. "Okay, goodnight."

Sacha laughed quietly into my skin, his hand stroking my lower back as he pressed his chest to mine. I could feel him tilting his head down to kiss the corner of my mouth. "Goodnight," he said, pressing those warm, warm lips to my sleepy ones.

How would he expect me to not reciprocate when that fantastic, full mouth touched mine?

Closed mouth, unhurried kisses piled on top of one another. Moments turned into minutes and soft pecks turned into softer, open-mouth kisses that had my heart racing. Sacha pulled back to let out a small breath, tucking me into him even more. His body was warm and firm; it took me all of thirty seconds to fall asleep after he kissed me one last time.

Mason's question haunted me for days.

What were Sacha and I?

We spent most of our time together. Okay, that was a fat, stinky lie. We spent all of our time together when it was possible. Between interviews, soundchecks, and my brother taking me places, we didn't get to spend all day joined at the hip but that was fine. When it was possible, it happened.

During shows, he'd sneak to the merch area with his hoodie disguising him and talk to me. I'd take my break strategically before he went on to wish him good luck. During shows, he usually said something directed toward me, like mentioning his attraction to brunettes. Then each night, he'd climb into my bunk and spend the night with me after we muffled our laughs over whatever we found funny in that moment.

It was a blinding kind of thing, this unbelievable friendship—this love—I had with and for him. It was mine and it made me happy, and I reveled in it.

But as much as his words and his kisses enveloped me, I still wondered. Calling us friends with benefits seemed so cheap, so unimportant. I knew he cared for me as more than just a friend. I could feel it in my bones.

A little over a week into the Europe tour, it seemed like someone upstairs in the white kingdom of harps and wings, decided that they wanted to help me out with this state of confusion that had taken over.

A friend of Julian's—why it was always Julian's friends that stirred things up was beyond me—

decided he liked his American meat.

That American meat being me.

All night, the guy had been flirting with me. That lilting English accent whispered to me how cute he thought I was when he checked out Ghost Orchid merch. It wasn't like I was going after his compliments or paying the guy any attention because I wasn't. When he first started, I just told him, "I'm dating someone." Simple enough, right? It didn't stop him, though.

He just kept coming back, and I found myself edging toward Carter and Gordo's company every time he made an appearance.

It was after the show when we were outside waiting to finish loading up, that I walked over to a group standing around. Sacha was standing in the loose circle with Julian and the little flirt from earlier. As soon as I saddled up a comfortable distance away from Sacha's side, he shot me a wide grin and took two steps over, throwing his arm over my shoulder. His chin was tipped down as he said, "Hi, Princess."

I slipped my arm around his waist and smiled. It wasn't like we were trying to hide the affection between us; he was free with his hugs and attention and so was I. But I wasn't the kind of girl who constantly needed someone holding my hand to feel special. Then again, that didn't say much because he could have stuck his finger in my ear and I would have thought it was cute. "Hi."

One of Julian's other friends visiting that day

cleared his throat, making Sacha rearrange us back in the direction of the rest of the group. He hauled me in closer and gestured in my direction with his head. "Guys, this is my Gaby. Princess, this is—"

Time stopped.

I couldn't remember anything after he said my name.

My Gaby.

My Gaby.

Not everyone's Gaby. Not Flabby. Not Eli's sister. Not just plain old Gaby.

Sacha's Gaby.

The only thing I managed to catch was The Flirt raising an eyebrow because I was in a damn dream world.

When Sacha slipped into my bunk later on, in what had become our routine, I raised an eyebrow. "I'm your Gaby?" I asked him first thing in a whisper as soon as we were settled under my sheets.

My friend grinned that earth-shattering smile that made my ovaries scream. "Yeah."

"Huh," I huffed.

Sacha dipped his mouth to mine, wrapping a flexed arm around me to pull us chest to chest. "You didn't know that you're my girl?" He pressed a long, lingering kiss on my lips.

I kissed him back, trying to leave a similar impression on him. "I didn't get the memo."

"You didn't?" he asked in a teasing voice. When I shook my head, he pressed his lips to the corner of my mouth. "You are."

"I am?"

He nodded. "Yup."

"So you're my Sassy?" I asked against his neck, brushing my mouth over the smooth skin right by his shoulder.

Sacha groaned when I kissed him there. "All yours," he clarified in a husky voice.

"Good."

"I think so."

I grinned at him and he grinned right back.

His index finger inched up to trace the shell of my ear. "I heard Sam was flirting with you all night."

My eyes were too busy being closed in response to his touch, to visibly take in whatever expression was on his face. "Was that Julian's friend?" I asked in a low, almost dreamy voice as he planted a kiss alongside my hairline.

"Mhmm," he replied, placing his lips in the same spot again.

"Then yes, he was." It took way more self-control than it should have to pry an eyelid open and peek.

His reply was a grumble that reached all the way to my toes. "Too bad for him."

It was just a flash flood of lips and more lips, hands on ribs and under T-shirts. He slanted his mouth over mine, brushing his tongue against me, over and over again. The hand I had on his hip, started to crawl under his T-shirt, smoothing over his hot skin and lean muscles.

Sacha's hand kneaded my hip before inching its way up my shirt, his fingertips brushing the skin of my stomach. It was such an innocent gesture but it made me freeze. It reminded me of what I'd been putting off telling him.

Wonderful Sacha must have sensed the change in tension coursing through me because he stopped and pulled away just slightly. "Too much?"

God bless him. I leaned up enough so that I could kiss his collarbone, my heart racing because of our kisses but mainly because I was worried about telling him the truth. Realistically, I knew that chances were, he wouldn't recoil in disgust or yell or anything dumb like that, but... the idea of sharing this small secret was still intimidating and a little scary. What if he did think it was weird? I was weird?

"I have something I need to tell you," I blurted out before I could change my mind.

He smiled gently. "Okay."

Okay? Well, all right. His fingertips brushed against the same bare spot on my stomach they'd been in when I'd freaked out. "I have breast implants." And, I went for it. Just went right on in without knocking, damn it.

Not a single word or sound came out of him for possibly five seconds. Then all of a sudden he hummed and kissed me. "Okay."

Another okay? That's it? "They were asymmetrical. I had surgery," I explained even though he hadn't asked but I wanted him to know, to understand. Not that it mattered but…

That had him pulling back all of two inches to look me right in the eye. "That sucks, Princess."

Uhh… Was I feeling let down that he wasn't reacting differently? "That's all you have to say?" I asked.

I could see him blink in the darkness of the bunk. "Yeah. I don't care if you have them or not. I'm sorry you went through that. I'm sure it was tough," he added, squeezing my hip.

And that was that. In that moment, I felt like I was relinquishing the rest of my life to this man. Gladly. Willingly. Effortlessly.

Neither one of us said anything after that for a long time.

At one point, as he made out, his hand cupped my breast over my shirt, his thumb grazing my nipple.

He rolled me onto my back, settling between my legs like he'd been there for years. We'd been keeping it easy and sweet in the nights before. He kept kissing me, but it was when I felt him dropping his weight so that our hips pressed together, that I almost cried tears of joy.

Sacha was hot and hard against me. When he started rolling his hips, pressing what felt like a nice, long cock against me, it was only because his mouth was glued to mine that I didn't whimper out loud.

"Jesus, Gaby," he whispered, rolling his pelvis so the ridged head between his legs rubbed the apex of mine through our thin clothing.

I knew that we needed to be quiet, but when his tongue licked my neck before he started sucking softly, I had to bite my lip to keep from moaning like a total porn star on camera. That didn't stop me from wrapping my legs around his waist and arching against him. My hands roamed up and down his spine, smoothing over the taut muscles that were flexing with his hips.

His thumb kept grazing my nipple, slow, steady circles that complimented the steady thrust of his hips and cock. Sacha's mouth was so warm and his tongue so sensual, I couldn't think. That blunt head kept rubbing against me so deliciously that I wished more than anything we weren't in my tiny bunk, surrounded by fifteen other people, fully clothed.

When I felt the start of my orgasm through the pit of my belly, I pressed my forehead to his shoulder as he kept thrusting his hips against my heat. There wasn't a doubt in my mind that I was so turned on I'd probably soaked through my underwear and my sweats. But when I came, with white spots dotting my vision and a silenced cry to his neck, I wouldn't have cared if we were in the middle of the street doing it.

With a few more grinds against me, I felt his whole body tighten under my hands. He shuddered, cursing so quietly it sounded like mumbling. My limbs felt loose and way too happy as Sacha's eyes met with mine and he gave me sly smile, kissing me slowly once more.

"You're killing me," I groaned before he rolled off of me. A huge smile took up my face. I put my head on my palm, and simply savored the sight that was this beautiful man.

Sacha blinked before rolling to his side, stroking his fingertips across my face with a smile. He sighed right before leaning in and sucking on my bottom lip for a moment. "That was better than—," he looked at my eyes and paused, probably thinking better of whatever was originally going to come out of his mouth. "Everything." Sacha gave me a goofy smile before slipping out of my bunk to change.

As I lay there, I smiled, totally blissed out. These next three weeks were going to be awesome. I just knew it.

~

"You get some of that pink zucchini yet?"

I burst out laughing at Laila's question. I'd borrowed Gordo's laptop to Skype with my bestest friend on the entire planet—not counting the Disciples of Doom and Sacha. It had been more than a month since the last time we'd talked, and I had a lot to tell her in "person" what I didn't want her to find out about via email. We'd already caught up on just about everything else, except the good stuff.

Specifically, my nightly grind sessions.

Just thinking about them got me all hot and

anxious.

"Not yet," I grumbled, smiling. "It's hard enough when there's fifteen other people a few feet away."

Laila shook her head as she grinned. "You hussy."

"I never said I wasn't," I laughed.

"But you're finally staying in hostels?"

We were traveling in a sprinter van now that we were in France and staying in hostels and cheap hotels. I was excited to sleep in a real bed. *Right.* 'A real bed.' We'd go with that. "Yes, we are."

"Good luck with that piece of vegetable!" She winked.

I snorted and gave her a thumbs-up. "I'm going to go vegetarian, just watch."

Her head ducked out of the screen shot, but her loud, rough laugh got clearly picked up by the microphone. Her "there's something seriously wrong with you" made me crack up.

"I'm teaching you my tricks, kid. Take notes."

That made her laugh even harder, the top of her head peeking up at the bottom of the screen. Slowly, she sat up, her dark skin pink and flushed as she wiped at her eyes. "I have my own tricks. The damsel in distress works every time."

I'd always thought that Laila's self-confidence was one of the greatest things about her. That girl knew she was something special.

"Did you tell him about Lucy and Ethel?" she asked.

The memory of that conversation was still fresh. "Oh yeah. He didn't even blink. Later on, he told me he'd thought I was just being modest—"

That had her screeching. "Modest? You?"

"Shut up," I hissed with an amused snicker. "So I like to wear shorts, leave me alone." My brother started bellowing my name out from down the hall, so I sighed. "I need to get going. Eli is hollering for 'Doctor Flabby,' and he sounds like he's dying. I'll email you soon, okay?"

She nodded and blew me a kiss that I blew back before we each logged off Skype. I was putting the computer to sleep when two large hands curved over my shoulders.

"Have fun talking to Laila?" Sacha's voice was low as he spoke.

I looked up at him, grinning. "Always. I miss her."

He smiled back at me before bending over to plant an upside-down kiss on my lips. "Your brother's looking for you. He has a splinter he can't reach, and he refuses to let anyone else try to get it out."

Of course. "Doctor Flabby is on her way."

He snickered. "If you were a doctor and your picture was online, I'd probably become a hypochondriac," he chuckled, taking a step back.

Getting off the chair and slipping the laptop under my arm, I smiled at the guy in front of me who was too good looking for his own good. "Thank you?" I blinked. "I think."

He slipped an arm over my shoulder and pulled me to him a little roughly. "I'd even let you give me a rectal exam."

We both laughed so loud it echoed down the hallway. Honestly, I'm surprised I didn't fall on the floor but that was probably because we were side-by-side.

"Let me go sign up for medical school right now," I told him, slapping his stomach with the back of my hand.

"I'm ready to spread them whenever you are."

Oh my God. I burst out laughing again, slapping my hand over my face. "Let me invest in a good flashlight then."

He dropped his arm and kissed my cheek all sloppy, wet and perfect as he laughed. "Where have you been all my life, huh?"

"In Texas?" I offered with a stupid face.

Sacha just shook his head, grinning, before squeezing my wrist and linking our fingers together. "In that case, I'm glad you got out of there."

It wasn't until we got to Zurich that we were able to stay in a hotel. The hostels we'd stayed in while the bands played Frankfurt and Stuttgart were fine, except I'd been stuck sharing a room with my brother, Mason, and Gordo both nights. The first day

I woke up, they'd drawn whiskers on my face with a marker. The second night, I made sure to sleep face down with a sheet over my head. Assholes.

"I have my own room," Sacha informed me when we were in the van heading to the hotel.

I raised my eyebrow at him, grinning. "Oh, really?"

He nodded, narrowing those gray-blue eyes in my direction. "Stay with me. I've missed your big butt up against me."

"Of course you have." I leaned into him. "I'll get Carter to share a room with me so I don't have to listen to Eli singing about you and me sitting in a tree tomorrow morning."

Sacha shook his head, smiling huge. "He told me earlier that if I knocked you up while on tour, we'd have to get married and name the baby after him."

I threw my head back and laughed. "Oh God."

He shrugged. "I'm okay with the terms." Sacha kissed my cheek before lowering his voice. "Let's get started tonight," he teased. At least I think it was a tease.

"What?" I squeaked because the whole baby thing kind of scared the shit out of me. I loved kids, I just wasn't sure if I wanted them anytime soon. Or ever.

"I'm kidding," he smiled gently, reaching out to hold my hand and squeeze it. "At least about the kids. We'll have to figure out something when I have to leave again."

The reminder that this between us was so new,

that he lived in one state and I lived in another, sat oddly in my chest. I was so used to seeing him nearly all-day every day that I wasn't sure what we were going to do once the tour was over in a couple weeks. I didn't want to bring it up right then. Sacha saying that we'd have to figure out something gave me a sort of reassurance that he was willing to have something to work on once life went back to normal.

When we got to the hotel, I followed Sacha to his room, flicking off my brother when he started moaning from down the hall, "I'm going to be sick."

I hadn't gotten used to how much smaller everything seemed to be in Europe. The rooms were more compact, and even the shower stall was narrower than I was used to. But I wasn't going to complain as I dropped my backpack on the floor next to the double-sized bed.

"You want to shower first?" Sacha asked.

"You can go first. You're faster than I am," I told him.

He nodded, digging through his backpack for his clothes and toiletries before slipping into the tiny bathroom. In less than ten minutes, he was out, and I thought I'd died. Wearing only a pair of his beloved black basketball shorts, it was a miracle I wasn't standing because I would have fallen over. Sacha had some serious definition to his upper body; there were planes and crevices of muscles over his frame had me drooling in approval.

And the bastard knew it because he just smirked

in my direction.

"Shut up," I mumbled as I slipped past him only to reach back and pinch his butt cheek before closing the door. I could hear him laughing from the other side while I showered quickly.

Once I finished getting dressed, I opened the door to find him sprawled on top of the bed, still shirtless, flipping through the channels on the small box television. I smiled before taking a seat next to him. He looked over at me before reaching out to place his hand on my thigh, rubbing up and down the length of it.

I took the time to count the solid bands of ink that striped up his arm. There were thirteen of them total, starting at his wrist and going up his shoulder in perfectly even spacing. "Was there a reason for these?" I asked, knowing his gaze was still on me.

Sacha took my hand with his free one, and placed it on his forearm. "Each band is a reminder of the number of labels that rejected us before we got a yes," he answered. "I like remembering that no matter how successful I might be now or in the future, it wasn't an easy journey." He paused for a moment. "Is that cheesy?"

"No," I snorted, because it wasn't. This was my pretty humble guy who didn't act or look in the way I'd expected him to in the beginning. "I think it's neat." I slid my fingertip around the band covering his elbow. "And the one on your chest?"

He looked down at the thick swirl of black on his

pectoral. "I just thought it looked good," he laughed.

I shook my head, snorting. "You're an idiot." I poked his taut stomach. "The one on your neck?" I grazed the piano keys with my fingers and watched as his tipped his head to the side to capture them against his skin.

"It's my favorite instrument. Did you know I started playing when I was three?" I shook my head. "I did. I'm classically trained. I remember my mom sitting behind me on the bench before I was old enough to reach the pedals, trying to teach me."

How cute would that have been? A pale-skinned little boy with crisp black hair and huge gray eyes? Bah. I kept that to myself and instead asked, "You have any more tattoos?"

"One," he said in a flat voice.

"Where?" I asked him suspiciously.

Pale eyes blinked. "On my ass."

"No way!"

"Yes way."

A second later, I was trying to roll him over to look at his ass cheek, but he grabbed onto my wrists to keep me from doing it. "Let me see it," I begged.

"No."

"Come *on*."

He shook his head, sternly.

"Why not?"

"It's the first tattoo I ever got," he admitted.

I smirked at him, reveling in the fact that he was still holding my wrists. "It can't be that bad." When he didn't say anything in response, I got a little scared. "Seriously. What is it? As long as it isn't a tribal tattoo, it can't be that horrible."

Sacha looked at me for what felt like a long time. "It's of my dog."

I blinked at him. "Shut up."

"It is," he snorted the answer out, smiling too wide for me to take him seriously.

I tried pulling my hands out of his hold, but I couldn't. "You're a damn liar."

He pulled me to him, kissing my throat softly. "Okay, I guess you can see," he murmured against me. A moment later, he was flipping over onto his hands and knees, and I was pulling down his shorts and boxer briefs to one side.

There was nothing there.

I pulled down the other side, and there was nothing there either.

"Liar!" I laughed at the same time I slapped the lower half of his butt cheek as hard as I could.

With a yelp, Sacha flipped over, wrapping an arm around my waist to pull me onto the bed beneath him. His long body stretched over mine until we were pelvis to pelvis. He shook his head. "Oh Gaby, Gaby. You want to play the spanking game?"

CHAPTER TWENTY-FOUR

Sacha got a single good spank in.

I don't know what I'd been thinking hitting him. This was Sacha. I should have known he was going to retaliate somehow. And he did. In the blink of an eye, he flipped me onto my stomach and smacked my butt so hard there was for sure going to be a bruise there tomorrow.

The special thing about my relationship with this guy, the thing that made us and what we were different, was that we were both laughing our asses off the entire time.

Not in a million years could I have ever imagined thinking that getting spanked by another person could be both funny and also pretty damn sexy. I could blame the latter on the fact that I'd seen his tight and cute butt cheeks seconds ago. My Sassy was something special. If there was a fraction of a doubt in my brain that I was crazy for this guy, that I felt a connection with him that trumped any other relationship I'd had in the past by leagues in the sea —it was smashed.

"You bitch!" I screeched against the bed cover, bucking my hips away.

Heavy weight fell over me, his chest pressed against my back, and I could feel his lips on my neck. "Princess," he said it with a snort.

"That hurt!"

He cracked up harder, kissing me over and over again. "Gaby," he murmured. "I'd say I'm sorry, but I'm not."

I howled in pain until his palm smoothed from my side over my lower back and slowly inched down to cup my still aching ass; I sucked in a rabid breath. That large palm stroked, rubbed and kneaded the flesh gently. What did I do? I arched my freaking back.

His free hand pushed up the back of my shirt, up, up, up until all the material bunched over my breasts and the middle of my back. "You're so smooth," he said in a husky voice right before hot, wet lips were dragged down my spine. "God, Gaby," he groaned as I curled into him even more.

"Hmm?" I mumbled incoherently, relishing in the sensation of his mouth and warm skin on mine.

I felt something infinitely times warmer than his lips and much more wet at the small of my back. He licked me. Oh my lord, Sacha—the most gorgeous man in every universe—was licking me. Both of his hands slipped around my waist. His fingers prodded at the elastic of my sleeping pants, before pulling it down erotically slowly.

It wasn't until I felt his mouth on my shoulder and his fingers dipping inside the front of my panties that I thought the earth shattered into a million fragments. "Sacha," his name hissed from my lips.

He moaned my name in return, those long, lightly callused fingertips brushing over my the lower seam of my body, not stopping until he swept over the slit there multiple times. "Fuck," he hummed into my ear. A single finger dipped into me at the same time he used his other hand to pull my back against his upright chest. The position gave him access to my neck, where he started sucking lightly.

I cried out when he slipped another finger in me, fingering me so slowly I couldn't breathe from the sweet anticipation. What the hell my hands were doing, I really had no clue. I think they'd landed on his thighs, squeezing them tightly. "That's so good."

He hummed, nipping me lightly on the slope between my neck and shoulder. "I want you so fucking bad."

The rocking of my hips against the twisting and scissoring of his fingers should have been enough of an answer to his request, but I turned my mouth to kiss him, long, deep and slow. It was only when I pulled away from his lips that I nodded. "Please."

Sacha yanked my shorts and underwear down

my legs a second later, giving me a light slap where his hand had been last. Moist lips kissed one cheek and then the other before I rolled over into a sitting position. His mouth covered mine again, kissing me slowly, sucking one lip and then the other into his mouth while his hands fiddled with the bunched material of my shirt, pulling it up and over my head.

His eyes swept their way down, a great breath of air filling his lungs as he did it. While I hadn't opted to get the biggest boobs in the universe, I liked Lucy and Ethel more than enough. They were now both a small C-cup with only tiny lines for scars on the bottom of each. They looked as natural as they possibly could. Sacha pushed me onto my back gently, dragging his open mouth and lips down my chin, over my jaw, neck, collarbones, before settling over my right nipple. It wasn't my imagination when I felt him shudder over me.

I was pulling his shorts and boxer briefs down his hips with my hands and then my feet when I couldn't reach anymore. My fingers roamed their way up and down his smooth back from shoulder to ass. Legs opened wider around his naked hips. The more skin I saw—both that smooth, lightly tanned skin and the one painted in black strokes of ink—the more I couldn't comprehend how lucky I was.

"You're driving me nuts," he groaned, lapping against my nipple. "I need you right now." The heavy, hot feel of his cock brushed against my inner thigh as he rolled his hips. "Can I?"

The "yes" exploded off my tongue in a rush.

Sacha pulled back. His heavy, beautiful green eyes were hooded with lust and something else I couldn't decipher. He slanted his mouth against mine before pulling back to press our foreheads together. One finger brushed over my breast while another one stroked across my jaw.

I closed my eyes because it all seemed like too much. The way he felt over me, the way his eyes made me feel like I wasn't my own proprietor. But I felt like a coward doing it, so I opened them again.

He smiled at me gently before reaching over me, digging into his backpack for a second, retrieving a small box from inside. "You're a dream come true," he said softly once he was back in place, kissing me over my heart.

Catching sight of the black and gold wrapper in his hand, I glanced back up at his face. "You're perfect," I told him.

Sacha kissed me, pulling away to look down. I could see his hands shaking as he tore open the condom and sat back on his heels. I don't know how I didn't babble something like "holy shit" or "oh my God." In the times we'd spent in my bunk before, everything we ever did was over clothing. I'd never put my hands on his naked flesh. So when I glanced down his bare, hard chest and the symmetrical, block-shaped muscles of his abs to see his thick, long cock hard and proud in the air, I sucked in a breath.

He rolled the condom over the broad, blunt head

between his thighs and over the thickening shaft that stretched wider at the base. Sacha wrapped his hands over my hips to pull me toward him once he was fully sheathed. The bulbous head slipped up and down my lower lips, the tip rubbing over me so nicely I whimpered.

One more kiss and he was dropping to his elbows, caging me in between his biceps. Another soft, gentle kiss and he was adjusting himself to press his smooth head in me. Slowly, he pushed. I spread and stretched around him, inch by inch until he was buried to the hilt. The short, brown hairs of his base were pressed to my smooth lips.

Sacha let out a noise that sounded strangled, but I pressed my forehead against his shoulder, trying to make it through how full he made me feel.

After a minute or five, he pulled out of me slowly before sliding back in at the same languid pace. Then again. And again. Slow, slow, slow, he worked his hips and organ deep in me. "I'm not going to last that long," he whispered, kissing the corner of my mouth.

"That's okay." It was more than okay. Better than okay.

"You feel so fucking good. I'm sorry," he panted, giving me a sharp thrust upward.

I cried out.

"Everyday. I want you everyday," he groaned. "You're the best thing in the world." He flipped us over after that, never pulling out of me or losing contact with our mouths as we rolled. "Ride me," he begged. "I want you to come."

I smiled at him, blissed out and feeling more amazing than any human being should be capable of. But I slid up and down his long cock slowly. It seemed like less than a minute later, I was sweating and riding him faster. "Oh my God."

His hips pumped up, out of rhythm and sync, and I came so hard, my abdominal muscles cramped. I'd barely come out of my orgasm, still seeing spots in my eyes, when he pushed into me even faster, panting into my neck. Sacha went tense all over, pressing his lips against my chest with a muffled, "Fuck!" He came, riding out his orgasm inside of me.

In the minutes after he'd calmed down, thrown away the condom and crawled back into bed, I felt like I was living in a dream. Sacha was curling around me, pushing my hair out of my face and grinning from ear to ear—a smile that put every other one to shame.

"What's that look for?" I asked him, running my hand over his tattooed arm.

His smile turned dopey and sweet. "You make me so fucking happy, Princess. You have no idea."

~

"You're dumb."

Sacha scoffed, slipping his hands over my feet to set them into his lap. We were sitting on his bed playing Uno in Berlin. Earlier that day, we'd walked around with Julian and Freddy and then followed that up by going to the venue for the show. Now that everything was over, we could finally allow exhaustion to hit full force. Almost three months of nonstop touring was finally taking its toll on all of us.

Eli and Gordo had been sick for the past week. Mason looked like he'd gotten into a fight with a chupacabra and lost. Poor Carter looked thinner and paler than normal. The other TCC guys weren't faring much better. Our bodies weren't made to be on the move so much on such erratic sleep and inconsistent diets, but our hearts were trying to keep up.

I think the only thing that kept me going was Sassy.

And the piece of Malykhin between his thighs.

Ever since that night in Zurich, we had turned into horny teenagers. No bathroom or hotel room was spared. It was fucking fantastical. *Magical.* A wet dream come true.

My heart and body weren't match for this man.

"It's not my fault that I know how to play the game," I laughed.

He flicked me on the forehead. "There's no strategy to it, you're just getting lucky."

Taking a card from the deck, I threw it at his face. "There is a strategy. You can't keep putting down all your Draw Fours and Draw Twos when you get them, duh. You need to wait until you only have a few cards left, and then make me eat shit."

"That doesn't make any sense," he frowned, poking me in the side before putting down a blue four.

I groaned and put down a blue Skip. "Says the man who hasn't beat me once."

Sacha laughed. "I can beat you at plenty of other things."

Which was the truth but I shrugged, smiling. "Maybe but not this, sucker."

Four moves later, I'd won again. He grabbed the messy pile of cards and tossed them in the air with a snort. "That's what I think about you winning."

"You suck."

He fell back onto the bed, pulling me down alongside him. "You suck way better than I do," he murmured, kissing my neck.

I shivered, tilting my head up so he could get a better angle for more skin. "True."

Sacha dragged his hot tongue over the shell of my ear. "Gaby?"

"Yes?"

His hand slowly stroked down my arm. "We only have a week left," he said in a soft voice, reminding me that our time together was coming to an end.

I moved my head to kiss his jaw, ignoring the anxiety it caused in my stomach. "I know."

"What are we going to do?"

Clear gray eyes met mine, something like worry or sadness filled in the edges of his lashes. I'd been meaning to ask him about it, but I was a chicken. In that moment, I regretted that I hadn't brought it up earlier.

"Make it work?" I offered him.

He threw his head back and laughed. "No shit." Fingers wrapped around my wrist, pulling my hand to his chest. "This has to work."

"Oh yeah?"

Sacha nodded, still smiling. "Yeah, Princess. It does."

I kissed his cheek, slinking one leg between his. "I know." I kissed his cheek again. "Who else is going keep you entertained if you don't have me?"

After a brief pause with no answer, we looked at each other and laughed.

"Julian?"

He kissed my nose while his chest vibrated with a rough chuckle. "I love you."

The admission crushed my heart, flattening it out and ruining it for the rest of my existence. "I know."

"You do?" he asked me softly.

"Yep." I pulled away from him to get a better glimpse at the smooth texture of the skin on his face and the long, dark lashes that framed his colored eyes. It wasn't necessary to think of all the things he did and had done to let me know he cared about me, mainly because for the first time in my life, I felt his affection. His attention. I felt Sacha in a way that had no explanation or reason. I knew love in its many forms. I knew how I loved Eli in a way that made perfect sense because we'd been stuck together for so long. I knew how I loved the other two baboons, but this… was nothing like that. It was undeniable, bright and massive.

It was a rainbow, a unicorn, a million-dollar lottery ticket and happiness incarnate all rolled into one thing.

"I love you. So much."

His smile was the size of Jupiter and brighter than the sun. "I—," he stuttered, flushing. "I—"

"You can get it out," I teased him.

Sacha smirked. "How much?"

"How much what?"

I rolled my eyes. "I just said 'so much.' A lot. Too much." I hummed in my throat. "Why?"

"Because if you don't love me very much, I have a lot more work to do until you do," he stated.

That was suspicious. "Why?"

"Because I don't think I'm going to like being away from you when the tour is over." He tugged on my earlobe, wrapping his arm around my waist to hoist me on top of him. He was hard already, pressing against the thin material of his boxer briefs.

"I don't think I'm going to either," I admitted to him, trying not to rock over his thick erection but failing miserably. "You don't have to tour again for at least a few months after this, right?"

He nodded against me. His fingers slipped underneath the hem of my shirt. "No. We're just writing until we're ready for the next album. This is the last tour for the cycle."

"We'll figure it out," I promised, letting him peel off my shirt. His thumbs brushed over my nipples slowly. Looking away from the movement of his fingers, I smiled, taking in that handsome face. "We have to."

$\sim$

"Twelve men?" The van driver, who was also our translator, confirmed with Julian our group number before relaying the information to the receptionist working at the front desk of the hotel in Muenster.

I shot a side-glance over to my brother, who was standing next to me. "Pretty sure I'm not a man," I whispered.

Eli snickered, throwing an elbow out to catch me on my lowest rib. "Notice how no one bothered to correct him?"

"Jerk."

"Just speaking the truth, Flabby. You're pretty much a dude." He laughed. "Except Sacha thinks you're pretty, and I guess you do have nice hair."

"I think your hair is nicer, you douchebag." I elbowed him back. "But thanks for telling me you like my hair."

Eliza rolled his eyes, poking me in the forehead before we followed Christof, our translator extraordinaire, down the hallway that led to our hotel rooms. "Want to go eat at that little restaurant we passed on the walk over here?"

I nodded at him, pausing at a door that Christof explained would be my room. My brother followed after him. I'd barely opened the door when a presence came up behind me. "Princess," Sacha said as he reached over me and pushed the door open wider.

"Sas," I grinned up him, stepping inside.

He followed in after me, dropping his bag right by the door. "I missed you today."

"Me too," I said, dropping my bag alongside his and wrapping my arms around his waist.

He'd been busy all day. There'd been two interviews with German magazines, a television interview, then a soundcheck in a venue with bad PA equipment that took twice as long as it should have. We'd only seen each other when we'd woken up and had breakfast, and then in passing during the day. I'd spent the afternoon at the *Prinzipalmarkt* and the Pablo Picasso museum with Carter before we headed back to set up merch.

How the hell was I supposed to cope with not being around him in a few days? Instead of being separated by doors and fans, it was going to be thousands of miles and mountain ranges that separated us. It made my heart ache thinking about it.

"I'm really tired," he murmured, kissing my nose. "My throat is starting to hurt, too."

I winced. "Eli said something about going to eat,

do you want me to bring you something back so you can stay here and rest?"

Sacha nodded, sighing. "Please. Just food. I'm just going to make some tea, shower and lay down—"

"Naked?" I asked him, waggling my eyebrows to get his mind away from feeling crappy.

He snickered. "For you, anything."

Planting another kiss on his lips that lingered decades, I dropped another one on his throat and started backing away toward the door before stopping. What the hell was I doing leaving? "Do you want me to stay?"

"I'll be fine. I'd rather stay here and you bring me something back."

I eyed him for a second before nodding. "Call Eli if you need me, okay?"

"I will," he scoffed halfheartedly. "Cheap-ass."

Still on my case about refusing to turn on my cell phone so that I could avoid roaming charges, I winked and walked out of the room. Eli stood down the hall with his hands buried in the pockets of his loose shorts. He waved me over before we made our way out of the hotel and toward an open restaurant.

"You all right?" I asked.

He nodded slowly, the growing curls on his head catching my attention. "I still feel like shit, and I'm ready to go home."

"I hear ya." Because I did. I was tired of hotels, little to no privacy, and always being on the move, but the idea of not seeing the people I'd grown so close to over the last three months regularly, bummed me out even more.

Opening the door before me, he narrowed his eyes. "Did you figure out what you're doing yet when we get back?"

I groaned. "No."

"No idea?" He didn't believe me. I usually had a plan for everything.

In this case, I only had the next four days planned. After that...

"Not a single one," I sighed.

"What about your honey boo?" His question was low and cautious.

Eliza and I hadn't really talked about the situation with Sacha very much. It was weird, at least with my brother. He knew how I felt about him, using that special sixth sense, and he'd been the first one to tell me that Sacha felt the same way in return, but still. I knew Sacha's intentions were pure and honest. That didn't mean the future still wasn't scary and full of variables.

"He's planning on visiting a week after we get home."

Eliza raised an eyebrow. "Huh."

"What?"

He shrugged too slowly. "That's... soon."

"And?"

"It's good," he explained. "It makes me happy, Flabby. That kid thinks you're the greatest thing on the planet, and I'm glad he does. You deserve somebody like that." When my eyes started to get watery at his commentary, he yanked on the end of my ponytail really hard. "No crying allowed. Stop it."

"You love me."

He groaned and looked away. "Yeah, I do, estupid. That's my nice deed of the year."

I laughed before wrapping both of my arms around his giant bicep. "Thanks, E. I'm glad you invited me to come on tour."

Eli shot me a sick glance before opening his mouth, sticking his finger part of the way inside in a gagging motion. "Trust me. We all know how thankful you are that you came on tour, you dirty whore."

He wasn't surprised at all when I punched him in the stomach.

"You two lovebirds will figure it out. I won't be touring for a while, but you're more than welcome to go out with us again when the next one is confirmed," he said. "We can still get a place together." I opened my mouth to say we should do it, but he put up a hand. "Think about it. Give it a few weeks to see what happens, Flabs. All right?"

I nodded at him, grateful for his offer but not sure if I'd want to go on tour again after all of this, even if it was months or years from this moment. Plus, if Sacha was gone and I was gone, we'd never get to see each other. Something deep in the pit of my stomach told me this long-distance crap was going to be hard.

But all the best things in life weren't exactly supposed to be easy either, right?

CHAPTER TWENTY-FIVE

"Why do you look like you just found out that Kulti guy got married again?" Mason asked me in a loud whisper. We were in Antwerp for the last day of the tour. The Cloud Collision was about to go back onstage for their encore performance, and in the meantime, while Eli and Gordo talked to fans in the audience, this baboon was keeping me company.

I remembered that he had in fact been around when I found out my longtime crush, Reiner Kulti the German soccer icon I'd adored once upon a fifteen-year-old day, had the nerve to get married to some actress. Ugh. It had been a bad day, to say the least. "I'm sad the tour is over."

He shrugged. "It was pretty fun, wasn't it?"

I nodded.

Mason gave me a goofy look. "You got to tour with the most attractive men in Prog—"

"I think that's kind of stretching it."

He frowned but kept going. "Got to see the world. See a kangaroo in person—"

"Saw you almost get punched by that same kangaroo—"

"Watched your brother get hit on by that transgender guy—"

I made a face at him, remembering the incident. "I'm pretty sure that was you."

Mason didn't even bother confirming or denying my statement. "Went to a bunch of boring museums —"

I groaned. Mase and I had very different standards for what fun was.

"Got to spend time with your best friends—"

He had me there.

"And you met your little snuggle bug," he cooed with fluttering eyelashes like an idiot.

I relaxed my facial expression to look at him with boredom. "You forgot something."

"Carter ripping his pants when we were in Stockholm?"

"Nope."

"Julian and Eli getting blow jobs from the same girl an hour apart?"

I gagged at the reminder of that little ditty. They'd both been grossed out, more so Julian than Eli because he'd been the second guy to mess around with the girl. Disgusting. "No."

Mason narrowed his eyes. "What, then?"

"Me punching you in the nuts for the first time," I told him while simultaneously swinging my fist in the general direction of his balls.

He jumped a foot back with a laugh. "Jesus! I'm glad I called the wedding off, you crazy." He whooped, but I couldn't hear him because the music started up again so loudly, it was impossible.

There were only a couple of songs in their encore repertoire. After three months of being on tour, listening to the bands night after night, I could probably sing to all of their songs and play all of the instruments from memory. And I didn't even know how to play any instrument very well. Or at all, whatever.

My heart ached a little knowing that this was the last time I'd get to see either band play for who knows how long. It seemed bittersweet that I'd agreed to come along reluctantly at first, only hoping to get away from crap back home. Now I was heartsick that the experience was coming to a close. Who would have known?

"We only have a few songs left, Antwerp! Before it gets fast and heavy, we'd like to thank all of you for coming out tonight on our tour closer! It's been an insane three months with our friends in Ghost Orchid, who have stuck it out with us. Thank you to our crew, and especially," Sacha put his hand over his heart, smiling a tiny playful grin, "to my beautiful girl, the greatest thing since the invention of air conditioning, My Gaby, for making this the best fucking tour ever." The people in the audience started whistling and yelling out things I didn't understand. "Are you guys fucking ready?"

"YES!" the audience yelled in response.

Sacha pointed out into the audience before jumping up high off of a speaker, at the same time the cymbals on the drum set crashed and the second to last song began.

Me.

Me.

I was the greatest thing since air conditioning, and who didn't love air conditioning?

When I looked over at Mason with what I'm sure was the dumbest, goofiest smile to ever exist, he grimaced and shoved at my head, which only made me smile more.

In that moment, I made that decision that there was nothing, and I mean nothing, that I'd let stand between Sassy and I. There would only ever be him. He was the end to my beginning.

An hour later, when we were standing around outside while the guys finished signing autographs and posing for pictures drenched in sweat and smelling like dirty socks, I let myself take it all in. Sacha walked over after ending a conversation with a couple of fans and grinned. The bastard knew I had the swoons for him and his words. Plus, he was still wearing his stage clothes, specifically the suspenders he'd added to his performance wardrobe.

"I love air conditioning," I told him, threading my

fingers through his when he stopped in front of me.

He nodded, smiling that same grin that I'm sure I'd replicated when he'd spoken to the audience earlier. "Me too, *Rocky*. Me too."

In twenty-four hours, we were going to be separated by thousands of miles. But distance was insignificant when you loved someone the way I loved Sacha. Like air conditioning. And laughter.

EPILOGUE

"Hiiii," I cooed into the camera on my laptop.

"Hi, Princess." The screen in front of me blurred while I figured Sacha moved around his hotel room. A second later the shot focused on the normally handsome man on the screen. He looked terrible. His pale eyes were dull, highlighted by the dark bags beneath them.

"You look like shit," I said, taking in the sickly, ashen shade of his skin. It was a telltale sign that the flu he'd come down with two days ago was still kicking his ass.

Sacha smiled weakly, chuckling. "Happy anniversary to you, my love."

I squeaked, temporarily forgetting about how sick he looked. "Happy anniversary!"

"I'm sorry I can't be there," he murmured, running a hand through his growing hair. The last time I'd seen him—almost four weeks ago—it'd been at its usual short buzz cut length on the sides. Recently, he'd been getting a lot lazier about shaving it meticulously, and I liked it. Then again, I'd probably still think he was beautiful if he had a mullet—the true sign of a perfect specimen.

I shrugged, smiling at him through the camera. "It's okay. My present showed up in the mail yesterday, but I waited until today to open it like the box said," I told him in a sing-song voice, with a wiggle to my eyebrows, holding up the cool bracelet he'd sent me from Indonesia. "I love it."

Sacha leaned forward to rest his chin on his hand, still looking out of sorts but happy. The plain white-gold band on his ring finger winked at me, reminding me that exactly a year ago, we'd decided at the last minute to go get hitched. We didn't even have rings when we did it. It had just been two random people at the courthouse who'd served as our witnesses, and us. Weeks later, we finally got around to getting some simple bands and couldn't have been happier.

We'd made it exactly two months living in different states before he stated the distance was killing him. In sixty days, he'd visited me three times, and I'd gone to see him twice in San Francisco before accepting that we didn't want to be so far away from each other. Correction: We couldn't be so far away from each other.

A game of paper-rock-scissors via video chat

decided that I'd be the one moving.

And I did.

"I thought of you when I saw it." He somehow managed to wink at me despite the fact that I knew he felt awful. "I have another one."

"Another present?"

He nodded.

I made an "ooh" noise. "Show me."

His tired face softened as he grinned wickedly. A moment later, he pulled his shirt over his head and gave me a perfect view of one side of his tattooed chest—

"You got my name tattooed!" I yelled it, leaning forward in my chair to get a better look at the pretty, loopy lettering on my screen, because that definitely worked.

"No, I got the other love of my life's name tattooed," he laughed hoarsely.

"Sassy," I sighed. The trance I was in was so powerful I couldn't think of a comeback to his dumb response. My eyes were glued to the fact that my name was permanently tattooed onto his skin, directly mirroring the black swirl on his other pec. There was a little turtle dove at the end of the 'y' and I suddenly had the urge to cry. "I miss you." The statement came out like a sad moan. "I have your present here, ready and waiting."

Sacha's smirk was a wasteful one. "You have no idea how much I miss you too, but I'll be home in three days." He sighed.

"Naked?"

He laughed. "Definitely—"

"Sachita!" Eli's booming, deep voice called out from over my shoulder.

I turned around to roll my eyes at my brother. He'd been staying with me for the last two weeks, but he spent more time with our twenty-year-old, single blonde neighbor than he did with his "favorite sister." Right after we'd gotten home from The Rhythm & Chord Tour, he'd committed himself to not going so long without seeing me. True to his word, Eli went out of his way to visit even after I moved halfway across the country. Hell, Mase and Gordo tagged along half the time. No distance was too far to strain those friendships.

"Hey, E," Sacha called out with a wave.

"Me and Gaby went to go see the new *Transformers* movie," my brother offered him the information, despite the fact that we'd said we wouldn't tell Sacha we'd gone unless he asked. The bastard. They were Sacha's favorite movies.

He gasped. "You went without me?"

I nodded at him slowly, gravely. "I'm sorry. We were really bored, and I promise to go watch it with you again when you get home."

"You're lucky I love you," he grinned. He loved his movies, but he loved me more.

"I know, Sassy." I smiled back at him, completely forgetting about Eli standing behind me.

"I'm gonna go puke now. Take care, man. I'll take

care of your old hag until you get home!" Eli yelled before throwing something at the back of my head and leaving the room.

I rolled my eyes and laughed. "Remind me why I went into business with him."

"Because you love him?" Sacha asked me with a raised eyebrow, like it was difficult for him to remember why I'd done it too.

A couple months after we'd moved in together, I still hadn't been able to find a job that I was crazy about. Sacha had offered to take me on tour with him as their merch girl, but I loved Carter. He cemented himself as one of my closest—and only—friends after my move, and I knew damn well he loved touring with TCC despite how little they helped him. There was no way I was going to screw him over like that. After mentioning it to Eliza one night over the phone, he asked me why I didn't just sell merch online. Ghost Orchid paid out of their butts to let a major company sell their things for them, apparently.

An idea, and a small loan from my brother because I refused to take money from Sacha, started The Merch Girl. It was an online website where I sold TCC, Ghost Orchid and eventually fifteen other bands' merch, thanks to contacts from my two favorite men. I charged less than most other big companies did and made sure to stay on top of everything. The ultimate bonus was being my own boss, so I could visit Sacha on tour whenever I wanted as long as I could get someone to take over the business for however long was needed.

We'd agreed when he left for the first time after my move, that we wouldn't go more than a month without seeing each other. It was long enough so that our reunions were the hottest thing in the universe, and not so long that we both turned into those lovesick morons that made us roll our eyes.

Love, at least our version of love, was little things. Intangible things. It was laughs and our three turtles named Mercury, Frank and Bumblebee. It was playing soccer at the park by our apartment, going for runs and trying to trip each other during them, and it was our video chats when we were on different continents. It was compromises and separation from each other, and in my case, from my family, the baboons and Laila.

But I loved him and for us to be together, it was nothing.

ACKNOWLEDGMENTS

To the greatest readers in the universe, thank you so much for your love and support. You all keep me going when I want to take a long walk off a short pier.

Thank you to my Bear, my mom and dad, Ale, Raul, Eddie, Isaac and Kaitlyn for keeping me sane. I'd also like to thank my Navarro and Letchford family for all their love.

Gabriella West and Dell Wilson—thank you for all your help in making RCM a finished product! Letitia Hasser with RBA Designs and Jeff Senter with Indie Formatting Services for doing all they do to make RCM better to look at than I ever could. A very big thank you to Lauren Abramo at Dystel & Goderich for helping me spread my work to audio. Amanda Brink, thank you for your never-ending friendship, patience and encouragement.

Last but never least, thank you to my two best friends on the planet, Dorian and Kaiser.

ABOUT THE AUTHOR

Mariana Zapata lives in a small town in Colorado with her husband and two oversized children—her beloved Great Danes, Dorian and Kaiser. When she's not writing, she's reading, hiking, forcing kisses on her boys, or pretending to write.

Please join my Mailing List (for New Release Information Only)

@marianazapata_

marianazapatawrites

www.marianazapata.com
marianazapata@live.com

ALSO BY MARIANA ZAPATA

Lingus

Under Locke

KULTI